MAD AS THE DICKENS

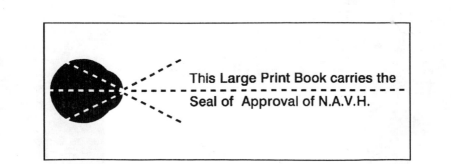

This Large Print Book carries the
Seal of Approval of N.A.V.H.

A LAURA FLEMING MYSTERY

MAD AS THE DICKENS

TONI L. P. KELNER

WHEELER PUBLISHING
A part of Gale, Cengage Learning

GALE
CENGAGE Learning

Detroit • New York • San Francisco • New Haven, Conn • Waterville, Maine • London

GALE
CENGAGE Learning

Copyright © 2001 by Toni L. P. Kelner.
Wheeler Publishing, a part of Gale, Cengage Learning.

LIBRARY OF CONGRESS CATALOGING-IN-PUBLICATION DATA

Kelner, Toni L. P.
  Mad as the Dickens : a Laura Fleming mystery / by Toni L.P.
Kelner.
    p. cm.
  ISBN-13: 978-1-59722-861-9 (pbk. : alk. paper)
  ISBN-10: 1-59722-861-3 (pbk. : alk. paper)
  1. Fleming, Laura (Fictitious character)—Fiction. 2. Women
detectives—North Carolina—Fiction. 3. Actors—Crimes
against—Fiction. 4. Amateur theater—Fiction. 5. North
Carolina—Fiction. 6. Large type books. I. Title.
PS3561.E39734M33 2008
813'.54—dc22   2008032224

Published in 2009 by arrangement with Kensington Books, an imprint
of Kensington Publishing Corp.

LT-M

Printed in the United States of America
1 2 3 4 5 6 7 13 12 11 10 09

To my mother-in-law,
Judith Ward Kelner,
who has always honored
Christmas in her heart
and tries to keep it all year!

ACKNOWLEDGMENTS

I want to thank:

My husband, Stephen P. Kelner, Jr., for providing his usual unfailing support, and for coming up with the title.

Fellow EMWA members Leo Du Lac, David Housewright, D. P. Lyle, MD., Steve Perry, and Mary V. Welk for answering my questions about blood spatters, natural gas poisoning, and moonshining.

Erik Abbott for assistance with theater lore.

Elizabeth Shaw for proofreading the manuscript in record time.

My daughters, Magdalene and Valerie, for not tearing the house down while I was busy writing.

Barbara Ikeda, Joan Rafferty, Joanmichelle

Rafferty, Ivie Skids, and Victoria Walker, for keeping Maggie and Valerie happily occupied.

CHAPTER ONE

"Stop, stop, STOP!" Richard paced back and forth in front of the stage, running his fingers through his hair hard enough to pull it out. "What are you people doing? Have any of you even read the play?"

The actors on stage looked at one another as if trying to decide who he was talking to.

"Don't look at each other. I'm the director!" Richard said, jabbing himself in the chest. "Look at me when I'm talking."

Their heads obediently turned toward him.

"I've been involved in theater for over twenty years, and this is the worst rehearsal I have ever seen. I've been to first readings that were more convincing than this so-called performance. It's less than a week until opening night; now is the time to polish blocking, to add nuances to your interpretations of characters. You people don't even know your lines yet."

I saw Seth Murdstone, the man playing Scrooge, trying to hide his copy of the script.

Richard went on. "*A Christmas Carol* is one of the most popular plays of all time. It's been performed in every variation possible, from traditional to musical to the Muppets. Yet somehow, you people have missed the entire point of the play!"

Richard stopped pacing to glare at them. "It can't be done — it just cannot be done." Then he stormed out the door. The cast just watched him go, as if a tornado had blown by.

Even my cousin Vasti, who could throw a mean tantrum herself, was speechless for nearly thirty seconds. Then she wailed, "Laurie Anne, you've got to do something!"

"He'll calm down in a minute," I said, trying to sound as if I believed it, but I'd never known Richard to act that way before. At least, I hadn't before this trip to Byerly. Since then, I'd seen several other explosions from him, each worse than the last.

I was the pregnant one; I was supposed to be the one with raging hormones. But ever since Vasti had called to talk Richard into taking over the production, he'd become as temperamental as John Huston and an Arabian stallion put together.

Vasti was still looking at me entreatingly, so I said, "I'll go talk to him." Then I levered myself out of the chair, once again surprised at how hard it was to maneuver while five months pregnant.

Seth came over and offered me a hand. "I'm sorry, Laurie Anne, I know I'm the reason Richard is so bent out of shape. I'm trying, I really am, but Scrooge has so many lines to learn. I'll keep at it; don't you worry."

"It's nothing to do with you, Seth," I said, which was at the very least a white lie. "Richard's just tired."

"Be sure and tell him how sorry I am," he said as I headed for the door.

I felt bad for him. No matter how hard Seth tried to act as nasty as Scrooge was written, he just didn't have it in him. When he said, "Bah, humbug," it sounded as if he were joking.

I couldn't imagine why Vasti had given him the part. Scrooge is usually portrayed as a skinny fellow, old and pinched-looking. Seth, on the other hand, was a well-built man with a full head of snow-white hair, and was always smiling and laughing. He was as old as Scrooge was supposed to be, but he sure didn't look it.

Had I been back in Boston, where Richard and I lived, I wouldn't have dreamed of going outside in December without a coat on, and I would probably have grabbed gloves, a hat, and a scarf, too. But after so many Massachusetts winters, North Carolina winters seem almost springlike. Besides which, being pregnant kept me warm, even in Boston. So it was a relief to leave the stuffy recreation center building for the brisk, sunny day waiting outside.

My usually mild-mannered husband was standing not far from the door, his hands jammed in his pockets as he kicked at the red clay dirt and muttered to himself.

"Hey," I said.

He didn't answer.

"Hello?"

There was still no answer.

"Richard, I think I'm in labor."

That got his attention. He turned white as a sheet and started toward me.

"Just kidding," I said.

He stopped short and thumped his chest, presumably to make sure his heart was still beating. "Laura, please don't joke about that."

"Sorry," I said, struggling to keep a smile off my face. "I had to get your attention somehow."

"You got it, all right."

"So do you want to go home now, or should we stay through Christmas?"

"What do you mean?" he said.

"We can either spend the rest of the holidays here relaxing, or fly back to Boston and spend Christmas alone the way we planned in the first place. You just said that there was no way you could whip the cast into shape in time. So why beat your head against a brick wall? Give it up now and let Vasti worry about it."

"That wouldn't be exactly kind to Vasti, would it?" he said hesitantly.

"Who cares?" I said. "She didn't tell you the whole story, or you'd never have agreed to come. You were supposed to have two weeks to rehearse, not just one. Besides, you can't stage a decent production with this cast — they're hopeless. I mean, Seth Murdstone is as nice a man as you'd ever want to meet, but he's a terrible actor."

"I know," Richard said. "I hate losing my temper at him, but I think he got that accent from listening to Dick Van Dyke in *Mary Poppins.*"

"What about the others? None of them can act."

"That's not true. Bob Cratchit keeps getting better, and Mrs. Cratchit is already wonderful. The Spirits of Christmas aren't too bad, and even though Scrooge's nephew needs work, I could coax it out of him."

"I suppose you could," I said, "but there's no way you can get it done by Friday night."

"Maybe I could," he said speculatively. "If we lose the phony British accents so we get a little authenticity . . . We'd have to rehearse morning, noon, and night, but maybe . . ."

"In less than a week?"

"Look, Laura," he said heatedly, "I've waited my whole life to direct. Do you really think I'd give up my only chance because the cast needs a little work?"

"A *little* work?"

"Okay, a lot of work. I can do it. They can do it. We can do it." He strode purposefully toward the door, then turned back. "I thought you were a programmer, not a psychologist."

I grinned. "I'm practicing for when the baby throws his or her first tantrum."

"Was I that bad?"

"Oh, yeah."

He looked at the door. "Do you think they'll take me back?"

"Of course. They'd be scared not to."

He looked sheepish. "I suppose I should get a grip on my temper."

"Does that mean that we're staying?"

"That's what it means," he said. "I'm going to give the people in Byerly a show they'll never forget!" He started back inside, his shoulders squared like a drill sergeant determined to whip a platoon of raw recruits into shape.

CHAPTER TWO

I sat down on the low brick wall at the entrance to the recreation center to enjoy the fresh air a little longer, rubbing my tummy automatically. I'd always wondered why pregnant women do that all the time, and I still didn't know, but I'd given up trying to stop myself. I did know why pregnant women speak to their unborn babies, or at least I'd read theories about how it would turn them into genuises. But I did it as instinctively as I rubbed my tummy.

"Don't worry, baby," I said. "Your daddy isn't usually so volatile." I was hoping the baby would inherit Richard's usual temperament, and maybe those deep-brown eyes. I didn't care if he was short like me or tall like Richard, but I did want a child who loved books as much as we did. Richard had voted for light-brown hair like mine, admittedly easier to control than his own, and it would be a lot easier to keep the little one

16

in shoes if his toes weren't as long as Richard's. Maybe I'd be able to see something of my parents in the baby's face, and I really wanted him or her to share my grandfather's musical talent and Aunt Nora's gift for cooking.

Then I started thinking about all the other traits the baby could get from my family: Aunt Maggie's orneriness or Aunt Ruby Lee's sweetness, Vasti's piercing voice or Willis's usual silence, Linwood's mean streak or Earl's gentleness. And that was just my side of the family! "Baby," I said, "with this gene pool, there's no telling how you'll turn out. But your mama and daddy are going to love you no matter what."

Eventually I went back inside, just in case Richard had exploded again. Though things seemed to be running smoothly, Vasti still looked nervous, so I said, "I think he's going to be all right now."

"I sure hope so," said Vasti. "Who'd have known Richard could be so much trouble?"

"It's your fault that he's so aggravated. You told us we had two weeks until opening night, and then you moved it up a week."

"I had to. The recreation center is already booked for that other night. We're just lucky I talked that group into rehearsing somewhere else."

"What about the theater at the high school?" I knew they had a decent one there. I'd bought candy bars and magazine subscriptions from younger cousins to help pay for it.

"It's already booked, too," Vasti said.

"The middle school? Or even the elementary school?"

"Holiday pageants." She indignantly added, "How was I supposed to know that everybody in Byerly was putting on a show this year?"

"Why didn't you set something up sooner?" Lack of planning wasn't one of Vasti's problems. Usually she had each minute of her day planned, and if I gave her a chance, she'd plan most of mine, too.

"I do have a new baby, you know," she said. "I'm breast-feeding, and Bitsy isn't even sleeping through the night yet. Just wait until your baby is born and see how much you manage to get done!"

"All right," I said, relenting. "Richard will do his best. But why didn't you tell us about all the practical jokes?"

"I didn't think it was worth mentioning," she said unconvincingly. "There are always mix-ups when you've got this many people around."

"Not like this! I've already lost track of

the mix-ups that have happened just in the two days we've been here." I used my fingers to count off. "The thermostat has gone haywire so we're either freezing or sweating, and the fire alarm has gone off twice. Then somebody tied most of the ropes backstage in knots that took us an hour to untie, and all the lightbulbs for the stage went out. Not to mention the fact that every single roll of toilet paper in the building disappeared overnight." Since my doctor had ordered me to drink lots of water, that last one was the worst as far as I was concerned. Even I was tired of the tricks, despite the fact that I'd attended MIT, where the pursuit of practical jokes was almost a religion.

"I've tried to find out who it is, but nobody will own up to it," she said. "I thought the Norton kids were doing it, but Junior questioned them herself and she swears it wasn't them."

Vasti had cast some of my friend Junior Norton's nieces and nephews as the Cratchit children. Though Junior was a devoted aunt, I knew she'd be the first to admit it if they'd been causing trouble.

She continued, "I was hoping that once Richard got here and things calmed down, the pranks would stop."

"I hope you don't think Richard is going to track down the joker," I warned. "He's got his hands full already. That's another thing — why didn't you warn him about how badly things were going? It's no wonder your other director quit." I saw a guilty expression flash across her face. "Vasti, who was the original director?"

She turned away. "Why do you ask?"

"It was you!" I guessed. "You were the director, weren't you?"

She hung her head, then nodded.

"You told us he quit because of a family emergency."

"It *was* a family emergency. Do you know what it's like trying to nurse a baby in the middle of rehearsal? I thought I had a director, but Sally Hendon got him for *her* show, so I figured I'd do it myself. I didn't think directing would be so hard, but nobody was learning their lines and the show was just awful. I had to do *something*."

"Maybe so, but you didn't have to lie to me and Richard."

"I didn't lie. I just didn't tell you every little detail."

"Vasti —"

"You're not going to tell Richard, are you? I don't want him to make another scene."

"If he asks me, I'll tell him the truth, but I

won't volunteer anything."

"Thank you, Laurie Anne. It's all for a good cause." Then she looked at her watch and said, "Look at the time! I've got to go pick up Bitsy at my in-laws' house. I only left one bottle of my milk, and it's nearly feeding time." She grabbed her purse and coat and stopped only long enough to say, "You'll keep an eye on things, won't you?"

"Sure," I said, but she was already out the door.

I looked around the room and sighed, mostly on my husband's behalf. Even though it was Richard's first crack at directing a play, I thought he deserved better than a stage in a worn-out recreation hall. The building was decades old, and over the years had hosted craft fairs, scout meetings, senior citizen's parties, and goodness knows what else. Half the chairs were broken, and I didn't completely trust the ones that weren't. The linoleum was worn near the doors and peeling up elsewhere. Somebody had decorated a dilapidated artificial Christmas tree with a dozen red satin balls, and hung a few straggly strands of garland around the walls, but that bit of holiday cheer only made the place look worse.

Of course, none of that would show once the house lights were out. What bothered

Richard was the fact that the stage was only a few feet off the ground, which meant that sight lines for the audience were going to be horrible. My makeup mirror at home was more advanced than the lighting system, and there must have been whole generations of moths raised on the curtain. On the plus side, the acoustics were surprisingly good and the backstage space was decent, despite the layers of dust.

Junior Norton saw me and waved me over to an empty chair next to her. Junior's a little bit shorter than my five feet, two inches, but there's something about the way she carries her sturdy build that gets people's attention. Andy Norton had had his heart set on a little boy to pass on his name, but when the fifth girl arrived, he gave up and named her Junior. Of course, later on he got his boy, but since "Junior" was taken, the new baby was Trey, for Andy III. Junior had taken over from Andy as police chief, with Trey as her part-time deputy while he finished college.

"I take it that Richard is sticking around," Junior said.

"For now, anyway."

We watched the players at work for a few minutes in companionable silence.

Then Junior said, "You know, this is about

as interesting as seeing grass grow."

"Or watching paint dry."

It was only my second day of rehearsal, but it seemed as if I'd been sitting in those hard plastic chairs for a month. I'd thought it would be fun to see Richard direct — nobody had told me how boring rehearsals are. Watching my husband run the cast through the same scenes over and over again was enough to drive me to drink.

I was just happy that I had a companion in boredom. Junior was spending some of her rare time off riding herd on the nieces and nephews who had parts in the show.

"Do you think Richard will throw another tantrum?" she said hopefully.

"It wasn't that bad," I said, defending him. "The cast is way behind where they should be. I don't blame Richard a bit for getting hot under the collar."

"I don't blame him either. I just wish it would happen again. If *something* doesn't happen, I'm going to fall sound asleep."

"I hear that," I said. "Maybe we should try to hunt down the practical joker."

"Hunt him down? I want to shake his hand. Those jokes and your husband's tantrums are the only things getting me through the day."

I was tempted to sneak off and go shopping or visiting or something, but I was afraid I might be needed to calm down the director again.

Back on stage, Richard stopped the action once more and ran his fingers through his already disheveled hair — a sign that agitation was building again. "David," he said, "can you try to look a little more cheerful? You're young Ebeneezer, Ebeneezer *before* he turns into a curmudgeon. It's Christmas, and you're having a wonderful time. You are not having root canal surgery!"

"Sorry," he said. "I'm trying my best." Other than his hair and bushy eyebrows still being reddish-brown, David Murdstone was the spitting image of his father, and his dual roles as Scrooge's nephew and Young Scrooge took advantage of the resemblance. David usually had his daddy's smile, too, but not right that minute.

"Just think happy thoughts," Richard said. "Florence, you make your entrance now."

Florence Easterly, in character as the young woman Ebeneezer was once in love with, floated onto the stage. Even as bored as I was, I could see David's face light up when he saw her. Though the two of them were fifty years old if they were a day, they'd only been married a few months, and it showed.

24

Richard must have seen the same thing I did, because he came up with a way to use it. "Here's an idea. Florence, I want you to be on stage when the Spirit of Christmas Past and Scrooge arrive."

"That's not in the book," David objected.

"If we were going to do exactly as the script says," Richard said patiently, "you people wouldn't need me. Just try it."

"Whatever you say, Richard," Florence said.

He said, "Let's start with Fezziwig shaking Young Ebeneezer's hand." They ran through the last part of the scene again, and this time it worked beautifully. Young Ebeneezer glowed with Christmas joy, and so did Richard.

Maybe he was going to pull it off after all. The players were still rough, but they'd improved so much already and they still had nearly a week before opening night. If Richard could just get Seth Murdstone to do a decent job with Scrooge, it might not be a total disaster.

Richard called out, "Spirit of Christmas Past and Scrooge, let's get you two into the picture."

Oliver Jarndyce, the round-faced man playing the first spirit to visit Scrooge, stepped out of the wings, but he was alone.

"Where's Scrooge?" Richard asked.

"He said he wanted a cigarette," Oliver said.

For a second it looked as if Junior might see her wish for another tantrum granted, but Richard swallowed whatever it was he wanted to say and instead said, "Mrs. Gamp, do you think you could find Seth and get him back on stage?"

"I sure will; Mrs. Harris probably knows just where he went," the cheerful, birdlike stage manager said, and she scooted away. Unlike most of the cast, she managed to be right where she needed to be whenever Richard called her.

Richard ran his fingers through his hair again. "While we're waiting for Scrooge, let's try something a little different."

My eyes glazed over at that, and I lost track of what was happening for the next few minutes. Then a scream rang out, and I jerked wide awake. Since when was there a scream in that scene?

The folks on stage looked as surprised as I was. I turned to ask Junior what had happened, but her reflexes had taken her nearly up onstage by then, and I took off after her as fast as five months of pregnancy would allow.

Richard saw me coming and helped hoist

me up, and then we followed Junior as she chased a second scream. How she'd been able to judge the direction it was coming from in that cave of a building, I'll never know. To me it seemed to echo everywhere.

We went stage left and down the narrow, dimly lit corridor that led past the dressing rooms and ended at the back door. We found Mrs. Gamp about halfway down the hall, her fist pressed against her mouth as if to hold in any more screams.

Lying on one side on the floor in front of her was Seth Murdstone, blood seeping from a swollen lump on his head. I could tell he was dead even before Junior knelt to touch his wrist.

"As dead as a doornail," Richard whispered, quoting from *A Christmas Carol.*

All I could think of was that he'd promised a show that Byerly would never forget. It looked as if he'd succeeded even before the curtain went up.

CHAPTER THREE

Junior barked, "All of y'all step back, and nobody touch anything!"

We obeyed, and I looked away from Seth's body. Mrs. Gamp had started sobbing, and I pulled her away, then let her hold on to me while she continued to cry. More members of the cast and crew came down the hall toward us, but Richard waved them away. I don't know if they realized how serious it was or if they were afraid of another one of Richard's tantrums, but they moved back without questioning him.

Junior reached into her pocket, pulled out a cell phone, and dialed. "Hey, Mark. I've got something for you."

At first I was surprised Junior would hand over a murder to her deputy, but then I remembered that she was on vacation. Even though Junior was there on the scene, investigating Seth's death was going to be Mark Pope's job, not hers.

"You've got yourself a situation at the recreation center," Junior was saying. "The fatal kind. You know we're rehearsing a play down here? One of our actors got himself killed. . . . Seth Murdstone . . . Of course, the scene is secured. . . . I *am* going to let you handle it. . . . Yes, I touched something — how do you think I knew he was dead?" Junior's sigh was loud enough for Mark to hear it. "I'll be here when you get here." Junior broke the connection and put the phone back in her pocket.

The people down the hall started asking questions, and I realized that Junior, Mrs. Gamp, Richard, and I were blocking their view of Seth's body. "Richard, we can't let David and Jake see their father like this," I whispered. Both of Seth's sons were in the play.

"We're not going to let *anybody* see him like this," Junior said firmly. "Not yet, anyway." In a louder voice, she called out, "People, we've had an accident."

My Aunt Maggie yelled back, "What kind of accident? Who is it?"

Junior ignored the questions. "Help is on the way, so y'all can go on back to the auditorium." She added, "Richard, take Laurie Anne and Mrs. Gamp out, too, and

29

make sure nobody leaves before Mark gets here."

"What do we tell them?" I asked.

"Exactly what I just said, and not one word more."

"They're going to figure out that Seth is missing," I pointed out.

"Probably, but it'll take them a while. Mark should be here by then, and he can worry about it."

Mrs. Gamp still had her head buried on my shoulder, and as I was wondering how I was going to extricate her, Junior said, "Mrs. Gamp, I sure would appreciate you looking after my sisters' children for me."

Once she had a job to do, Mrs. Gamp promptly dried her eyes, and said, "Don't you worry. Mrs. Harris and I will take care of them." She started marching down the hall, fluttering her hands to herd people in front of her. Richard followed, holding himself as wide as he could to block as much of the line of sight as possible.

I stayed long enough to look around. The wall of the hall was lined with shiny off-white tiles up to eye level, and then with beige-painted concrete blocks the rest of the way to the ceiling. The flat ceiling was painted a darker color and punctuated with ceiling fixtures. There were no new marks on the walls or elsewhere on the well-scuffed linoleum floor, and other than Seth's body, there was nothing in the hall but Junior and me.

"Junior, how did Seth hit his head?"

"You tell me."

"Maybe he slipped and ran into . . ." I looked around, but there was nothing he could have run into. "Maybe he hit the floor . . . or the wall."

"Look at the shape of that knot on his head. He didn't get that from a flat surface. I'm guessing it was something long and not too wide."

"But there's nothing like that in here."

"That's right. So unless whatever it was he hit himself on walked away afterward . . ."

"Then somebody killed him," I finished for her.

"That's what I'm thinking."

"But who?" I knew that nice people get murdered as often as nasty ones, but I couldn't imagine why anybody would have wanted Seth Murdstone dead. "Did the killer come in that way?" I asked, nodding at the door to the back parking lot. The smokers had been going out that way for cigarette breaks.

"Whoever it was had to have come

through one of these doors," she said neutrally. "It's too soon to say which one."

I'd really wanted her to say that the killer must have come from outside, meaning that it wasn't somebody involved in the play.

"Laurie Anne, are you all right?" Junior asked.

"This isn't my first dead body," I reminded her.

"I know, but you've never been pregnant before. Mark will never let me hear the end of it if I let you get sick all over his crime scene."

"I'll have you know that I quit having morning sickness months ago."

"In that case, do me a favor and wait outside for Mark to get here, and send him in my direction."

"All right." Despite what I'd said to Junior, I was just as glad to get away from Seth's body.

Richard had everybody out of the hall by then, and I had to tap on the door at the end to get him out of the way so I could get through.

"Junior wants me to go meet Mark," I whispered to him.

"I'll hold the fort here." He leaned down to give me a quick peck on the cheek. "Are you all right?"

"I'm fine," I said firmly.

My great-aunt pounced on me then. Nobody is quite sure how old Aunt Maggie is. Her hair had been salt-and-pepper for as long as I could remember, though maybe there was a bit more salt than there used to be. I didn't know how Vasti had talked her into supplying props for the play, since she wasn't known for her willingness to volunteer or for her Christmas spirit. Her sweatshirt said, "BAH! HUMBUG!" in bright green letters, and she'd owned it long before she started working on the play.

She said, "Laurie Anne, what in the Sam Hill is going on? I heard Sarah Gamp scream like she'd seen a ghost, but all she'll say is that I shouldn't frighten the children."

I might have been tempted to tell Aunt Maggie the truth, just to ensure family peace, but there were too many people listening in. The entire cast and crew were clustered in the auditorium, and I could see Florence looking around as if trying to decide who was missing.

"There's been an accident," I said, going toward the door to the parking lot. "Just like Junior said."

"What kind of accident?" Aunt Maggie asked, walking along beside me.

"Help is on the way," I said, still moving.

"Laurie Anne . . ." Aunt Maggie said.

I dropped my voice to a whisper. "Junior asked me not to say anything until Mark Pope gets here."

"Why did she call her deputy for an accident?"

"Please, Aunt Maggie. Junior doesn't want people getting worked up."

"They're already getting worked up."

I just shrugged. She was right, but there wasn't anything I could do other than what Junior had asked me to do.

"All right," Aunt Maggie said, "but I expect you to tell me the whole story later."

"I will," I promised, and I finally made it out the door.

I stood on the sidewalk in front of the building to wait, again rubbing my tummy. "Well, baby," I said, "you've seen your first dead body. Okay, not seen, but been around. They do pop up now and again." That was true enough, but it sounded too flippant for the circumstances. "Not that Mama and Daddy go looking for murder victims, mind you, but we have gotten mixed up with this kind of thing before." That wasn't much of an improvement. "Sometimes Mama and Daddy solve mysteries." Great, the kid was going to think that her parents rode around in a van with a Great Dane named Scooby Doo.

Before I could confuse my unborn child further, a blue-and-white police cruiser tore into the parking lot, siren blaring. The driver didn't so much park as screech to a halt, blocking three parking places in the process. Then Mark Pope got out of the car.

Mark Pope is one of the most forgettable-looking men I've ever met. Medium height and build, with medium brown eyes and hair. If his job had ever called for following somebody on foot, he'd have been great, because nobody would remember him ten minutes after seeing him. He strode over to me, his hand perched on the handle of the nightstick at his belt.

"Where's the alleged body?"

I was tempted to tell him it was allegedly in the alleged recreation center, but I settled for, "Inside. Junior asked me to take you there."

"Good enough." Then he stopped, and looked me over. "You're one of the Burnettes."

"That's right." Actually, it was my mother who'd been a Burnette, but people around Byerly and Rocky Shoals tend to trace people back at least two generations in order

35

to place them correctly. "I'm Laura Fleming."

"Right. Laurie Anne."

I winced, but I knew it wasn't worth the trouble to correct him any more than I could correct my family.

"You're the one who keeps butting into police business."

"You might say that." Richard and I had clashed with Mark after a flea market dealer was murdered. Mark had been on the wrong track entirely and hadn't been pleased when we beat him to the killer.[1]

"Is that what you're doing now?"

"No, I'm here because my husband is directing the play."

He didn't look convinced, but he said, "Let's get on with it," and started toward the door.

"There's something I should tell you. Mr. Murdstone's sons are inside, and they don't know he's been — that he's been hurt. I don't know how you want to handle it, but —"

"Well *I* know how I want to handle it."

"Whatever you say." I hadn't been trying to help him anyway — I'd only wanted to make things easier for David and Jake.

[1] *Tight as a Tick*

All conversation stopped when I led Mark into the auditorium. He swiveled his head around like a spotlight, as if relishing the attention. David and Jake were standing together, with Florence's hand in David's, and I was sure that they'd realized Seth was missing. Everybody watched while I showed Mark the way, but it seemed to me that the Murdstones were watching us more closely than the rest.

Richard was still guarding the door to the hall, but he stepped aside when he saw us coming.

"Junior is down —" I started to say, but Mark cut me off.

"I'll take it from here." He turned back to the people in the room and raised his voice much louder than was necessary. "I don't want any of you people leaving the premises until we sort out the situation, and nobody is to come down this way unless I tell them to. Is that understood?"

When nobody answered, he took that to mean that it was, and he went into the hall, shutting the door in our faces.

CHAPTER FOUR

" 'Secret, and self-contained, and solitary as an oyster,' " Richard said.

"That Shakespeare had something to say about everything, didn't he?" Aunt Maggie said, coming up to us.

"Actually, that wasn't the Bard. It was Charles Dickens in *A Christmas Carol.* Stave One, if I'm not mistaken."

Aunt Maggie raised one eyebrow. "Since when do you quote Dickens?"

"Since he decided to direct this play," I explained. As a Shakespeare professor at Boston College, Richard didn't know all the Bard's work by heart, but he came close, and was usually more than willing to share that knowledge. "You see, it's an old theater superstition that it's bad luck to quote *Mac*—"

"Don't say it!" Richard nearly shouted.

"Sorry. It's bad luck to quote that Scottish play, or even to say its name."

"The Scottish play?" Aunt Maggie asked.

Richard was still looking at me in alarm, and short of spelling it out, there wasn't any way I could think of to tell Aunt Maggie that we weren't supposed to say *Macbeth*. "I'll tell you which one I mean later. Anyway, just to make sure he doesn't accidentally quote from *that* play, he's sworn off quoting Shakespeare for the duration."

"Hence the use of Dickens, in honor of our production," Richard added.

Aunt Maggie shook her head. "Richard, did you ever think of just saying things like normal people?"

"Did you ever think of wearing shirts that don't tell people what's on your mind?"

"Fat chance," she said with a snort.

"My sentiments exactly."

She looked as if she wanted to say more, but she must have decided it wouldn't do any good, so she changed the subject. "Are you two going to tell me what's going on around here? It's Seth, isn't it?"

I hesitated, but decided it wasn't going to be a secret much longer anyway. Keeping my voice low so that nobody else could hear, I said, "Yes, ma'am. He's dead."

She nodded, her suspicions confirmed. "What happened? Florence says he had a bad heart. Was that it?"

"I don't think it was a heart attack," I said, but before I could say more, Mark stepped out of the door from the hall. "Is Mr. Murdstone's family here?" he said.

David stepped forward. "Deputy Pope, I believe you know my brother Jake and my wife Florence."

Mark nodded in acknowledgment. "I'm afraid I've got bad news for you," he said.

The two men stiffened and Florence gasped. I've known other women to gasp for effect, but with her it sounded genuine.

"Is Daddy . . . ?" Jake couldn't finish the question.

Mark nodded.

"Was it his heart?" David wanted to know. "Chief Norton said something about an accident, but my father does have a bad heart."

Mark hesitated, then said, "I'm not sure. Once the medical examiner gets here, I may be able to tell you more."

"Can I see him?" Jake asked.

"Not yet, but I'll tell you when you can. If y'all will excuse me, I need to notify the proper authorities." Closing the hall door quietly but firmly, he went back toward Seth's body.

Though we should have given them some privacy, I don't think anybody could resist watching the Murdstones. Florence grabbed hold of David, who was staring straight ahead, then reached out and pulled Jake into the embrace, too. Jake started to cry, deep sobs that must have hurt him.

That's when I turned away, rubbing my tummy again.

"I guess he broke it to them as best he could," Aunt Maggie allowed, "but he should have gotten them alone first."

"It wouldn't have made any difference," I said.

"Well, I think —" Aunt Maggie started to say; then she stopped. "I guess you know what you're talking about."

Junior's father, Chief Andy Norton, had been the one to tell me when my parents were killed in a car accident. I'd been visiting my grandfather Paw, and Chief Norton had asked Paw out onto the porch to tell him, giving Paw a chance to recover before they told me. But it hadn't really mattered. I'd known from the expression on Chief Norton's face that something was bad wrong.

"Sometimes being alone is worse," said a voice from behind us. It was Tim Topper, who was playing Bob Cratchit, and like me, he had reason to know. His mother had been murdered when he was just a little boy, so Chief Norton had come to visit him, too. Since Tim's father had been long gone, Tim was left to be raised by his aunt and uncle.

I looked down at my tummy, feeling the baby's kicks. Suddenly I was terrified that something would happen to me or Richard before our child could grow up — that some police officer would be wearing that same expression to give that awful news someday.

Richard somehow knew I was close to tears before I did myself, and he wrapped his arms around me. "It's okay, Laura," he murmured.

"It's just the damn hormones," I said angrily. "I didn't even hardly know Seth."

"I know," Richard said, rubbing my back. "Let's sit down." He led me to as quiet a corner as he could find, and made me put my feet up while Aunt Maggie got me one of the bottles of cold water I'd brought to rehearsal.

Part of me appreciated the attention, while part of me hated the feelings of weakness that pregnancy caused. The rest of me was watching the other people in the auditorium. They were probably starting to realize that Seth Murdstone hadn't died of a heart attack or from an accident — that he'd been murdered. I couldn't help thinking that there was a good chance that the murderer was in the room with us.

CHAPTER FIVE

Though Richard had known a fair amount about Dickens before he decided to direct *A Christmas Carol,* ever since then he'd been reading exhaustively, and as usual, he'd shared tidbits. That's how I knew that it's pretty easy to tell the villains in Dickens's books. They tend to be grotesque like Fagin, or repellent like Uriah Heep. Unfortunately, real-life murderers don't always look or act like murderers, but knowing that didn't stop me from looking over the cast and crew.

There was Aunt Maggie, of course, but as far as I knew, she'd liked Seth. Lord knows that she would have let us know if she hadn't, and even then, she would have been more likely to subject him to a tongue-lashing than to a bludgeoning.

She noticed me looking around and said, "Was it an accident, Laurie Anne?"

"It doesn't look like it."

She nodded, absorbing it more easily than most people would have. Maybe it was her age, but I've always thought that Aunt Maggie must have been born unflappable. "Do you think that somebody here did it?"

"I don't know enough to say. I don't even know these people that well." There hadn't been much time to meet everybody yet, and after Richard's tantrums, I thought some of them had been avoiding me. "Other than the triplets, of course."

Nearby were my cousins Idelle, Odelle, and Carlelle Holt. Though they don't always dress alike, they do it often enough that the rest of the family has gotten used to being confused. That day it was snug blue jeans and matching Christmas-colored sweaters: Idelle in red, Odelle in green, and Carlelle in green and red stripes. Vasti had brought them in to do costumes and makeup for the show, and since they have more clothes and wear more makeup than anybody else I've ever met, I thought they'd do a good job.

"What do you think, Richard?" I asked. "You know everybody."

"Only through their parts," he said.

Aunt Maggie said, "Y'all are talking like this is Boston. This is Byerly, Laurie Anne. You must know these folks."

"I don't know *everybody* in Byerly," I

protested. "I haven't lived here in ten years." I'd gone up North to go to college and had ended up marrying Richard and staying there. "I only just met Seth." And I wasn't going to get a chance to get to know him any better, I thought sadly.

"You know Big Bill," Aunt Maggie said, nodding at an older man in a flannel shirt and blue jeans.

I nodded, though I could hardly believe that he was there. Big Bill Walters owned Walters Mill, which employed a good proportion of the people in Byerly. He also owned the bank, several apartment buildings, and I wasn't sure how much more of the town. Anything he didn't own, he ran by means of being head of the city council. I'd never seen him in anything less formal than a sport jacket, and I certainly would never have thought that he owned a pair of blue jeans, let alone would wear them in public.

I'd been hearing rumors about him and Aunt Maggie, but this was the first chance I'd had to ask her about them. "So are you two — ?"

"We two aren't anything," she said emphatically. "He thinks he can make it up to me after trying to sell the mill to a bunch of no-good Yankees.[2] He just happened to be at the flea market when Vasti tricked me into doing props for the show, and when he said he'd be glad to help out, Vasti couldn't wait to give him a part."

Richard said, "He's playing Jacob Marley, Scrooge's dead partner."

"I hear he only took the part to be around you, Aunt Maggie," I teased. "It must be —"

"Don't say it!" she snapped.

"Yes, ma'am. I mean, no ma'am."

She gave me a look. "Anyway, he's been helping me out with the props." She glanced back in his direction. "He looks pretty darned good in those blue jeans, don't you think?"

I blinked. Though I knew that a person's sex life didn't come to a screeching halt at age sixty, I wasn't sure I was up to hearing my great-aunt critique Big Bill Walters's tail end.

Aunt Maggie said, "Did you meet the Murdstone brothers?"

"Briefly. Vasti introduced us yesterday, but David's been busy onstage and Jake's been backstage."

Jake was playing the charity collector and

[2] *Death of a Damn Yankee*

building sets. He was in the furniture business with his father, which was why he'd been tapped to make sets. He didn't look much like his brother or his father. He was much thinner, which made him look taller, and his hair was jet black.

"Jake must take after their mother," I said.

"I don't remember what she looked like. She died when Jake was just a little thing," Aunt Maggie said. "You know Jake's boy Barnaby is the reason we're doing this play."

"I thought it was for charity." Most of Vasti's endeavors were for charity, though she was usually pretty vague about the actual cause involved. For some people, this would have meant that the work was its own reward. In Vasti's case, the reward was having a chance to order people around and make a big show.

"It *is* for charity. The money is going to the Shriners' Burn Hospital in memory of Barnaby. He died last month."

"There was another fire in Byerly?" I asked. The previous spring there'd been a rash of them.[3] What with the Burnette home place being firebombed and my coming uncomfortably close to burning to death myself, I was a little sensitive on the subject.

[3] *Death of a Damn Yankee*

"Don't tell me there's another arsonist at work."

"Nothing like that. Barnaby was hurt in an accident, one of those propane space heaters. I hear there were burns all over his body." She shook her head. "He wasn't but nine years old."

Richard solemnly said, " 'When Death strikes down the innocent and young, for every fragile form from which he lets the panting spirit free, a hundred virtues rise, in shapes of mercy, charity, and love, to work the world, and bless it.' *The Old Curiosity Shop,* Chapter Forty."

"So it's just the two of them now," I said. Though I didn't have any brothers or sisters, I had enough cousins, aunts, uncles, and other relatives that I couldn't imagine not being surrounded by family.

"And David's wife, Florence," Aunt Maggie said.

"Scrooge's girlfriend in the past, and Mrs. Cratchit in the present," Richard put in.

The petite blonde was sitting between Jake and David, but her eyes were only for her husband. Most women her age would look silly in pastels, but the fuzzy rose-colored sweater suited her fine. I knew she was tougher than she looked — she was the lawyer who'd helped my cousin Ilene when she was in trouble.[4] "I heard they got married. It must have been quite the shindig, with her family connections and all."

Aunt Maggie snorted. "Not hardly! She and David eloped, and the Junior League is still buzzing about it."

"Why? Because they didn't get another chance to dress up?"

"That and the fact that Florence married beneath herself." She must have seen the look on my face because she added, "I'm just repeating what they're saying. This 'marrying up' and 'marrying down' business is nothing but foolishness."

I nodded, though technically I'd "married up" myself. Richard was a full head taller than I was.

"Florence is one of the few people Vasti didn't have to drag into this kicking and screaming," Aunt Maggie said.

"Since when does anybody need to drag in performers in Byerly?" I didn't know if all small towns had as many aspiring actors, musicians, singers, and dancers as Byerly did, or if we were just lucky. That didn't mean that people were good, but they were darned enthusiastic, and there'd never been a show without hotly contested roles.

[4] *Trouble Looking for a Place to Happen*

"All the usual folks were already working for the competition," Aunt Maggie said.

"What competition?"

"The Byerly Holiday Follies. Since they got going early, they got the cream of the crop. No offense, Richard."

"None taken," he said with a grin.

"Even Dorcas Walters is going to be in the Follies," Aunt Maggie added.

"Really? Who's in charge of it?" I asked.

"Sally Hendon."

Ouch! Sally Hendon was a distant cousin of mine and Vasti's, and as far as Vasti was concerned, she wasn't distant enough. Once she became the county's leading saleswoman for Mary Kay cosmetics, Sally had set her sights on being the biggest social climber, too. She'd jumped onto any committee that would have her, helped with every charity event that came down the pike, and ingratiated herself with the society columnist in Byerly's twice-weekly newspaper. Since Vasti used the same techniques, they'd butted heads more than once.

For Sally to have gotten the jump on Vasti's theatrical aspirations must have been galling, and I realized now that it was probably Sally's show that had the high school auditorium booked up. Even worse, Vasti and Sally were both dying to get into the

51

Junior League, and Dorcas Walters was the reigning president. Everybody in town knew Dorcas couldn't act, sing, or dance, but she still lusted after the spotlight. That Sally had managed to find something for her to do on stage was quite a coup, sure to improve her chances of getting into the coveted organization.

Aunt Maggie said, "Vasti's lucky she got Florence. She and David were on their honeymoon when Sally Hendon put out the word that she wanted performers, so her show was already full up when they got back. In fact, Vasti had been thinking of not even doing a show until she heard Florence was available."

"Is she that good an actress?" I asked.

"Excellent," Richard said. "One of the bright spots in the cast."

"You don't think Vasti picked her for that, do you?" Aunt Maggie asked. "All Vasti cares about is that Florence is the membership secretary of the Junior League."

Then Vasti wasn't completely off her game after all. "Did Vasti choose all the actors by what they can do for her?"

"Naturally. Not that some of those folks aren't good, but that's not why she picked them. You know how she got Florence, and when Florence said she thought her new husband would be interested, Vasti gave him a part, too."

I asked, "What about Seth as Scrooge? Was it because he's Florence's father-in-law?"

"That and the fact that the show's in honor of his grandson. Which is why Jake is in on it. You already know that a bunch of the Norton girls' kids are playing Tiny Tim and the other little Cratchits."

"So Vasti can get Junior and Trey to direct traffic?" I guessed.

"Got it in one."

"What about Bob Cratchit?" I asked.

"Tim Topper?" Richard said. "I thought it was quite brave of Vasti to cast a black man as Cratchit next to a white Scrooge, using American racism as an analogy for the British class system."

Aunt Maggie looked at him pityingly.

"It was the barbecue, wasn't it?" I said. Tim ran Pigwick's, one of Byerly's two barbecue houses. "Refreshments for the intermission? Catering for the cast party?"

Richard said, "You're serious, aren't you? Did Vasti even bother to hold auditions?"

"What for?" Aunt Maggie said.

"How could Vasti do this to a perfectly good play?" he moaned.

"What other favors is she after?" I asked

Aunt Maggie.

"See if you can guess."

"Oliver Jarndyce is the Spirit of Christmas Past. He's in real estate, isn't he? Is Vasti still talking about buying a bigger house because of the baby?"

Aunt Maggie nodded.

Sid Honeywell, the plump and usually jolly man playing the Spirit of Christmas Present, had a gas station. "Door prizes from Sid?"

Aunt Maggie nodded again.

Pete Fredericks was one of Byerly's morticians and was all too appropriately cast as the Spirit of Christmas Yet to Come. "Do I want to know what she wants from Pete?"

"Don't worry. He's just bringing extra chairs for the show."

"That's a relief." I had to wonder if he was going to be taking care of Seth Murdstone. "What about Mrs. Gamp? She's not in the Junior League, is she?"

"Not hardly. They'd choke on their cucumber sandwiches before they'd let a trucker's widow in their precious club."

" 'Be wery careful o' vidders all your life,' " Richard quoted. "*Pickwick Papers,* Chapter Twenty."

Aunt Maggie ignored him. "Besides which, she probably wouldn't have time.

54

She's too busy volunteering. At church, and at the schools, and up at the hospital in Hickory. She even volunteered to work on the play without Vasti having to chase her down. Mrs. Gamp does good work, even if she is a mite strange."

"What do you mean?" Richard said. "She and Mrs. Harris are the only things holding this play together."

"Richard," I said, "have you actually seen Mrs. Harris?"

"Not yet. Is there something wrong with her?"

"Not at all — other than the fact that she doesn't exist. There is no Mrs. Harris — Mrs. Gamp invented her."

"Are you serious?"

I nodded.

"Is she seeing a professional about that?" he asked.

Aunt Maggie looked at him as if he were the one with the imaginary friend. "What on earth for? Mrs. Gamp doesn't bother anybody. Neither does Mrs. Harris."

Before we could speculate further, we heard the sound of sirens. I think all of us jumped at the noise, but I wondered if one of us in the room was afraid to know that more police were coming.

CHAPTER SIX

Mark ushered a procession of medical and police personnel past us on their way to and from the hallway where Seth still lay. A county officer was stationed at the front door to make sure nobody unauthorized went in or out — and probably to keep an eye on us, too.

Eventually Junior came out from the hallway, looking as disgusted as I'd ever seen her.

"Junior?" I said, but she walked past me to where her nieces and nephews were still under Mrs. Gamp's wing.

"Thanks, Mrs. Gamp," she said. "I'll take over now."

Florence said, "Chief Norton, can you tell us anything more?"

"No, ma'am, I can't. This is a police investigation and I'm staying out of it."

"Don't be foolish!" Aunt Maggie said. "You *are* the police around here."

"Not this month," Mark said. He'd followed Junior out the door, and it seemed to me that I heard more than a little satisfaction in his voice as he said, "Chief Norton is off duty until the end of the year. Though I appreciate her help in securing the scene until the appropriate personnel could arrive, she's now welcome to go about her business as a private citizen." Actually, the way Mark said it made it sound as if Junior was *required* to do so.

Then he turned to the Murdstones and said, "If one of you could come with me, I need a formal identification of the deceased."

"I'll go," Jake said immediately.

"Let me do it, little brother," David said.

"We'll *all* go," Florence announced, and she took the two men by the hand to follow Mark.

There was dead silence for a few seconds, and then people started chattering, probably trying not to think about what the Murdstones were going through. I took advantage of the distraction to escape Aunt Maggie and Richard long enough to go to Junior. Her nieces and nephews seemed relatively unaffected and were playing with brightly colored Gameboys.

"Junior, what's going on?" I asked her.

"You heard Deputy Pope," Junior said, with extra-heavy emphasis on Mark's title. "He's in charge here — I'm just a private citizen."

"I heard it; I just didn't believe it. Since when do you let personal time get in the way of police business?" Usually it was the other way around. Junior had been using official excuses to get out of unwanted family and social obligations for years.

Junior frowned. "This vacation wasn't exactly my idea. I got a memo from the city council that I had some accrued vacation, and if I didn't take it I'd lose it at the end of the year. I wasn't going to worry about it, but Mark found out."

"Why did he care?"

"Didn't you know he's angling for my job?"

"You're kidding."

"Apparently he's been nursing a grudge ever since I took over for Daddy — he just did a good job of hiding it up until recently. He figures the more time he has in charge, the better his chances are of proving to the city council that they need a real man in the job."

"Is anybody dumb enough to buy that?"

"I hope not, but you know the council. Some of them think I'm going to up and quit as soon as I find myself a man to marry."

"Oh, please," I said, rolling my eyes.

"Anyway, Mark called my mama and told her I was working too hard. Mama has been complaining for years that I don't take enough time off at Christmas, and when she found out how much vacation I was going to lose, she tore into me about it. I tried to tell her about the mess that people get into over the holidays, like drunk driving and shoplifting and domestic problems, but she was a police chief's wife too long to be impressed. She said Mark can handle the drunks by himself, and he can get my brother to help with the domestics, and that nobody bothers to shoplift in Byerly when they can go to the mall in Hickory instead. So to make her happy, I told her I'd take the time off. Which means that, short of a major emergency, I'm not to even set foot in the station until after New Year's."

I know there are people who would think Junior was insane for letting her mother push her around like that, but those people don't have families. Or maybe their families aren't run by anybody as strong-willed as Mrs. Norton. I said, "We can always hope for an earthquake."

"Even that might not be enough to convince Mama. Though I might have been able to change her mind if we'd known you were coming down."

"What's that supposed to mean?"

"Laurie Anne, do you know how few homicides we get in Byerly, and what percentage of those homicides take place when you're in town?"

"Ha, ha," was the best response I could come up with. "Anyway, can't you get away with helping Mark on the sly? Without telling your mama?"

"I might could, but Mark won't accept so much as a suggestion from me while he's trying to impress the city council with how good he'd be as police chief."

"Isn't catching a killer more important than making points?"

"Of course it is, but Mark's bound and determined to prove what a big man he is."

"Playing politics shouldn't come between the police and solving murders."

"It happens all the time," Junior said. "I hear it's even worse in big departments, not to mention competition between the county mounties and state troopers, and federal versus local, and every other kind of authority. Fighting over turf is a fact of life. Besides which . . ." I waited for her to go on, but all she did was to shake her head and mutter,

"It's probably nothing."

I knew I wouldn't get anything more out of her until she was ready, so I changed the subject. "Do you think Mark is up to handling the case?"

"We'll have to wait and see," was all she would say.

Vasti burst in then, completely ignoring the officer who was trying to stop her. "What in the Sam Hill is going on?" she said, looking at all of us accusingly. Then she saw me. "Laurie Anne, I told you to keep an eye on things. What did Richard do now? I saw an ambulance out there. Don't tell me he hit somebody!"

"Of course he didn't hit anybody!" I snapped.

Mark Pope appeared and said, "What's this about somebody hitting people?"

"Nobody hit anybody," I said; then I realized how ridiculous that was, considering what had happened to Seth. "I mean —"

"What she means is that her husband has been repeatedly losing his temper ever since he got here," Vasti said, "but I'd never have left him alone if I'd known he was going to get violent."

Mark actually pulled out a pad of paper and a pen. "Would you say Mr. Fleming had

61

any particular animosity toward Seth Murdstone?"

"Lord, yes," Vasti said, rolling her eyes. "He's been picking on Seth ever since he got into town."

"Was the late Mr. Murdstone acquainted with Mr. Fleming before then?"

"I don't think so. Why —" She stopped. "What do you mean, 'the *late* Mr. Murdstone'?"

I said, "That's what I've been trying to tell you, Vasti. Somebody killed Seth."

"What?"

"Chief Norton said she'd told everyone it was an accident," Mark said, his attention suddenly on me.

"A child could have seen it wasn't an accident," I said in as scathing a tone as I could manage. "Besides which, Junior and I already discussed it."

"I wasn't aware Chief Norton was sharing information about the investigation," Mark said.

"Just one private citizen talking to another," Junior said.

Mark narrowed his eyes. "Then let's get back to Mr. Fleming. Mrs. Bumgarner, you were explaining how Mr. Fleming came to know Mr. Murdstone."

"I didn't even know they knew each

other," Vasti said, flustered. "Laurie Anne never told me."

"They didn't know each other!" I said. The baby picked that moment to start kicking, and I was about ready to join in.

"Mark," Junior said, "if you ever get around to questioning witnesses, you'll find out that Richard was on stage when Seth was killed. I can vouch for him myself."

"Is that right?" Mark said, sounding disappointed as he shoved the note pad back into his pocket. "Then if you'll excuse me, I'll get back to the investigation." He stalked off.

"Thanks a lot, Vasti," I said. "You almost got Richard arrested for murder."

"Did I hear that correctly?" Richard said, joining us.

That led to two rounds of explanations: one to tell Vasti what had happened to Seth; and a second to tell Richard the ridiculous conclusion Mark Pope had come to.

"That idiot," I seethed. "How dare he think that about Richard!"

"It is his job to explore every possibility," Richard said mildly, "though I must admit I'd never considered myself the murderous type."

Then Vasti said, "But what are we going to do about the play?"

"Vasti!" I said. "A man's been killed."

"I know that, Laurie Anne, but we've made a commitment to the community, and to the Shriners' Hospital. Let's not forget about that."

"You mean, let's not forget about your getting into the Junior League!" I shot back. I was planning to keep going when Junior reached out and touched my arm.

"Y'all might want to hold off on that for now," she said. "They're bringing out Seth."

We quieted down and turned to watch as ambulance attendants rolled out a gurney with a black body bag on top. David, Jake, and Florence followed after, their eyes red from crying.

Feeling awful for arguing with my own cousin at a time like that, I reached out and rubbed Vasti's shoulders in silent apology. She nodded back and squeezed my hand as we watched the Murdstones accompany Seth outside. There were plenty of tears then, and I wasn't ashamed that I was one of the ones crying.

After that, I thought the question of the play would be moot, considering that we'd just lost our Scrooge and figuring that surely the other Murdstones wouldn't want to go on. But I'd underestimated Vasti.

At least she wasn't rude enough to bring

it up again right then. Not that she had a chance. Once Seth's body was gone, a crew of county police officers started pulling people aside to question us about what had happened during rehearsal.

The humorless officer who interviewed me wouldn't tell me a thing, and at first I wondered if Mark had warned him about me. Then I realized that as far as he was concerned, I was a murder suspect. After all, I'd been outside alone for a while, and that could have been when Seth was killed. Maybe I should have been gratified that he would think a pregnant woman capable of murder, but I wasn't.

After having me go over my whereabouts about a dozen times, and then those of Richard, he wanted to know where everybody else in the crew had been at every moment of the rehearsal. I was more than a little embarrassed to have to tell him that I had no idea. I knew Richard had been on stage, and that Vasti and Junior had spoken to me at various points, but otherwise, it was just a blur. People had been wandering onstage, and backstage, and into the kitchen, and all over. When it came down to it, the only person I could really vouch for was myself, and I didn't have anybody to give me an alibi.

When he finally gave up on me, I was sent to sit down at a table with the other witnesses. Or maybe we were suspects, because an officer was standing over us, watching and listening. Mark was still questioning Jake, but everybody else was sitting around, looking bored, disgusted, or annoyed. Needless to say, Vasti was one of the annoyed ones.

"Can you believe that that officer had the nerve to ask if I went straight to my in-laws' house?" she said. "I told her that it was Bitsy's feeding time, but she seemed to think I could have snuck around back and killed Seth."

"It's theoretically possible," I said, "assuming you had a reason to want Seth dead."

She glared at me.

"I know you didn't do it, Vasti, but they don't." I'd been just as mad at the officer who interviewed me, but I did understand why he was acting that way. "They're just determining who could have killed Seth. Isn't that right, Junior?"

"That's what they're trying to do, anyway," she said, "but I don't think they'll have much luck. We all compared notes a minute ago, and nobody's in the clear except your husband."

"Really?"

There were nods all around.

Before I could ask anything else, Mark brought Jake back over. I was expecting Mark to say something about the case, but all he said was that the investigation was proceeding and that none of us should leave town. If I hadn't been worn slap out, I'd have tried to get more out of him, but it was awfully late and I was starving. So when he said we could go, I went.

My next thought was to talk things over with somebody in the family, but Aunt Maggie said she was going straight to an auction where she was supposed to sell, Vasti had to go get Bitsy, and the triplets had dates. So Richard and I made a quick stop at Hardee's for dinner, and though he and I halfheartedly rehashed the whole mess, neither of us really had anything to say that we hadn't heard already. I was relieved to fall into bed.

CHAPTER SEVEN

Richard and I stay with Aunt Maggie when we're in Byerly, in the Burnette home place where I'd grown up. I don't know how many Burnettes have lived in that old white clapboard house, but going there makes me feel like I'm surrounded by family. When my parents were alive, we were always there visiting, and after they died, I'd gone to live there with Paw. Years later, when Paw died,[5] the house had passed on to Aunt Maggie, but she'd never hesitated to open the doors to me. She'd even left my bedroom the same as it had been when I left, so when I awoke late the next morning, it was in comfortably familiar surroundings.

I stumbled downstairs to the den in the basement, found Richard reading, and joined him on the flower-patterned couch.

[5] *Down Home Murder*

"Where's Aunt Maggie?" I said around a yawn.

"She was up at the crack of dawn as usual, pursuing her appointed rounds."

Though the flea market where she sold was only open on weekends, Aunt Maggie spent most of the rest of the week tracking down new merchandise at auctions, yard sales, thrift stores, and who knew where else.

"I should have known." Then I caught a glimpse of the cover of the book in his hand. "What are you reading?"

He looked sheepish as he held it up. "It's one of Aunt Maggie's romances. I didn't bring anything to read other than Dickens and related material, and there doesn't seem to be any reason to finish them now."

"I'm sorry you won't get to direct the play," I said, hugging him, "but you'll get another chance."

"I suppose," he said. "It's not important now."

"Maybe you can hook up with one of the local theater groups when we get back home."

"I don't think there's going to be time before the baby arrives." He patted my tummy. "And I have a hunch this little one is going to be taking up a lot of my energy for the next few years."

"He or she sure is taking up a lot of mine now," I said, stifling another yawn. "What time is it?"

"Nearly eleven. You better hurry up. Junior will be here soon."

"Shoot, I'd forgotten about getting together with Junior," I said. Before everything had gone crazy the day before, Junior had asked me to go to lunch with her. "Do you think she still wants to go?"

"She called to confirm a little while ago."

"Don't you want to come with us?" I asked, not wanting to leave him there by himself.

"No, thanks."

"Then maybe I'll call her and cancel. I'm kind of tired after yesterday."

"No, you're not," he said with a knowing smile. "You just don't want me to brood about the play. But I'm not brooding — I just want to finish this book. Romances are really underrated. The plot of this one is incredibly complicated and I want to see how the author ties it all together."

I let him get away with it for two reasons. First, I was pretty sure that he'd say so if he needed me to stay. And second, he loved reading enough that he probably really did want to see how the book ended. So I headed upstairs to shower, dress, do my hair, and take my prenatal vitamin. When I heard Junior honking her car horn from the driveway, I asked again if he wanted to come, but by that point he was so immersed in the book that all he did was wave.

When I got into Junior's battered Jeep, the first thing I noticed was her outfit. I rarely saw her in anything but her police uniform and cowboy boots, but today she had on winter white slacks with a matching blazer, a pretty blue blouse, and flats. "You're looking spiffy today. I feel underdressed." Actually I'd felt underdressed most of the time I'd been pregnant. I had a couple of nice maternity outfits for work, but mostly I was relying on stretch pants and oversized sweatshirts like what I was wearing. "Is that makeup?"

"I don't get many excuses to dress up. Besides, I was up early and didn't have anything better to do."

"This vacation is pretty hard on you, isn't it?" I said sympathetically.

"You don't know the half of it. Now that the play's been canceled, Mama wants me to help with the baking and wrapping and shopping and I don't know what all."

"Don't you enjoy getting into the Christmas spirit?" I teased.

"About as much as getting a tooth pulled.

71

I like Christmas fine, but I've burnt every Christmas cookie I've ever tried to make, my presents have to be rewrapped before they're fit to be seen under a tree, and I'd rather face a riot than a mall at Christmastime. Riding herd on the kids at rehearsals was boring, but it beat the heck out of the alternatives."

"Any word about the investigation?"

"I'm just a private citizen, remember?" she said.

I quickly changed the subject. "Where are we going to eat?"

"Wherever you want."

"I'm dying for some barbecue," I said. "How about Fork-in-the-Road? It's closer than Pigwick's, and I'm about to starve."

She snickered. "Does being pregnant really make women that hungry?"

"Junior, I swear I dream of food. I wonder if Aunt Nora has started her Christmas baking yet; I could really go for some of her double-butter cookies."

"You can find out later. My mama asked me to drop by her house later and pick something up."

"Why don't we go now? I can wait that long for barbecue." Besides which, Aunt Nora's house was closer than Fork-in-the-Road and she always had food around.

"Let's not. I know you Burnettes — if y'all get to talking, we won't get out of there for an hour."

"Good point. Barbecue now, double-butter cookies later."

We made small talk about old friends from high school along the way, and in no time we were sitting at a table with a plastic red-and-white checked tablecloth, with iced tea, heaping plates of pulled-pork barbecue, and a basket of hush puppies in front of us.

I took a big bite of barbecue and sighed happily. "I really ought to take some of this home with me and let my Boston friends taste what they've been missing. They grill beef, put some ketchup or barbecue sauce on it, and think they've got something. They look at me like I'm crazy when I try to tell them they need a vinegar sauce, but if they had just one bite of this . . ."

"Laurie Anne, you know as well as I do that if you took any of this up North, you'd have it all eaten yourself before anybody knew you were back."

"Assuming that I didn't eat it on the airplane," I agreed.

After a few minutes of serious eating, Junior asked, "Are you and Richard going to be staying in town for the holidays? I mean, since he doesn't have a play to direct."

"We haven't talked about it, but I think we will. The family would be mighty disappointed if we didn't, and I hate to think what it would cost to change our plane tickets this time of year. How about you? Other than helping your mother, what are you going to do with the rest of your vacation?"

"That's up to you."

"It is?"

"I thought I might give you a hand."

"Give me a hand doing what?"

"Solving Seth Murdstone's murder."

I blinked. "What makes you think that I'm getting mixed up with that?"

"He's dead. You're here."

"I don't always spend my trips home chasing killers."

Junior didn't say anything, just raised one eyebrow.

I tried to come up with a time Richard and I had come to Byerly without a murder intervening, but I couldn't, so I took another approach. "I've had good reasons for getting involved before, but not this time. Nobody in my family is a suspect, and no one has asked me to step in, and I didn't even know Seth that long. Murder isn't a game to me, Junior."

"I know it's not, Laurie Anne. That's why I figured you'd want to investigate. You hate the idea of somebody getting away with murder as much as I do."

"You're right about that," I said. When my own grandfather was murdered, I'd started taking all murders more personally. I knew darned well that Paw's murderer would probably never have been caught without Richard and me.

Junior said, "I realize that Seth wasn't a friend of yours, and maybe nobody in your family is directly involved, but somebody is asking you to step in — me."

"Why?"

"Because Mark Pope is going to screw it up if you don't help."

"Mark's not that bad," I said halfheartedly. "I mean, he's not stupid or anything."

"No, he's not stupid, but I've got a hunch that he's going the wrong way on this one."

"Really?" Junior's hunches were legendary in Byerly — I'd never known her to have a wrong one — but still I wasn't convinced. "I don't know, Junior. I mean, look at me. I'm as big as a house, and my feet swell if I'm on them for more than ten minutes at a time. I spend half my time eating and the other half in the bathroom. Then there are my mood swings — if you think Richard's tantrums are bad, you really don't want to see one of my hormone attacks. This might not be the best time for me to go snooping."

"Your brain still works, doesn't it?"

"You tell me."

"And your mouth still works."

"Is that a comment on how many hush puppies I've eaten?"

Junior refused to rise to the bait. "So you can still go around and ask people questions and think about what they say. Most of the time that's all you do, isn't it? It's not like you go on stakeout or try to tail people or break into houses, so I don't see why your being pregnant makes any difference."

"Spoken like somebody who's never been pregnant."

"Look, Laurie Anne, I'm not going to try to talk you into anything you don't want to do. If you can sleep at night knowing that you've let Seth's murderer go free —"

"Like heck you're not trying to talk me into it!"

"Okay, I am trying to talk you into it. Is it working?"

"I'm not sure," I said. "I want to think about it."

"That's fine."

We ate for a few minutes without talking, and I figured that Junior had given up for the time being. I should have known better. I was just about to finish my barbecue when she said, "Would it help you any to know more about Seth?"

"Like what?" I said cautiously. "I know he was a widower with two sons, and his grandson recently died in an accident. And that he was a nice man, of course."

"Do you know what line of work he was in?"

"He made furniture, didn't he?"

"Yep, but when he wasn't making furniture he was making moonshine."

"Moonshine!" I yelped. When I saw heads turn my way, I lowered my voice. "That sweet old man was a moonshiner?"

"That's right."

"How on earth could I have missed hearing about that?"

"Very few people know, and I'd just as soon it stayed that way, just in case I'm wrong."

"What do you mean?"

"My daddy has suspected Seth was running a still since before I was born. He just never managed to catch him at it."

"Really?" As good a police chief as Junior was, there were those in Byerly who insisted that Andy Norton had been better. I wasn't willing to go that far, but I knew that most of what Junior knew, she'd learned from her father. "I didn't think your daddy ever gave up."

"He didn't give up. That's why he passed the case on to me when he retired."

"Is he sure Seth was a moonshiner? I just can't picture it."

"Years back, Daddy started getting hints that somebody in Byerly was shipping shine up North. So he started hunting around, and more than once he came across spots where stills had been, but all that was left was bits of copper tubing and such. He even found an intact still once and kept watch to see who came back to it, but the moonshiner must have gotten wind of him being there, because he never showed. And he hadn't left a fingerprint or anything else to identify him. Eventually Seth Murdstone's name got attached to the rumors, and Daddy started keeping an eye on Seth.

"The problem was, Seth had too much sense to put the still on his own land. So even though Daddy managed to look over his property a few times, there was nothing to find. He tried watching Seth to see where he went, but every time he did, Seth spent all day in his workshop, making chairs. Or he'd manage to sneak out despite Daddy watching him, and the moonshine would go through just like before."

"I'd never have thought Seth was smart enough to stay away from your father," I said.

Junior shrugged. "He was either smart or lucky."

"You say he shipped the stuff up North?"

"That's right. There are plenty of bars that would rather buy illegal booze for cheap, charge regular prices, and pocket the difference. Daddy figured Seth was sending it up in the trucks with his furniture, but he could never catch him at it, no matter how many times he stopped the trucks."

"I can't believe word of this never got around town."

"Daddy was careful. He knew that if the rumor got out, it would hurt his chances of catching Seth. Not to mention the fact that without proof, Seth could have sued him for slander."

"Is he sure Seth was the one? Maybe somebody was trying to make it look like it was Seth."

"Daddy said he had a hunch."

There was no arguing with that. Like Junior's, Andy Norton's hunches were never wrong.

Junior said, "I've been sniffing around Seth ever since I became police chief, but I haven't had a bit more luck than Daddy did."

"Do Jake and David know about it?"

"They must. Those chairs of Seth's didn't put David through business school, and Jake was in business with his daddy."

"It's hard for me to get my mind around this," I said. "I wouldn't have suspected Seth of doing anything worse than speeding."

"He probably did that, too, when it was time to get his product to market."

"Do you think Jake is going to keep the business going? The moonshining part, I mean."

"Probably, though I can't ask him."

I shook my head, amazed that none of this had ever made it into the Byerly rumor mill. There were other bootleggers around, but people knew who they were, and who had the best product and prices. Even I knew some of them, though the one time I'd tasted moonshine had been more than enough for me. "How on earth did he ever keep it a secret all these years?"

"Seth may not have been a good actor on-stage, but he could play parts offstage like nobody's business."

"Do you think the moonshining had something to do with his death?"

"Could be. There's money in moonshine, and when you mix money and criminals, you tend to get killings."

"Rival moonshiners? Seth not delivering the booze on time?"

"Something like that. Maybe he was shipping watered booze, or not greasing the right palms along the way, or even running into bigger sharks in the water."

Now Junior was starting to scare me. I could understand personal killings. Revenge or jealousy or fear — those things I'd run into before. Killing for business was something different. "If that's what it was, I don't want to get anywhere near this one," I said flatly. "Dealing with organized crime is not my idea of a good time."

"Hey, that's just one possibility, and if that's what it was, you're right to stay away. Solving that kind of killing is best left to the professionals."

"Is Mark investigating from that angle?"

"That's what I suggested to him. Of course, he knows about Seth, because he was in on the original investigation with Daddy, and he's been involved in mine. But he didn't seem to think much of the idea."

"Why not?"

"I don't know. Mark isn't telling me any more than he has to. Besides, he could be right. People get killed all the time without having anything to do with moonshining. I just wanted to let you know what you're getting yourself into."

"I appreciate that, but I still haven't made up my mind."

"Right. I imagine you'll want to talk to Richard. I know y'all work together, but I don't have a problem with being a third wheel." The waitress dropped our check on the table and Junior reached for it. "Let me pick this up."

"Are you trying to bribe me?"

"Will it work?"

I took the last hush puppy. "With food as good as this, it just might."

Chapter Eight

I was considering Junior's request as we drove to Aunt Nora's, so we didn't talk much. The idea that Seth's murderer might go free did bother me. I'd been worried about it ever since I found out Junior was letting Mark handle the case. I still didn't quite understand why she didn't just tell her mother the situation had changed and go back to work, but since I'd foregone my own Christmas plans for my family, I couldn't very well criticize Junior.

Still, I wasn't sure if I should even be thinking about murder while carrying a baby. The doctor had told me to stick as closely as possible to my normal routine, but I didn't think she expected murder to be part of that routine. Though I'd never really been hurt during my investigations, I'd come close, and Richard had been shot. Did it make sense for me to risk my baby's life? And the baby was Richard's too. I had to speak to him before I decided anything.

"Junior," I said, "do you mind dropping me off at Aunt Maggie's before you go to Aunt Nora's? I really need to talk to Richard." As Junior had said before lunch, we were likely to be over there a while, especially since I hadn't seen Aunt Nora since I'd been in town.

"I would, Laurie Anne, but Mama told your aunt I'd be there by two. It's nearly that now, and Nora knows you're with me."

"Rats!" If we didn't go straight there, Aunt Nora would think we'd been in a car crash or there was a problem with the baby or who knows what.

"Besides, I thought you wanted some of her cookies."

"That's right," I said, brightening. Talking to Richard could wait. I spent the rest of the drive happily imagining those cookies and hoping that Aunt Nora would pack me a box of them to take with me. Maybe I'd even save a couple for Richard.

With cookies on the brain, I was moving pretty fast when we got to Aunt Nora's house, and I didn't notice that Junior was letting me go ahead of her. The door was unlocked as usual and I went on in, meaning to call for Aunt Nora on my way to the kitchen.

before. "Let's give it a shot."

"That would be great," she said. "The fact is, I've always wanted to see how it is you go about solving a case."

"Really? I always figured you thought I was going about everything ass-backwards."

"I never argue with results, and you've gotten them time and time again — even when I've been completely in the dark."

"Thank you," I said, but now I was getting suspicious. Though Christmastime is usually green in North Carolina, I was smelling snow. A snow *job,* that is. "Junior, you're not just wanting to do this because you're bored with vacation, are you?"

"That's part of it."

"And part of it's because you want to get back at Mark Pope for trying to get your job?"

"You bet," she said, not at all repentant.

Something was still niggling at me, but I didn't know what. "There's more to it, isn't there?"

Now she stopped smiling. "If I told you that there was, but that I couldn't tell you what, would you back out?"

I thought about it for a minute. I'd known Junior a long time, and we'd been through a lot together. There'd been times when I'd asked her to trust me and she'd done it.

Except Aunt Nora was in the hall waiting for me. So was Aunt Daphine, Aunt Edna, Aunt Ruby Lee, Aunt Nellie, and Aunt Maggie. As soon as I stepped in, they yelled, "Surprise!"

Beyond the aunts, I saw a cluster of female cousins and other lady relatives and friends. Pink and baby blue streamers were everywhere, with matching balloons stuck in every conceivable niche. There was a table stacked high with presents wrapped in pastel-colored paper, and every available surface had some sort of party favor: miniature baby carriages, giant baby bottles and pacifiers, plush storks, and cardboard rocking horses. If it wasn't a baby shower, it was an awfully good imitation.

"Junior, were you in on this?" I said.

She just smiled. Now I knew why she was dressed so nicely.

I happily hugged everybody who came within reach: motherly Aunt Nora; tall Aunt Nellie, dressed dramatically as always; buxom, blue-eyed Aunt Ruby Lee; Aunt Edna, who'd only recently transformed from drab to vivacious; and the always smiling Aunt Daphine. Then I assured everybody that I was completely taken by surprise, and started the time-consuming process of catching up on family gossip.

We were expecting a lot of weddings over the next few years, and the family was trying to decide who'd go first: Aunt Nora's boy Thaddeous, Aunt Ruby Lee's son Clifford, or maybe Aunt Ruby Lee's daughter Ilene. Aunt Edna had a head start on all of them because she was already engaged to her beau, Caleb, and had a beautiful diamond to prove it.

Unsurprisingly, Uncle Ruben and Aunt Nellie had a new business. Their previous businesses, of which there'd been more than I could remember, had lasted an average of three months. This time they'd joined the Internet revolution. Though folks were vague on the details, it sounded to me as if they were sending spam all over the world.

Everybody told me how wonderful I looked, and asked whether I'd picked out names, and said the other things people say to pregnant women. And of course, they had to pat my tummy and compare my size to how big Vasti had been at that point of her pregnancy.

"Where is Vasti?" I asked, finally realizing we were a cousin short.

"She's running behind," Aunt Daphine said. "Bitsy slept late, and Vasti had to feed her before she could get dressed."

Talk about feeding babies reminded Aunt

Nora that I hadn't eaten yet, and even though I protested that I'd just come from lunch, she pushed me into a big armchair so she could fill up a plate for me. Obviously she believed in eating for two. She brought tiny pimento-cheese sandwiches, little country ham biscuits, carrot sticks with creamy onion dip, fruit salad, potato salad, hunks of cheese on crackers, some of the double-butter cookies I'd been hoping for, and a big glass of milk to wash it all down. Then she actually said, "Don't forget to save room for dessert."

Not wanting to hurt her feelings, I ate every smidgeon of it, and had just finished when Aunt Daphine said, "Who's ready for party games?" We spent the next hour or so playing a ludicrous assortment of games including a baby-diapering race using dolls borrowed from Sue's youngest girl; coming up with baby names using the letters from the parents' names; and the baby-bottle-sucking relay race. I'd never seen so many grown women making such fools of themselves, and I've rarely laughed so much.

When I thought nobody could hear me, I patted my tummy and said, "See all the fuss people are making over you?" Then I looked up and saw Junior grinning at me. So much for not being heard.

"I bet y'all have been playing Mozart to your belly to make the baby a genius," she said.

"We have not," I said, seeing no reason to admit that Richard had been reading Shakespeare out loud ever since I'd found out I was pregnant.

"I've seen expecting parents do sillier things," she said.

"Since when are you an expert on babies?" Junior had started helping out her daddy at the police station almost as soon as she could walk, so she hadn't worked as a babysitter like most of the girls in Byerly.

"Are you serious? I've delivered a baby, which is more than you can say."

"That's right. I haven't even gone to childbirth classes yet."

"Besides which, I've got four big sisters, and they all have kids. I've been to every one of their baby showers, and since I've got friends with babies, I've been to most of their showers, too. Do you have any idea of how many showers that makes?"

"Quite a few," I said, wondering if I'd be able to survive eating that many pieces of pastel pink-and-blue cake.

"So I've heard every old wives' tale, newfangled improvement, and cockamamie theory about babies that you can imagine."

"I had no idea. Now I understand how you did so well in the bottle-drinking contest." I only wished I had a picture of Junior sucking down apple juice through a rubber nipple.

"It's all in the way you hold the bottle," she said loftily.

"You were pretty fast with those diapers, too."

"I've had plenty of practice. But only with the girls. It's too nerve-racking with a boy. You never know when he's going to cut loose."

"I hadn't thought of that," I said, wincing. "Aunt Maggie says mine is a girl, so I'm safe."

"This time, anyway."

"This time?" I said, thinking about the five months I'd already gone through and the four still to come. "I don't even want to think about going through this again."

"You'll feel differently when you hold that baby in your arms," Aunt Nora said, bringing me another glass of milk. "You'll forget all about the stretch marks and swollen feet once you look in that little face and hold those little hands."

"Are you sure?" I asked doubtfully.

She just laughed and patted my tummy before heading back toward the kitchen.

"Junior, with all your vast experience, can you tell me why is it that everybody wants to pat my tummy?"

"To make sure you're not faking?"

I had to laugh.

We were about to start in on the stack of presents when Vasti burst in the front door, looking more than a little harried. There was a run in her stockings, she'd forgotten to put on lipstick, and her shoes didn't match her skirt. Instead of an extravagantly wrapped gift, she was carrying a wrinkled Belk's shopping bag. Motherhood was really taking its toll on my cousin.

"I'm sorry I'm late," she said, though she made it sound as if it was our fault for starting without her. "I was on the phone all morning, and Bitsy was so cranky that it took me forever to get her fed, and Grandmama was late getting to my house." She stopped just long enough to take a breath. "Then Bitsy threw up all over my dress, and I had to change into the first thing I could find."

"You look fine," Aunt Daphine said. "Come sit down and I'll get you a cup of punch."

Vasti let herself be led to the couch, and in an aggrieved tone said, "I suppose Laurie

Anne has told you all about Seth Murdstone."

No wonder she was aggravated. She wasn't worried about being beaten to the punch bowl; she was worried about being beaten to the punch with the news.

"Actually, I hadn't mentioned it," I said, trying not to smile when her face lit up. "I wasn't sure it was appropriate to talk about it at a baby shower."

Her face fell again. "Maybe I shouldn't talk about it either —"

"We've already heard the news," Aunt Nora said, "but we don't know all the details." She and Vasti looked at me hopefully.

"It's not going to bother me to talk about it," I said — especially since Junior and I had already discussed it over lunch. Besides, I was afraid that Vasti would burst if she didn't get a chance to tell the tale.

Everybody listened in as Vasti told us about Seth's death, and I was impressed that she gave such an accurate recitation of the facts. She hadn't even been there when Seth was found, and besides, she usually embroidered the facts to make a better story. Of course, knowing that several of the rest of us had been there may have kept her on the straight and narrow.

"That's awful," Aunt Ruby Lee said. "Seth was such a nice man. To have that happen in broad daylight . . ."

"Do they have any idea of who might have done it?" Aunt Nora asked.

"I talked to Mark Pope a little while ago," Vasti said. "He hasn't made any arrests yet, but he thinks it's mighty interesting that Seth was found right next to a door to the outside."

I knew Vasti was waiting for a cue, but I had to ask, "Meaning what?"

"Isn't it obvious?" Vasti asked. "Somebody came in that door, thinking there was nobody around. Must have meant to make off with whatever he could find. When he saw Seth standing there, he panicked and hit him. Or maybe Seth caught him in the act."

I looked over at Junior to see her reaction to this piece of speculation, but she avoided my eyes. "Is that the best Mark can do?" I asked. "Somebody just happened to come by — in broad daylight, like Aunt Ruby Lee said — and walked in the door at the exact moment when Seth was standing there. And he just happened to be carrying something heavy enough to hit Seth with, which he did so quickly and quietly that nobody noticed it."

"Maybe nobody heard anything because Richard was having one of his tantrums," Vasti shot back.

"Maybe," I said through gritted teeth, "but I think it's darned unlikely that a thief would be stupid enough to break into a building with all our cars parked outside."

"Then why do you think the killer came in that door?"

"Maybe he didn't come in the door."

"You don't think it was somebody in the play, do you?" Aunt Nora asked anxiously.

"I don't know," I said, "but if it was somebody from outside, Seth must have arranged to meet him there."

"What do you think, Junior?" Aunt Daphine asked.

Junior said, "Haven't you heard? I'm on vacation, so I'm not entitled to an opinion."

I think everybody was so surprised that Junior was really going to stay away from a murder investigation that nobody had anything else to say. After a minute or two of uncomfortable silence, Aunt Nora said, "I'm just sorry that it ruined your play, Vasti."

"Oh, don't be sorry," Vasti said. "The play is back on!"

"Are you serious?" I said. "There's no way the Murdstones are going to want to be in that play now."

"Yes, they are," Vasti said triumphantly. "That's part of the reason I was on the phone so long this morning."

"Vasti!" Aunt Daphine said. "You shouldn't have bothered them about a silly play at a time like this."

"I didn't bother them," she said, trying to look innocent. "I only called Florence to make a condolence call, and to see when the services were going to be. Then we got to talking about what a shame it was that the play couldn't go on now, what with it being in honor of poor Barnaby. Florence said she wished there was something she could do, but I said that of course nobody would expect her and Jake and David to take part after what had happened. Then I told her I had to go because I had to call the Shriners' Hospital. I'd promised free tickets for the show to some of the children there, and I needed to tell them they couldn't come. Well, Florence said not to say anything to them right away, and that she'd call me back in a little while."

She stopped and took a swallow of punch. "A few minutes later, Florence called back. She'd spoken to David and Jake and said that when they thought about Barnaby, they just couldn't stand to let him down. They knew that Seth would have hated to have been the cause of canceling a play in his own grandson's honor, so they decided to do their best to keep going." Seeing the expressions of everybody else in the room, Vasti added, "Naturally, we'll take time off for the funeral."

Aunt Daphine just shook her head, but she couldn't have been all that surprised. It was vintage Vasti.

"I've called everybody else in the show and they're all willing. It took a while to convince Junior's sisters that the kids would be safe, but I told them that Junior would be there and that she wouldn't let anybody else get killed. Right, Junior?"

"I'll do my best," Junior said dryly.

Vasti said, "The only folks I haven't called are y'all here at the shower, but now we're all set!"

"Haven't you forgotten something?" I asked.

"What? I called Mark Pope to make sure he was done at the recreation center so we could get back in for rehearsal this evening." She checked her watch. "You better hurry up and open your presents, Laurie Anne; I've got lots to do before then."

"What about . . . ?"

"Oh, don't worry about Richard. He's

ready and raring to go. Though he's got to do something about that temper of his."

"Vasti," I said, "we don't have anybody to play Scrooge."

She waved the objection away. "Oh, we'll find somebody."

"Who? I thought that Sally had everybody else in town committed."

"Then we'll shuffle around the people we've got. You're being a Scrooge yourself, Laurie Anne. Don't you want your husband's play to be a success?"

"Of course I do, but —" I stopped because there wasn't any real reason to argue. If anybody could produce a Scrooge out of thin air, it was Vasti.

After that, Aunt Nora steered us to opening presents, and talk turned to sleepers, booties, and rattles. It's amazing how a pair of sneakers suddenly becomes adorable when sized for a newborn. I'd never said, "Oh, how cute!" so many times in my life. The present I liked best was the bassinet I'd slept in myself. It had been freshly sanded, painted, and cushioned, and it matched perfectly the baby furniture Richard and I had picked out.

Once the presents were opened, I caught Aunt Ruby Lee cuddling the stuffed bear dressed like Sherlock Holmes that Junior had given me. She said, "You ought to put this up for yourself, as a memento. I know you're going to miss solving mysteries once the baby gets here."

"What do you mean?" Though I knew I had to take it easy while pregnant, I hadn't been worried about changes to my life after that. But Aunt Ruby Lee looked shocked, as did the other mothers nearby.

"You won't have the energy, for one," Vasti said. "You have no idea how rough night-time feedings are."

"And forget about spare time, especially if you keep working," my cousin Sue put in. "By the time you put the baby to bed, and maybe clean up a little, you're not going to want to do anything but sleep."

"You and Linwood must do something other than sleep," Ilene said with a giggle, "or you wouldn't have but the one kid!"

Everybody laughed at that, but even though I joined in, I felt unhappy. Was it really going to be that bad?

Aunt Nora must have realized what I was thinking. She put an arm around me and said, "Don't you worry. You know Vasti and Sue always make things out to sound worse than they are. Your life isn't going to change that much."

"Did things stay pretty much the same for

you and Uncle Buddy when y'all started having babies?" I asked.

"Lord, Laurie Anne, that was so long ago I can hardly remember," she said with a laugh. "Sure, the boys kept me busy, but I knew then they wouldn't be little forever, and once they got big enough, I'd be able to do whatever I wanted to."

"How big is big enough?" I asked. Richard and I liked going to movies, and to plays, and to all kinds of places. Were we going to have to put all of that on hold until the baby hit high school? What if we had another baby? How many years would that add to our sentence?

"Now don't get yourself worked up," Aunt Nora said. "Look at Vasti. She's still doing what she likes to do."

"True." Of course, she didn't work full-time, and goodness knows the play wasn't up to her usual standards.

"What are you two looking so serious about?" Aunt Daphine asked.

"Laurie Anne's worried that she won't have any time to herself once the baby shows up," Aunt Nora said.

"Y'all are the ones who said I wouldn't be able to do the things I've been doing," I objected.

"You don't mean messing with killers, do

you?" Aunt Daphine said. "Why would you want to do that once you've got a baby?"

Now they were making it sound as if my helping people in trouble had been a twisted replacement for motherhood. "All I'm saying is that I don't see why having a baby will change everything. I'm going to be the same person, aren't I?"

"Of course you are," Aunt Daphine said. "It's just that you're going to be a lot busier than you are now. Your priorities are going to be different."

"So other than me having no time to sleep or do what I like to do, and suddenly having a completely different set of goals, everything will be the same. Is that right?"

My two aunts looked at each other uneasily. Aunt Nora said, "You knew things were going to change once you had a baby, didn't you? You and Richard did plan this baby."

"Of course we did, and we knew things were going to be different." I looked down at my tummy, thinking how Richard had said that the play might be his last chance to direct for a long time. "I guess I'm just starting to realize how different. I'm not sure I'm up to it." Despite myself, my eyes started to tear.

The two of them converged on me in a double hug.

"Don't even think that!" Aunt Daphine said. "You're going to be a wonderful mama."

"You bet you are," Aunt Nora said, nodding vigorously. "You're just tired out from all the excitement. Carrying a baby is hard on a body, you know. Vasti says she read that when you're pregnant, just sitting down is as much work as climbing a mountain when you're not."

Aunt Daphine said, "My moods were up and down the whole time I was pregnant with Vasti — that's all that's happening with you."

"Pregnant women worry about everything, especially the first time," Aunt Nora said. "You just need something to take your mind off yourself."

Aunt Daphine snapped her fingers. "I know just the thing! What about Seth's murder? You've got one last chance to go after a killer!" She said it the way you'd suggest a trip to the park to a bored child during summer vacation, but before I could complain, Aunt Nora broke in.

"I don't know if that's a good idea, what with Laurie Anne being as far along as she is."

"She's made it through the first trimester, which is the worst time," Aunt Daphine

100

pointed out, "and she'll have Richard with her to make sure she stays out of trouble."

"But Daphine, Richard is going to be busy with the play!"

"That's right. What about Thaddeous? Laurie Anne said he was a big help when he was in Boston."[6]

Aunt Nora shook her head. "Don't you remember? He's gone to Boston with Michelle to visit her family and won't be back until Christmas morning."

The two of them turned toward me as if I were a particularly sticky problem they had to solve, but they still didn't bother to ask what I thought. I was trying to come up with a polite way to tell them to mind their own business when Junior walked up.

"How are y'all doing?" she asked, far too innocently. I'd lay odds that she'd heard our entire conversation.

"Junior?" Aunt Nora said, looking at Aunt Daphine.

"Junior!" Aunt Daphine replied, nodding.

"Yes?" Junior said, looking from one to the other.

Aunt Nora said, "Junior, you're just the person we want to talk to. Seth Murdstone's killing might be Laurie Anne's last chance

[6] *Country Comes to Town*

101

to solve a murder for a while, but Richard's going to be busy with the play, and in her condition, she doesn't need to be running around on her own. We were thinking that you and she could work together on this one, seeing as you're on vacation."

Junior pretended to consider it. "I'm supposed to be keeping an eye on my nieces and nephews. . . ."

"That's no problem; the triplets can help. Those children are as good as gold anyway."

"It might work," Junior said, rubbing her chin. "If it's all right with Laurie Anne, I'd be glad to help out."

"Of course it's all right," Aunt Nora said, beaming. "Doesn't that make you feel better, Laurie Anne?"

"Much better," I said. I don't know if the smile on my face looked at all real, because I was steaming on the inside.

The two aunts went to tell Idelle, Odelle, and Carlelle what they'd just committed them to, and once they were out of earshot, I said, "Junior, did you put them up to this?"

"Not me," she said, still trying to look innocent.

"Can you believe this? First they say I won't be able to do this anymore. Then they decide I can, but only this one last time and only if I have a chaperon. Since when does being pregnant mean that I don't get to make my own decisions?"

"They're just worried about you."

"I know that, but it's still aggravating."

"Families are like that. So don't feel like you have to tackle this if you don't feel up to it."

"Of course I feel up to it," I snapped. "I'm pregnant, not an invalid." I knew I was contradicting what I'd said to Junior over lunch, but I was too mad to care.

"That's fine," Junior said. "Of course, you don't have to work with me. I'll come up with an excuse for your aunts, and you can go ahead on your own."

"Come on, Junior, maybe you didn't orchestrate this with my aunts, but you sure as heck laid the groundwork. If I don't let you in on this, I'll never hear the end of it — from them or you."

"That's true." She grinned, abandoning all pretense of innocence.

I glared at her. Of course it was a good idea. Even if I hadn't been pregnant, it wouldn't have been smart to go asking possibly dangerous questions without backup, and with Richard back at work on the play, Junior was the best candidate around. It could even be fun to work with her; goodness knows we'd worked *against* each other

Surely I owed her the same. "No, Junior, I wouldn't back out."

"Then let's leave it at that."

"Okay," I said, and I stuck out my hand. "Partners?"

Junior gave my hand a firm shake. "Partners."

CHAPTER NINE

I would have liked to corner Aunt Nora then. Since she'd pushed me so hard, the least she could do was provide gossip on Seth and his family. But the shower was winding down, so everybody pitched in to load the presents into Aunt Maggie's battered Dodge Caravan. Of course, Aunt Nora couldn't resist sending along enough leftovers to feed a small army. Or one pregnant Burnette, I thought to myself as I snagged another deviled egg. Maybe my child was going to be born up North, but I was going to do my best to make sure she ate like a Southerner.

Richard met Aunt Maggie and me at the door, smiling widely.

"You knew about the shower, didn't you?" I said accusingly.

"Of course," he said as we started unloading the car. "But that's not why I'm so happy. Have you heard the good news?"

"That the play's back on?" I asked. "Vasti couldn't wait to tell us. But what are you going to do about Scrooge?"

"I'm not sure," he admitted. "Vasti seems to think it will work out."

"Vasti assumes things will work out because she can't imagine the world spinning in any direction other than hers."

"Generally speaking, she's right."

I had to admit that he had a point.

Once everything was inside, naturally I had to show it all off to him. He admired everything, but then he said, "Laura, do we need all this stuff for one little baby?"

"Are you kidding? There's more stuff being shipped up North, and Vasti said this isn't nearly as much as she got at her baby shower."

"How kind of her to point it out," Richard said. "Are we going to fit it into the new place?"

"We'll manage. By the way, I've got some other news for you." I explained how Junior and I had decided to tackle Seth's murder.

"I must admit that I assumed you'd be going after Seth's killer sooner or later," he said when I was finished.

"Why does everybody think I'm dying to go after every killer that comes around?"

"Why won't you admit that you like it?"

Richard countered. "You don't even admit it to me."

"I don't like . . ." In all honesty, I had to stop. "Okay, maybe I do like it. At least, I get some sort of satisfaction out of it. That's weird, isn't it?"

"No more so than for cops and private eyes to get satisfaction out of their work."

"They get paid for it."

"Lots of people enjoy things they don't get paid for. My directing this play is a case in point."

"I guess." For a minute I wondered why I liked chasing killers so much, and then I wondered why liking it bothered me.

Richard said, "Anyway, I'm glad you're not going at it alone."

"Why's that?" I said, tensing. If Richard said one word about my not being able to handle it while I was pregnant, I was going to have a mood swing that would turn his hair white.

"Because with the play back on, I'm not going to be able to do research or run around and question people with you."

"Don't you think I could work alone?"

"You probably could, but I wouldn't be able to concentrate on the play if you were." Before I could take offense, he added, "No more than you could concentrate if I were working without backup."

"True enough."

"And if the killer is in the cast or crew, I want a competent set of eyes keeping watch. Having two competent sets of eyes is even better."

As usual, he'd given exactly the right answers. If having an undiscovered killer in Byerly worried me, having one locked in a recreation center with my husband and various members of my family made me downright nervous. "That's me, the defender of the innocent," I said more lightly than I felt.

"I don't know that I'm exactly innocent," he said, putting his hand on my tummy, "but Laura, you can defend me anytime."

We cuddled for a few minutes after that. It's more awkward to cuddle when you're five months pregnant, but just as much fun.

Richard said, "You and Junior working together . . . Oh, to be a fly on the wall."

"Why do you say that?" I said. "I think we'll be a good team."

"If you don't kill each other."

"We're not the ones who've been throwing tantrums."

"Touché. But you two are strong-willed women."

"Since when are strong-willed women a problem?"

"When both of them are trying to be in charge. I can't picture Junior blithely following your lead, and I'm sure you won't follow anybody's but your own."

"I'm not sure how it's going to work either," I said. "I just wanted to make sure you weren't going to make any jokes about cat fights or hormones."

"What kind of sexist pig do you think I am?"

"No kind at all," I said, "or I'd never have let you knock me up."

"That's better," he said, mollified.

We cuddled a while longer, but when I caught Richard peeking at the wall clock, I realized that it was nearly time to head to rehearsal. We both had work to do.

CHAPTER TEN

It was a subdued crowd that night at the recreation center, and I saw more than one person sneaking glances at the door to the hallway where Seth had been killed. Still, it looked as if Vasti really had convinced everybody to come back. Admittedly, everybody jumped every time there was a loud noise, but they were there.

I'd expected Junior's nieces and nephews to be nervous, but they seemed fine. I didn't know if it was because death didn't mean as much to them at their age, or if having a deputy, a police chief, and several former police chiefs in the family had given them a different viewpoint. Instead, it was Sarah Gamp who showed the most strain, but then again, she'd been the one to find Seth's body. I thought it was awfully brave of her to come back at all.

Unless . . . Hadn't I read that the person to find a body is frequently involved? I tried to remember how long Mrs. Gamp had been gone when she went looking for Seth. Surely she'd had enough time to bludgeon him to death, and it wouldn't have taken her but a minute to hide the weapon. Then all she would have had to do is scream for help and pretend to be upset. Heck, she would probably have been upset if she'd just killed a man.

I didn't know why she would have wanted to kill Seth, but then again, I didn't know why anybody would have wanted to. Somebody had, so why not Mrs. Gamp? That's when I noticed Junior standing by my chair.

"Checking out the field?" she said as she sat down next to me.

"Just speculating," I said, a little embarrassed for suspecting a little old lady.

Richard hopped up onto the stage, and once everybody quieted down, he said, "The show must go on. We've all heard that. The show must go on." He paused, making eye contact with various people. "The fact is, the show doesn't have to go on. As much as I love the theater, there are countless good reasons to cancel a performance. The loss we've had is as strong a reason as I've ever known." He nodded at the Murdstones. "Yet every one of you has decided to get past that loss, to come back in here to do the job you promised to do. For that I applaud you." He actually clapped, and when he said, "Now applaud yourselves," darned if we didn't join in, even the Murdstones. As the sound started to dwindle, he said, "I hope you all get used to that sound, because that's what you're going to be hearing on opening night."

"This is almost as much fun as one of his tantrums," Junior whispered, but I shushed her. I'd sat in on enough of Richard's lectures to know he was a good teacher, and I'd seen him on stage so I knew he was a decent actor, but this was the first time I realized that he would have made a dandy preacher.

Then David Murdstone stood up. "Richard, may I say something?"

"Of course."

David turned to face the room. "I know some of you are surprised that Jake, Florence, and I are here tonight. Quite frankly, it was very difficult to come back. But this is what Dad would have wanted. He loved his grandson Barnaby, as did we all, and honoring him this way was extremely important to him. So for Dad's sake, and for Barnaby's, we decided to go on. In their names, thank you for being here with us."

There was no applause as David sat down,

but there were some wet eyes.

"Thank you, David," Richard said. "Now I won't lie to you people. We have a monumental task in front of us. Not only have we suffered the personal loss of Seth, we've also lost our leading man. If we're going to continue, we have to find another actor willing to take on the role of Scrooge."

There were murmurs and people looking around the room. As for me, I glared at Vasti. She'd implied that finding another Scrooge would be easy; now it was time for her to pull a rabbit out of her hat. Unfortunately, from the expression on her face, she was fresh out of rabbits.

"Why don't you do it, Richard?" Carlelle said. "I bet you've got all the lines memorized already."

I could tell he was flattered, but Vasti burst in. "Oh, no, you don't! We need Richard right where he is."

"Vasti's right," Richard said. "Directing you people is more than enough work for me."

"What about Sid? Or Oliver?" Tim asked.

Sid shook his head vigorously. "I couldn't do that. I've got all I can do to remember my own lines." I'm sure Richard was relieved. The roly-poly man was perfectly cast as the Spirit of Christmas Present, but he was a worse fit for Scrooge than Seth had been.

Oliver Jarndyce, who mangled his lines terribly, stood up eagerly, and I was sure I saw Richard flinch. "I'd be happy to jump in," he said. I had to wonder if he'd be as eager once he realized he wasn't going to be able to wear his reddish-brown toupee for the role.

"That's generous of you, Oliver," Richard said, "but that would still leave us with a hole in the cast. We need a Spirit of Christmas Past."

Oliver started to say something else, but Aunt Maggie piped up, using that tone of voice that carries over and through other voices. "What about Big Bill? He's been training for the part of Scrooge for years."

There were laughs, but to give Big Bill credit, he joined in.

"But he's already got a part, too," Oliver said indignantly. "He's Marley's ghost."

"True," Richard said. "Of course, Marley is a small role; somebody else could double up."

Oliver brightened up again. "In that case, perhaps I could —"

"Why not let Pete Fredericks play Marley?" Idelle said. "He doesn't have any lines as the Spirit of Christmas Yet to Come, and

115

you can't see his face in the robe I made him, so nobody will know he's doubling up."

There was agreement from everybody but Oliver. All he seemed able to manage was, "But . . . but . . ."

Richard took pity on him. "Oliver, if you're really willing to take on another part . . ."

"Anything!" Oliver said.

"Vasti only cast one charity collector, but generally two are used. There aren't any additional lines, but —"

"I'll do it!" Oliver said, and he sat down, looking quite pleased with himself.

"Then we have our cast. Big Bill, I realize you'll have to work from a script tonight, but —"

"Actually," Big Bill said, "before I agree to the part, I have one condition."

"Oh?" Richard said. He looked concerned, and Vasti looked downright panic-striken.

"As some of you may know, I've been trying to regain the affections of this lady here." Big Bill put his hand on Aunt Maggie's shoulder, and she promptly pushed it off again. "If she agrees to go out to dinner with me, I'll play Scrooge."

"Oh for pity's sake," Aunt Maggie said, "are you that desperate for a date?"

He didn't answer, just smiled.

Aunt Maggie could see that everybody was looking at her, and in Vasti's and Richard's case, they were staring beseechingly. "I suppose one dinner couldn't hurt anything," she finally said.

"One dinner for each curtain call," Big Bill persisted.

She rolled her eyes, but said, "All right, one dinner for each curtain call, whatever that is. But don't expect me to dress up!"

"Maggie, you look fetching no matter what you wear."

Aunt Maggie snorted particularly loudly.

Big Bill turned back to Richard and said, "Mr. Director, I accept the role with pleasure." For the second time that night there was applause.

Richard brought Big Bill onto the stage so they could discuss the part, and the other people either mingled or started work on whatever it was they were doing for the play. That meant that it was as good a time as any for Junior and me to get going. Only when we turned around, Mark Pope was standing right behind us. I hadn't even realized he was in the building; he must have come in during Richard's pep talk.

"Hey there, Mark," Junior said.

"Junior," he said. "I'm kind of surprised to see all of y'all here. When Mrs. Bumgar-

117

ner called about my releasing the crime scene, I thought she just wanted a chance for everybody to get their belongings, but now I hear that y'all are going through with this thing after all."

"Apparently so."

"Do you think that's a good idea? A man was murdered here."

"It's not my decision," she said. "Besides, I heard that you decided it was a burglar who killed Seth, and no sneak thief would come back here now." She lifted one eyebrow. "Or have you changed your mind?"

"I haven't closed the investigation yet," Mark said stiffly.

"Then I guess it's a good thing you're here to protect us."

"What about you?"

"You said you wanted to handle this case on your own — you go ahead and handle it."

"And Mrs. Fleming?" Mark asked.

"What about her?"

"Is she planning to interfere in my investigation?"

"What Mrs. Fleming does is her own business," Junior said firmly.

"Not if she hinders a police investigation."

"She's never hindered an investigation in

118

Byerly before. I don't expect her to start now."

Mark looked at me suspiciously, but all I did was smile. Though I didn't like being talked about as if I weren't there, I thought I'd do better to stay out of the conversation.

Mark must have realized that he wasn't going to get anything else out of us, because he nodded and said, "I think I'll take another look outside."

"Keep an eye out for sneak thieves," Junior said. "Or maybe you can catch that practical joker that's been bothering us."

He stiffened but didn't answer as he left.

Once I was sure he was out of earshot, I said, "Junior, what in the Sam Hill is going on?"

"What do you mean?"

"Since when does Mark talk to you like that, and since when do you put up with it?"

"Remember what you said at your aunt's house today? About your not backing out even if there was something I couldn't tell you?"

I didn't like it, but I said, "I remember. But let me get this straight: we're not telling Mark we're investigating?"

"Right."

"Even though he's going to figure it out soon enough?"

"That's right."

I looked at her, hoping she'd tell me something more. She didn't. So I said, "Well, if we're going to interfere in a police investigation, let's get going."

CHAPTER ELEVEN

"What do we do first?" Junior asked.

"What would you do if you were officially on the case?" I countered. Despite what Junior had said about wanting to see me in action, I was feeling a little self-conscious about working with an actual police officer.

"I'd examine the crime scene. Which Mark has released, if you want to take a look."

I didn't, but it was the logical place to start. "Let's go." As Junior and I made our way to the hallway, I saw Mark watching us with a frown on his face. Junior saw him too, but she didn't say anything as she pulled the last scrap of yellow crime-scene tape off the door.

The hall was empty. I suspected the rest of the cast was avoiding that part of the building. I would have too, given a choice. Other than Seth's body being gone, it looked pretty much the same as it had the day before. Thankfully, somebody had cleaned up the stains on the floor.

"Can I safely assume that you looked around while waiting for Mark to show up?" I asked.

Junior just grinned.

"So what exactly do you look for in a crime scene?"

"Anything I can find," she said, "though most of what I find doesn't mean a thing. In this case, I didn't have much time. I didn't want to move Seth's body around before the coroner got here, but I did make sure there was nothing under him that wasn't supposed to be there. Then I looked around for a murder weapon, but couldn't find one or even a good place to hide one. I was starting to think about how the killer got into and out of the hall when Mark showed up."

"Did you come to any conclusions?"

"Not a one."

There were six doors leading from the hallway: one to the auditorium, four to other rooms, and one to the outside. I looked longingly at the door leading outside. Despite what I'd said to Vasti at my baby shower, I really hoped the killer had come through that door. Though I knew it would make investigating a lot harder, I preferred that to having to suspect somebody I knew. "Was the back door unlocked?"

"Yes, though that doesn't tell us much. The smokers in the cast had been coming in and out all day, so it was left unlocked. I locked up after we found Seth, to make sure nobody could sneak in behind me."

"Was there any sign of anybody coming in that way?"

"Mark didn't tell me."

I just looked at her.

"Okay, I took a peek, but I didn't see anything that would help. There were a lot of cigarette butts on the ground, but none of them were still burning. It's all paved out there, so there couldn't be any footprints, and there was no blood trail or sign of a murder weapon. We could go look again, but the forensic people have been all over it, so there's not going to be anything left."

"Let's not bother." Next I tried to remember exactly where Seth's body had been.

Junior said, "The door wasn't what hit him, if that's what you're thinking."

"Just a thought." I had another one. "If Seth was there," I said, pointing, "doesn't that mean that he was between the door and the killer?"

"That's how it looks," Junior said, "but the killer could have walked past him and turned around. Why?"

"I was just wondering about these other rooms. Did you look in them?"

"Just to make sure there was nobody hiding in there, so it wouldn't hurt to look again."

The first two doors had hand-printed signs identifying them as "Men's Dressing Room" and "Women's Dressing Room"; the third was being used to store props and scenery flats; and the fourth was tiny — barely big enough for the sink and cleaning equipment it held.

"All of the windows are intact," Junior said.

"The locks have been painted shut," I added, looking them over. "Nobody came in or out that way. What about the kitchen?" The door that led from the auditorium to the kitchen was just a few feet away from the door to the hallway.

But Junior shook her head. "I looked in there the first day of rehearsal to make sure there wasn't anything in there my nieces and nephews could get into. There's an emergency exit, but it's got an alarm on it. All the windows are the louvered kind; they're not big enough for anybody to get through."

I looked up at the solid ceiling. "No way

124

to get through the roof."

"Not without a wrecking ball," Junior agreed.

"That means that whoever it was either came from outside or through the auditorium." I was still hoping to blame somebody from the outside if I could come up with something halfway reasonable. "Are we both agreed that Mark's idea of a sneak thief is completely bogus?"

"Do you even have to ask?" Junior said dryly. "I'll admit there are some pretty dumb criminals out there, but I don't think that we have any that dumb running around in Byerly."

"Seth could have set up a meeting with somebody, and told him to come to the door."

"I suppose, but I don't see how Seth could have known he was going to be free at that particular moment. He would have still been on stage if Richard hadn't thrown that tantrum."

"Could he have provoked Richard just to make sure he was free?"

Junior just looked at me.

"Never mind. Still, it's possible he set something up."

"Or another cast member could have gone outside and come back in again."

"Good point," though I wasn't thrilled about more evidence pointing to the cast. "I suppose it's theoretically possible that somebody snuck in the front door. . . ."

"Without anybody noticing?" Junior said skeptically.

"You're right; I don't believe it, either." I wasn't happy about it, but I was going to have to face facts. "So it does look like the killer was somebody involved with the play."

"That's what I think, unless we find something to point us in another direction," Junior said.

With that decided, I moved on. "Was there anything about Seth's body I should know?"

"Just what you already know: he was hit over the head with something. I'm no medical examiner, but it looks to me like it was long, like a bar or a stick, rather than round like a ball or square like a brick. Whatever it was, the killer probably brought it with him, because there wasn't anything that would fit the bill in the hallway beforehand or afterward."

"Then Mark hasn't found the murder weapon?"

"I don't think so, but I don't know for sure. Not only is he not telling me anything; he's doing all the work himself so even Trey doesn't know anything."

"Rats!" I'd been hoping we could use Junior's little brother as a source of information.

"Laurie Anne, you're going to have to stop using such strong language after the baby comes."

"Don't start, Junior," I said. "So we've examined the scene, and we've learned absolutely nothing. What would you do next?"

"Normally I'd have witness statements, and possibly the autopsy report. Had any physical evidence been found, I'd usually have more information on that."

"It must be nice to have so much to work with."

"How do you manage without it?"

I carefully kept my face straight. "Oh, I usually break into your office at night and take a peek at the files. Or hack into your computer and get the information."

She blinked. "Are you serious?"

"Of course I'm not serious," I said, laughing. "If I can't get it from you, I do without."

She relaxed. "Lord, you scared me there for a minute."

"Though if you want me to hack into Mark's computer —"

"I'd just as soon you didn't."

"Suit yourself."

"As I was saying, I'd have a lot of information to go through, but I'm not sure that any of it would help in this case. Maybe I don't have the autopsy report, but I was there when the doctor gave his preliminary opinion that Seth died from a blow to the head — possibly in combination with a bad heart — and I know about when he died. Whoever hit him did it from the front and was right-handed. It was a hard blow, but not so hard that any adult couldn't have done it."

"That lets your nieces and nephews out."

"I was kind of leaving them off the list, anyway," she said. "I don't think there was any useful trace evidence. No muddy footprints or blood drops or anything like that. Any fingerprints on the walls and door knob and such would be meaningless, because so many people have gone up and down that hall."

"If there were anything obvious, Mark would have made an arrest by now."

"I would hope so. Now, I haven't talked to everybody who was here when Seth was killed, but I've talked to enough of them to know that everybody was moving around so much that we can't rule out anybody as the killer."

"Except Richard."

"Right. He was on the stage pretty much the whole day, except when he stomped outside, and Vasti was watching y'all then because she was afraid he was going to leave. But the rest of us were milling around like ants on an anthill. There's not a single alibi that would hold up."

"Wonderful."

"It's not that bad. It would be better if we could eliminate some of the possibilities, but I do hate playing the alibi game. Who left where when, and whose watch is set fast, and all that mess. What we've got is this: nobody knows exactly when Seth came down this hall, and that means that pretty much anybody in the building could have come after him."

"Great."

"Though I'm assuming that you're in the clear, too."

"Thanks," I said. "I'll return the favor. While we're at it, I'd just as soon we leave the rest of my family off the list."

"I can go along with that. That leaves us with everybody else in the cast and crew."

"I guess we should be grateful that the cast isn't any bigger than it is. So, having exhausted all your reports, what would you do next?"

"I'd go talk to the folks who knew the

victim: his family, friends, neighbors, and so on. So I'd start with the Murdstones."

"What if they won't talk to you?"

"Laurie Anne, I'm chief of police. People talk to me, or I'll know the reason why."

"That definitely gives you an advantage," I said. "People can blow me off anytime they want to, and they don't have to give me a reason. So I start by talking to people who will talk to me, and hope that they know something about the victim."

"What if they don't?"

"I talk to somebody else. Eventually I find somebody who both knows something and will talk to me."

Junior looked doubtful and I didn't blame her. "What can I say? It's haphazard, but it's worked before."

"That it has. Since I'm just a citizen this time around, we'll try it your way. I take it this means we won't be talking to the Murdstones right off."

"Lord, no. They've just had a murder in the family. I wouldn't want to intrude at a time like this."

"What if one of them is the killer?"

"Then I don't want to talk to them before I know more." We left the hall and went back into the auditorium, where I surveyed the prospects. Aunt Nora and Aunt Daphine were usually my best sources of gossip, but neither of them was there. Vasti knew lots of gossip too, but she got as much wrong as she got right. "Let's go talk to the triplets," I finally decided. "They've been around the rehearsals long enough to have gotten a feel for everybody."

"I'll just listen in if that's all right."

"Richard usually takes notes for me."

She didn't say anything, but the look she gave me was answer enough.

"Okay, we'll skip the notes," I said.

Idelle, Odelle, and Carlelle had taken over a corner of the auditorium for their costumes and sewing equipment, with a long rack to hang clothes on. When Junior and I got there, Idelle was consulting a stack of papers on a clipboard while Odelle pulled a coat off the rack and Carlelle put together a stack of shoes, socks, and other garments.

Odelle held a tattered morning coat up for her sisters to see. "We're going to have to completely remake this."

Carlelle threw her hands up. "When am I supposed to do with that?"

"Problems?" I asked.

"Hey, Laurie Anne, Junior," Idelle said, looking up from her clipboard. "We just realized how much work it's going to be to make Scrooge's costume fit Big Bill."

131

"I hadn't thought about that," I admitted. Seth had been a big man, in height and in girth. Big Bill, despite his nickname, was shorter and much trimmer, which was why he looked so good in blue jeans.

"And we're going to have to come up with a whole new costume for Oliver to be a collector," Odelle said.

"That's right," Idelle said, flipping furiously through her papers. "It's all well and good for Richard to hand out parts like they were candy; he doesn't have to dress everybody!"

"Vasti told me y'all were renting costumes," I said.

Idelle rolled her eyes. "Don't get us started! We ordered from Morris's Costumes in Charlotte, and don't you know it took some sweet-talking! Do you know how many productions of *A Christmas Carol* there are at this time of year? But they promised us they'd get them to us — even claimed it was the last available set in the state. Only the costumes never showed up."

"Personally, I think they took something under the table to rent them to somebody else," Odelle put in.

"I wouldn't be surprised," Idelle said. "In the meantime, they're claiming the costumes were delivered, and even faxed us a copy of the signature of the person who signed for them. It's completely illegible, so it wasn't one of us."

I nodded sympathetically. Everybody knew that the triplets had beautiful hand-writing. I'd gotten them to address the invitations to my wedding.

"So with us going round and round with them, we decided to bite the bullet and make the costumes ourselves," Odelle said. "Which wasn't as bad as it could have been because we'd already planned to make some of them."

"Easy for you to say," Carlelle grumbled as she started picking at the seams in Scrooge's coat. "You're not the one doing the sewing."

"Who was it who spent half a day with a glue gun putting chains on Jacob Marley's costume?" Odelle retorted.

Then the three of them stared at one another in horror. "Marley! We've got to redo his costume, too!"

Idelle frantically consulted her list. "Maybe not. Pete Fredericks is only a little smaller around than Big Bill. We can pin him in if we have to."

"Maybe we won't even have to do that!" Carlelle said excitedly. "He's dead, isn't he? His clothes should be hanging on him."

"You're right!" Idelle said.

"What about the length on the pants?" Odelle wanted to know. "He's a couple of inches taller than Big Bill."

Carlelle's face fell again.

"Can you fray the hems?" I suggested. "If you've got enough threads hanging loose, people won't be able to tell it's too short."

"That might do it," Idelle said speculatively. "Odelle, go get Pete to try on the pants and see if it will work." While one sister rushed off, the other two went back to their respective lists and sewing.

"I had no idea that doing the costumes was so much work," I said.

"It wouldn't be so bad if we were doing something modern," Idelle said. "Sally Hendon's show is all contemporary costumes. They're buying most of them off the rack. We had to do research on Victorian clothes, and figure out what colors we could use, track down patterns, and all kinds of trouble. Plus making everything from scratch."

"Which would be a whole lot easier if I could use my sewing machine when I need to," Carlelle said, glaring up at the stage. "But every time I get going good, Richard makes me stop because I'm disturbing his concentration."

I really didn't want to have to apologize for my husband again, so I sidestepped the issue. "Why don't y'all use one of the back rooms so the noise won't bother anybody?"

"We tried that," Idelle said. "But after *somebody* wadded up a stack of costumes that I'd just finished ironing, and *somebody* hid every cotton picking spool of thread so we couldn't find them for an hour, we decided to keep our things out here where we can keep an eye on them."

"That prankster is getting pretty bad," I said. "Any idea of who it could be?"

Idelle shook her head. "If we did, we'd have a word or two with him. I like fun as much as the next person, but we don't have time for this!"

"You sure don't," I said sympathetically. "Is there anything I can do to help?" Admittedly, I was doing well to sew on a button, but surely there was something suitable for unskilled labor.

"Aren't you sweet to ask?" Idelle said. "But don't you worry about us. You know doing something like this isn't any fun unless we fuss about it. Aunt Daphine, Aunt Edna, and Aunt Nora have volunteered to come over to our place tonight and finish up the sewing."

"Besides," Carlelle said, "don't y'all have

135

another project?" She looked at us significantly.

"We were hoping y'all would be too distracted with the play to notice," I said.

"Laurie Anne, you've been living up North too long if you believe that."

"I said we were hoping, not that we believed it." I wasn't really surprised. It's not like a five months pregnant woman and a police chief aren't noticeable. Besides, the triplets had been at the baby shower, and I was sure that everybody there knew what we were up to.

"Assuming that y'all didn't come over here just to chat, what do you want to know?" Carlelle said.

"Are you sure you're not too busy?" I asked.

"Lord, Laurie Anne, I can sew in my sleep; sewing and talking at the same time is nothing."

"Good enough." I pulled a chair over next to Carlelle's, and Junior did the same. "I want to know about the Murdstones. You must have seen a lot of them since the show started. Starting with Seth."

Carlelle said, "I spent right much time with him when I was working on his costume. I liked him, too. He was an awfully nice man — friendly and easy to talk to."

136

"What did y'all talk about?"

"This and that. He was a bit of a flirt, to tell you the truth, though I think he'd have passed out from shock if I'd taken him up on it."

"What about his business?"

"You know he makes porch chairs and little tables to go with them? I was thinking about getting a set for Mama and Daddy's anniversary, and he said he'd do them for me for nothing. Isn't that sweet? Only I'd have to let him know right away, because he was thinking of retiring soon."

"How come? He wasn't that old, was he?"

"He turned sixty-four in June," Junior said.

"I guess that's nearly retirement age," I said, "but so many people work later these days. He must have done well to have put away enough money to retire early."

"He talked like he did," Idelle said, "but I imagine the real reason was because of what happened to his grandson. I think Seth blamed himself."

"I thought it was an accident," I said.

"It was, but Seth said he'd told Jake that old space heater wasn't safe to use around an active boy like Barnaby. He said he should have tossed it out himself before anything could happen. Besides, Seth was the only adult there when it happened. He and Jake shared a house, with Seth upstairs and Jake and Barnaby downstairs.

"Anyway, Seth heard Barnaby scream, and ran down and found him. Then he panicked. He realized afterward that he should have called an ambulance, but all he could think of was getting the boy to the hospital. So he wrapped him up in a blanket, put him in the truck, and took off for Hickory."

"Would it have made any difference if he'd called the ambulance?" I asked.

"Not a bit," Idelle said, "and Seth knew that, but he said he kept going over and over it all in his head, thinking that he could have done something to save the boy."

I could understand that; I'd spent plenty of late nights replaying mistakes in my head. At least none of mine had ever led to a child's death. Then I put my hand on my tummy, wondering what mistakes I would make with the baby.

"What about Jake?" I asked. "He's the one who left his nine-year-old son alone with a dangerous space heater."

"He didn't know the heater wasn't safe," Carlelle objected, "and he wouldn't have left Barnaby if Seth hadn't been there. Seth said he tried to get Barnaby to come upstairs with him, but Barnaby was playing computer games and didn't want to. Nobody could have known that would happen."

"I suppose not," I said.

"Poor Jake was so torn up about it," Idelle said. "The little fellow didn't die right away, you know. He was in the hospital for nearly a week, suffering. Mrs. Gamp volunteers up there, and she said he was just the bravest thing she ever saw. They thought he was going to make it, but he got an infection and that's really what killed him. It was just terrible."

I nodded, resolving never to leave my child alone or own a space heater. Then, eager to change the subject, I said, "Jake and Seth must have gotten along well to have worked together and lived in the same house."

"They seemed to," Carlelle said.

But Idelle added, "Most of the time, anyway. I saw them going at it one time last week."

"What were they arguing about?" I asked.

"I wasn't close enough to hear much of it," she said, sounding regretful, "but I think it was something to do with business. Seth said something about local competition, and Jake said they couldn't afford to just give everything up. It didn't last long, and they seemed all right the next day, so it must not have been all that serious."

"What would Jake have done if Seth had retired?" I said. "For that matter, what will he do now that Seth is gone?"

Carlelle said, "I would think he'd keep the business going, since that's the only job he's got, but I don't really know."

Though killing one's father to gain ownership of a chair company didn't seem like a compelling motive to me, it might look different from Jake's perspective. Or had they been arguing about moonshine and not chairs? "Seth didn't seem bothered by anything from what I saw of him. Did he say anything to y'all about being worried, or being in danger?"

The two sisters looked at one another, then shook their heads.

"What about David and Seth?" I asked. "Did they get along?"

"I guess," Carlelle said hesitantly.

"But?" I prompted.

"It's not like I saw them fighting, but they were awfully different. David being in business and being married to Florence Easterly and all. He's so serious, and Seth was so funny. Listening to the two of them together was like listening to two acquaintances talking, not a father and son. They didn't seem to have much in common."

"Same planet, different worlds," I said.

Sometimes I felt that way myself. Goodness knows I'd led a very different life from the rest of my family. Not only was I the first Burnette to go to college; I was the first to move up North and the first to marry a Yankee. There'd been a time when I wasn't close to any of my relatives, and it had taken work on all of our parts to get over that. It was a shame that Seth and David weren't going to have that chance.

I looked at Junior to see if she had any other questions, but she shook her head. So I thanked Idelle and Carlelle for their help and left them to their costumes.

CHAPTER TWELVE

"I don't get it, Junior," I said. "Killing Seth was like killing Santa Claus."

"Seth wasn't a saint, Laurie Anne, and Santa Claus doesn't run a still."

"I know, but it still seems nuts to me."

I was trying to decide who to talk to next when the door opened and a woman came in. Her hair was platinum blond and permed, and though the coat slung over one arm was navy blue, everything else she had on was the same shade of pink: skirt, blouse, purse, even her boots. It had been a while since I'd seen Sally Hendon, but a color scheme like that was impossible to forget.

"It's true!" she exclaimed in a voice loud enough to draw the attention of everybody in the room. "I didn't believe it, but it's true."

Vasti dropped whatever project she'd been supervising and rushed over to stand in front of Sally, her hands on her hips. "What do *you* want?" she demanded.

"Vasti, aren't you looking well? How's that baby of yours? How can you *stand* to leave her alone? I'd have thought you'd want to spend as much of her first Christmas season with her as you could."

Vasti refused to rise to the bait. "What are you doing here, Sally? I thought you had a show to put on."

Sally waved a hand in the air. "We've got everything under control over at the high school. I swear, my people are so organized, we could go on tonight." She looked pointedly at the chaos that reigned around us. "I heard that you hadn't given up on your little play after all, and thought I'd come over to see if I could help."

"We don't need any help from you!" Vasti said. "We're doing just fine."

"Oh, Vasti, we're family. You don't have to put on a brave face in front of me. I know things must be falling completely apart."

I could see the steam starting to shoot from Vasti's ears, and I wondered how long it would be before she threw a tantrum that would completely erase the memory of Richard's outbursts. I didn't think she'd get physical, but just in case, I moved closer to the two of them. Junior came, too, but I

143

suspect she just didn't want to miss anything.

Vasti must have realized that others were watching — particularly Florence. So instead of the verbal attack I was expecting, she adopted a syrupy tone to match Sally's. "That's so sweet, but I just can't imagine what help you could be here. You better head right back to your own rehearsal before things get out of hand. You know what they say: while the cat's away, the mice will play."

Other than a slight emphasis on the word *cat,* I thought Vasti had done a fine job of insulting Sally sweetly — just the kind of performance that the Junior League expected of its members. But Sally wasn't giving up.

"Vasti, everybody knows that you can't put on a show without a leading man. The loss of poor Mr. Murdstone is tragic in so many ways." She pulled a sad face for a few seconds, then snapped her fingers as if something had just occurred to her. "I know! Why don't we combine shows? We'll add a skit to my show, something short so your people won't have any trouble learning their lines. And you'll be able to go back home and tend to that darling daughter of yours."

Junior League or not, Vasti was about to lose it, so I thought I'd better step in. "That's kind of you to offer," I said, "but we've found a replacement for Seth."

"Who?" Sally snapped. Then she forced a smile. "I mean, I understood that all the town's capable actors were already busy."

"Hadn't you heard?" Vasti said, knowing that even Byerly's rumor mill couldn't have spread the word yet. "Big Bill Walters is going to play Scrooge."

Sally's mouth opened, but nothing came out for a good thirty seconds. Finally she visibly pulled herself together and said, "Is that right? How wonderful." There wasn't anything else Sally could say without implying criticism of the leading family in town, and as a dedicated social climber, she knew better than to do that. "Are you sure there isn't something I can do to help? You must be worn out. I can tell your little girl isn't sleeping through the night."

Ouch. Vasti was so good with makeup, I hadn't really noticed the bags under her eyes until then. After all her years selling Mary Kay, Sally must have learned how to spot the signs.

"I'm just fine," Vasti said through gritted teeth.

"But surely —"

Before Sally could repeat herself, I heard Aunt Maggie bellow, "Sally, if you really want something to do, come help me unload these boxes of props. And bring a rag with you — the dust on some of this stuff must be an inch thick."

Sally froze, then reached into her purse. "Oh, darn, there goes my pager."

"I didn't hear anything," Vasti said suspiciously.

Sally made a show of looking at the display of her beeper, though I noticed she held it so that nobody else could see it. "I've got to run. Vasti, you be sure and call when you need my help."

She hurried out the door, but not before Vasti muttered under her breath, "When pigs fly." I knew Sally must have heard it, because the color that rushed to her face didn't come from Mary Kay.

People got back to work after that, but even though I'd had a good dinner, I was hungry again. So I excused myself from Junior and went to find the package of snacks I'd left in the kitchen. I ate the fruit and drank water for the baby, then had a cookie for myself. I was coming back into the auditorium, wiping crumbs from my shirt, when Sid Honeywell came in the front door and called out, "Did anybody ask for something to get delivered here?"

"Like what?" Vasti asked.

Sid said, "There are some big old boxes out here that I don't think were here before."

Looking mystified, Vasti followed him outside. Junior and I went along, too.

Sure enough, three large cardboard boxes were stuck in an alcove outside, not too far from the nook the play's cigarette smokers had taken over since Seth's murder.

"I could have missed them," Sid said, "but I swear I think I'd have noticed something this big."

"What in the Sam Hill is this?" Vasti said, and reached out to grab one.

"Hold it," Junior said. "Why don't you let me take a look first?"

Vasti jumped back. "You don't think it's a bomb, do you?"

Junior said, "Bombs aren't usually this big," but I noticed that she didn't touch anything right away. Instead she pulled a tiny pocket flashlight and let the light shine onto the ground around the boxes. "The ground's too hard to hold prints, but it looks like somebody dragged them over from the parking lot."

Once she pointed it out, I could see the bent grass and scuff marks on the hard red clay that covered most of the area.

Junior moved closer, still not touching anything, and looked at the side opposite us. "According to this label, these boxes were supposed to be delivered to the Byerly Auditorium."

There was no Byerly Auditorium; the high school auditorium and the recreation center itself were the closest we had to such a thing. "Does it say who sent them?" I asked.

"Morris Costumes in Charlotte."

"Morris Costumes!" said a voice behind us. I hadn't realized it, but a crowd had gathered behind us. Idelle burst out and, if Junior hadn't stopped her, would have opened the boxes right then and there. "These are the costumes we ordered!"

"Where did they come from?" Odelle wanted to know. "They were supposed to have been delivered a week and a half ago."

"There's no way they've been here all this time," Carlelle declared. "We'd have seen them."

"Besides which," Junior added, "it rained late last week, and these boxes are bone dry."

"It's safe to open them, isn't it, Junior?" Idelle asked.

"Give me a minute first." She walked around all three boxes, looking closely at

148

them. "They should be all right. It doesn't look like the tape's been messed with since they left Charlotte."

The triplets gleefully ripped open the boxes and, after making sure they'd finally gotten what they'd ordered, drafted a couple of helpers and gleefully carted off their prize.

Vasti just stood there with her arms folded tightly across her chest, tapping her foot. "It was that Sally Hendon. I bet they got delivered to her show by mistake, and she didn't bother to tell anybody. She must have dumped them off when she was here."

"Why do you say that?" said a voice.

I jumped as Mark Pope stepped out. The way the man appeared from nowhere was getting on my nerves.

"Isn't it obvious?" Vasti said. "She shows up without being invited, and as soon as she's gone, we find these boxes. Do you know how much time's been wasted making new costumes?" She sounded as indignant as if it had been her own time that had been wasted. "Not having costumes could have ruined the show, which is what Sally wants. She thought the play was canceled, so she must have figured it wouldn't hurt to give them back now." She wagged a finger at Mark. "You ought to arrest her."

149

Aunt Maggie, who'd come out with the others, said, "Maybe it wasn't Sally. It could have been our practical joker." She turned to Mark, too. "It seems to me that you ought to be able to do something about this troublemaker before somebody gets hurt."

"In case y'all have forgotten, I've got a murder investigation to tend to. I don't have time for playing games with . . ." He paused. "On second thought, tell me more about these jokes."

Between them, Vasti and Aunt Maggie gave him a rundown on all the pranks I'd heard about, plus a few others, and Mark actually took notes. I looked at Junior, but she looked as confused as I was that Mark would take it so seriously.

"It seems to me that we've got a pattern here," Mark finally said.

"What kind of pattern?" Junior asked.

"The way these pranks have been escalating. You've been worried that somebody might get hurt. Maybe somebody already did. Maybe what happened to Seth Murdstone wasn't a murder after all."

"You think he died because of a practical joke?" Junior said, not bothering to hide her skepticism. "The man wasn't hit over the head with a whoopee cushion."

Mark shot her a look. "Even an innocent

bucket of water propped on a door can cause harm if it falls the wrong way."

"I didn't see any bucket near Seth's body."

"I didn't say it was a bucket, only that it could have been. There are all kinds of ways it could have been rigged. Obviously the prankster found Seth first, and removed the evidence."

"Maybe it's obvious to you —" Junior started to say. Then she stopped herself. "Never mind me. You go ahead and handle this however you want."

Mark looked as if he wasn't sure he could take her at her word, but he turned back to Vasti. "Is there anything else you can tell me?"

"I've already told you who it is," Vasti said. "Sally Hendon must be behind all the pranks. I want you to arrest her!"

"I can't do that," Mark said slowly.

"Why not?" Vasti said.

"Because Mrs. Hendon didn't leave these boxes here."

"How do you know?"

"It just so happens that I was examining the grounds when she arrived, and I was still here when she left. At no time did she unload any boxes."

"Are you sure?" Vasti said, clearly deflated. "Maybe she left them earlier. It was nearly

151

dark when we got here; maybe we missed them."

"Possibly," Mark allowed, "but there are other possibilities. If you don't mind, I think I'll go inside and see what I can find out about these so-called practical jokes."

Most of the others followed him inside, with Vasti speculating loudly that everything from a broken nail to low air in her tires could have been sabotage.

I waited with Junior until they were gone, then said, "What do you think? Could Seth have died by accident?"

"It's possible," Junior said, "but it doesn't seem to fit. All of the other practical jokes were pretty easily fixed. It was a pain untying those ropes, but it's not like any of them were cut. In fact, none of the other practical jokes have been dangerous. Missing thread and toilet paper isn't the kind of thing to get anybody hurt. Offhand, I can't think of any practical joke that would have killed Seth without leaving some sign of it."

"What about what Mark said? The prankster could have found Seth first and then removed the evidence."

"That's mighty cold-blooded for a practical joker."

"True," I said, "and come to think of it,

this new prank kind of blows the idea, anyway."

"How's that?"

"Suppose I was a practical joker, and even though one of my stunts had gone so badly wrong as to kill somebody, I'd managed to get away with it. The last thing I'd want to do is to play another joke. I'd swear off them for life!"

"Then again, you might develop a taste for killing, the way serial killers do."

"In that case, I'd set up something else that could kill somebody. I wouldn't bother messing with costumes."

"That makes sense to me. So what do you say we leave the practical jokes to Mark? He probably won't catch the killer, but maybe the joker will get nervous and find somebody else to bother."

CHAPTER THIRTEEN

Junior and I had intended to corner somebody else when we got back inside, but Richard had all of the cast onstage to give them comments on their performances, and most of the crew was helping the triplets unpack the newly delivered costumes. Besides which, Mark was poking around, and the way he kept looking our way made me nervous.

"Do you suppose he's going to be hanging around like that tomorrow?" I asked Junior.

"There's no telling."

"Maybe we could go someplace where we won't have him around."

"What did you have in mind?"

"We could go visit Aunt Nora. She might have gossip about Seth. Or we could go to Aunt Daphine's beauty parlor. A lot of good stuff gets told there."

"That might be interesting," Junior said,

but she didn't sound enthusiastic.

"You think it would be a waste of time, don't you?"

"I wouldn't say that exactly."

"What *would* you say?"

"I'd say that I'm tired, and kind of discouraged."

"I'm doing my best, Junior."

"It's not you, Laurie Anne. It's me. I'm used to doing things a certain way; that's all."

"And I'm used to doing things my way," I said, feeling a bit discouraged myself. "Maybe I'm the wrong person for this murder, what with Seth being a moonshiner. I don't know the first thing about moonshine."

"Officially, moonshine is any corn whiskey that hasn't been aged, but generally speaking, it's the illegal kind that gets people's attention," Junior said with a grin.

"Ha, ha. I know what it is, but I don't know anything about the business."

"I'm glad to hear that, Laurie Anne." She was still grinning.

"All right, laugh it up. But since you obviously know all about it, wouldn't you like to enlighten poor ignorant me?"

"As a matter of fact, I don't know a whole lot about the nuts and bolts of bootlegging myself, but there is somebody who might help us."

"Your daddy?"

"No, I'm talking about somebody in the business. When does rehearsal start tomorrow?"

"Richard wants everybody who can to come in first thing in the morning."

"Do you suppose anybody will mind if we're not here?"

"Probably not. I'll just tell folks I've got morning sickness. Nobody will question that."

"I thought you weren't having morning sickness anymore."

"You know that and I know that, but not everybody else needs to know."

Junior and I decided to meet at the recreation center after she'd dropped off her nieces and nephews, and she recruited Mrs. Gamp to watch the kids while we were gone. By the time that was settled, Vasti was impatiently waiting to lock up, and we all headed home.

I'd hoped to be able to talk things over with Richard on the way back to Aunt Maggie's and then in bed, but though he tried his best to pay attention, clearly his mind was still on stage. Finally I took pity on him, kissed him good night, and let him go to sleep.

I tried to wrestle the facts into a pattern myself, but I just couldn't come up with anything without my usual sounding board. Like Junior, I was used to doing things a certain way. I eventually gave up and went to sleep myself.

Junior was waiting for me when we got to the recreation center the next morning, and after a quick good-bye kiss for Richard before he started rehearsal, I climbed into her Jeep and we headed out.

Despite what I'd told Junior the night before, I did know a little about moonshine. I don't suppose there are many Southerners who don't. Most good-sized gatherings I'd attended in Byerly, whether wedding or funeral or family reunion, included a questionable bottle of corn whiskey being passed about. I'd even tasted the contents of one of those bottles. I could still remember how it burned its way through my body, and the way my cousin Linwood had laughed when tears ran down my face. After that, I'd been happy to stick to beer and mixed drinks, so I'd never bothered to learn exactly how people went about obtaining the stuff.

Still, there was something vaguely romantic about bootleggers, as if they were the

Southern versions of Robin Hood or Zorro. I'd listened to the tales of their pulling the wool over the eyes of government agents — invariably Yankees who were rude to Southern women — and then dashing through back routes and dirt roads to get their product into the willing hands of other independent men. The sport of stock-car racing had evolved from those midnight chases; Junior Johnson, one of the all-time greats, had spent time in jail for making moonshine runs.

With all that cultural history, I was looking forward to seeing just what kind of man Junior was taking me to see. Admittedly, Seth Murdstone hadn't fit my notions of what a moonshiner should be, but I felt sure that Junior's connection would be the rogue of my imagination.

I was glad Junior was driving, because even with her directing, I don't know that I would ever have found the place. She took us down roads I'd never been on before, and had to turn around twice before getting us on the right one.

"Are we still in Byerly?" I asked her once she seemed satisfied that we were on the right path.

"This patch isn't part of any town," she said. "That's the way the Todger family likes it: nobody local has any interest in shutting them down, and nobody federal can find them."

"Is that why you haven't shut them down yourself? Because they're not in Byerly?"

"Nope. It's because they're retired. They used to go through an awful lot of corn, but these days all they make is wine: elderberry wine, blackberry wine, and so on."

"Is that legal?"

"It would be, with the proper paperwork, which they don't have. But the wine isn't for sale anyway. It's all given away to family and friends. Of course, family and friends like to return the favor with a load of groceries or a tank of heating oil or whatever they happen to have on hand."

"Making it technically legal."

"Just barely."

Junior stopped the car, but all I could see was a wide spot in the road. "Are we there? I don't see anything."

"It's not polite to show up without announcing ourselves." She pulled her cell phone out of her pocket and dialed a number. "This is Junior Norton. I was wondering if I could come pay my respects. . . . No, I'm not alone. A friend of mine is with me. Laurie Anne Fleming. Her mama was Alice McCrary, one of the Burnette girls. . . .

That's right, she's expecting."

"Can they see us?" I said, looking around nervously.

Junior pointed up above the car. Darned if there wasn't a security camera aimed in our direction. She waved at it and nudged me until I did the same.

"Yes, I'm sure she'd like some molasses cookies. Is it all right if we come up to the house? . . . No, we don't mind if you finish up what you're doing first. Just give me a call when you're free. You've got my cell phone number, don't you? . . . Then we'll wait to hear from you." She broke the connection.

"Do they want us to come back another time?"

"No, they just want us to sit here until whoever is in there leaves. Which means that we've got to close our eyes."

"You're kidding."

"They're watching us through that camera, and if we don't cover up our eyes until a car goes by, not only will we not get inside their place today, but I'll never get in there again."

"Junior, you're scaring me."

"Don't worry. They're just private, and a bit ornery. They know I don't have any jurisdiction here, so they don't have to let me on their land if they don't want to. That means that I play by their rules if I want to talk to them."

It wasn't the strangest situation I'd ever been in, but it was darned close. Still, if Junior trusted them, I would too. "What do I do?"

"Close your eyes and then put your hands up over them." She demonstrated.

I obeyed but had to say, "What's to keep me from peeking?"

"Two things: One, they've got a zoom lens on that camera, and chances are that you'd get caught. And two, I gave my word years ago that I'd never peek and that nobody I ever brought with me would peek."

I got the message; I wasn't even tempted to peek after that. Well, I was tempted, but not enough to actually do it.

We stayed like that for what seemed like an awful long time, though it was probably no more than five or ten minutes. "Is it all right to talk?" I asked Junior.

"Sure, though I can't guarantee that they don't have a mike set up. What do you want to know?"

"Do you come up here often?"

"No, but every now and again I can get information from the Todgers that I can't get anywhere else. That camera up in the trees isn't the only one they've got, and they keep a close eye on this part of the woods."

"Are you sure they're not a militia group? Or a cult?"

She chuckled. "Just a mite more eccentric than most. Which I've got to admit is saying something around Byerly."

"I can't believe I've never heard of these folks."

"You're too young," Junior said. "Years ago, Todgers' liquor was all over these parts. When they got out of the business, they got more intent on privacy."

"You mean paranoid."

"Call it whatever you want."

Just then we heard a car approach ours, then pass on by.

"Can we open our eyes now?" I asked.

"Not yet." Maybe a minute later, Junior's phone bleeped, and she answered it with her eyes closed as far as I knew. "This is Junior. . . . Thank you kindly. We'll be right there." I guessed that she hung up, because she said, "All right, Laurie Anne, you can look now."

I did so, blinking a bit at the morning glare. "Junior, you do know the most interesting people."

"Somebody recently said that same thing to me. Only we were talking about you."

I tried to decide if I'd been insulted, complimented, or just accurately described, as we drove on through the woods, emerging in front of a fence that must have been ten feet tall. "How many bottles of wine did it take to pay for this?" I asked as the gate opened.

Even after we'd driven through, I couldn't see any buildings. The land inside the fence was as thickly wooded as the land outside. It wasn't until we'd driven another full minute that the house came into sight. After all the build-up, I'd been expecting something along the lines of Robin Hood's tree house, or even a castle. In fact, it was an ordinary split-level brick house with yellow shutters, and it would have fit in perfectly in any suburb in the country. There was a lawn surrounding it, with bushes and a collection of cheerful lawn gnomes. I could see a normal assortment of tools, hoses, and clutter inside the open garage door. Even the wreath on the door and the electric candles in the window screamed *"normal."*

I still didn't give up on my dreams of a dashing bootlegger until the front door opened and a fiftyish woman in jeans, a burnt-orange-striped blouse, and Keds waved at us.

"Don't tell me that's the moonshiner," I

said to Junior.

"That's Clara Todger," Junior said. "What were you expecting?"

I was so glad I hadn't said anything about Zorro or Robin Hood. "From what you said, I thought she'd be older."

"She's the granddaughter and daughter of the real moonshiners," Junior said. "They made some good shine in their day and delivered it themselves a lot of the time. Daddy says the Todger women are the best drivers he's ever seen."

As I climbed out of Junior's car, I rubbed my tummy and silently promised the baby that I'd try to stop making assumptions about people I hadn't met.

Clara Todger met us at the door. "Hey there, Junior."

"Hey there. Clara, this is my friend Laura Fleming."

Clara's response struck me as oddly formal. "Any friend of Junior's is welcome here."

"Thank you," I said.

Junior and I followed her through the house to the kitchen. I only caught glimpses of the other rooms, but everything seemed ordinary to me, from the furniture to the messy stacks of Christmas cards. The kitchen wasn't at all ordinary. It was huge, for one thing, and had the biggest stove I'd ever seen outside a restaurant. There were big copper pots and pans hung on one wall, and I could tell they were there for easy access, not decoration. The counters were covered with bowls of berries and various gadgets for removing seeds, stems, and such. Obviously this was where the Todgers made their wine.

Clara waved us toward chairs around the solid oak table, where glasses and a plate full of cookies were already waiting.

"It's just grape juice," Clara said when I hesitated. "I know you shouldn't drink anything stronger in your condition, and Junior is driving."

I took a swallow. It was delicious, and I didn't have any idea that it came from a grocery store.

"When are you due?" Clara asked.

"Around the middle of April," I said.

"Boy or girl?"

"We haven't found out."

She nodded in approval. I'd noticed that most people thought it was a good idea to wait, but most people found out early when it was their own baby. I had no idea why.

We all took cookies, which were just as good as the grape juice, and talked babies for a little while. Clara said she had three daughters of her own, but I was happy to find out that she wasn't one of those who thought it was necessary to share every detail of labor. I'd already heard enough gruesome tales to make me wonder why anybody ever had a second child.

Eventually Clara said, "This is lovely, but I'm guessing y'all didn't come all this way to eat cookies and discuss potty training."

"Not that these cookies wouldn't be worth the trip," Junior said politely, "but actually, we want to talk to you about the family business. The former family business, that is."

"Then either Laurie Anne here is thinking about getting into that business, which I doubt, or this is about Seth Murdstone."

"It's about Seth," Junior said. "I imagine you heard about him getting killed."

Clara nodded.

"I was wondering if you'd heard anything else about that through the grapevine. I know you wouldn't tell us anything if Seth were still operating, but since he's gone . . ." She let her sentence trail off, giving Clara a chance to think about it.

"There's been some talk," she said slowly. "You know that Seth was in the habit of sending the fruits of his labor up North?"

"I could never prove it, but that's what I

figured."

"There are others in the state who do the same thing, and some of them have mentioned problems up there. Someone is trying to take over all the available venues, and they're hoping to cut out everybody else."

"Who?"

"I've heard that they were Italian, but somebody else said Puerto Rican," Clara said. "Whoever they are, they're a lot more organized than the run-of-the-mill small-time operators."

"Like Seth?"

"Exactly. Seth stayed as far down the food chain as he could and still make a decent living. So I don't think he would have wanted to go head-to-head with the big boys. It would have been too much of a gamble for him."

"Did they threaten him?" I asked. "Physically, I mean."

"I don't know about Seth specifically, but there have been threats made. Everything from destruction of property to breaking legs. Makes me glad to be out of the business."

Junior looked pointedly at the open pantry door, where we could see rows and rows of neatly labeled bottles, but she didn't say anything about them. Instead she asked,

167

"Have any of the organized types come down here?"

"That I don't know. People are spooked right now, so they're seeing Al Capone with a tommy gun behind every tree. Every time there's an accident at a still, somebody claims it's mob sabotage, when probably it's nothing more than sloppy maintenance." To me she added, "Moonshiners in general aren't known for their common sense."

Junior asked, "Do you know what Seth was planning to do? Was he going to retire?"

"Rumor has it that he had been advised to switch to distributing locally, but that he hadn't decided one way or the other."

"Wouldn't that hurt business for the people already distributing around here?" I wanted to know. "Did any of them threaten Seth?"

Clara said, "Not that I know of. Which isn't to say that they might not have done something later, but right now they're more concerned with the people from up North."

"Did any of them have any feuds with Seth?"

"No. As I said, Seth stayed out of trouble. He had a handful of distribution deals and was happy with them. He stayed friends with everybody and made sure not to cut into anybody else's business, so nobody had

168

any quarrels with him that I knew about."

I shook my head ruefully. "Who would kill a man that everybody likes?"

"I didn't say I liked him," Clara said.

"Didn't you?"

"As a matter of fact, I didn't."

"Why not?"

"It was something that happened a long time ago. Lord, it must be twenty years now." She stopped, but I waited her out. Eventually she went on. "It was one of those icy winter nights when sensible people stay home, and one of our men was out on a delivery. To keep from being seen, he was driving one of the back roads with no lights on. Unfortunately, Seth Murdstone was doing the same thing on the same road. He rear-ended our man's car, and sent it into a tree. Our driver was killed."

"What about Seth?" I asked.

"Only bruised, so he could have stayed to help."

"He didn't stop?"

"He didn't even admit it until he had to. When my sisters and I went to check on the delivery, we found the car, but it wasn't until we asked around that we found out that Seth had been out that same night. When we tracked him down, he said he'd stopped, but when he saw the driver was

169

dead, he thought he better leave before the police came. He even said he thought he heard sirens. Which would have been reasonable — if he'd really heard sirens."

"You don't think he did?"

"I can't say, but I do know the police didn't find the wrecked car. Of course, it was certainly an accident, and it looked as if our man died instantly, so there was no real harm done. But I never quite trusted Seth after that." She gave me a tight smile. "I didn't decide to avenge our driver all these years later, if that's what you're thinking. If I'd wanted Seth Murdstone dead, he'd have been buried a long time ago."

Junior didn't comment, and there was something about Clara's tone that made me believe her. "What about the driver's family?" I asked.

"His wife never knew Seth had anything to do with it. There didn't seem to be any reason to stir up trouble."

I nodded. As much effort as the Todgers went to in ensuring their privacy, I could see why they wouldn't have done anything else.

Junior finished up her grape juice. "One other thing, Clara. Do you know where Seth's still is? I don't want it laying around to be found."

"I'm afraid I can't tell you."

I noticed that she hadn't said that she didn't know — only that she couldn't tell — and I was surprised that Junior didn't call her on it. Obviously the two of them had rules when dealing with each other.

Clara looked at the two of us. "Can I get either of you anything else before you go?"

It was a polite dismissal, made even more so when she offered us both bundles of molasses cookies to take with us. Junior refused just as politely, probably so it wouldn't look as if she was taking a bribe. As for me, I took both bundles.

The three of us chatted just a bit more about babies on the way out, and then I asked something I'd been wanting to know ever since Junior told me about the Todgers. "This doesn't have anything to do with Seth, and I know it's none of my business, but why did y'all quit bootlegging?"

Clara got still, and for a moment I expected her to order us off her property, or at least take back her cookies. Instead she said, "I decided it wasn't worth the risks. We didn't have the problems with Northerners then, but there was always the ATF to worry about. And the police, of course."

"Glad to hear that we hindered you a little," Junior said.

Clara went on, "But the real reason is that dead man I told you about. I was the one who had to break the news to his wife. She was pregnant at the time, and she lost the baby afterward."

I felt a cold breeze, and wasn't sure whether it was real or not.

"I decided then that it was time for a change. It took a while to talk the rest of the family into it, but eventually they agreed it was for the best."

"But if y'all aren't in the business anymore, why the cameras and fences?"

"After generations of being moonshiners, we Todgers prefer our privacy." Her smile told me that was all the answer I was going to get.

CHAPTER FOURTEEN

Once Junior had driven us out the gate, and I was reasonably sure that there weren't any cameras aimed so that anybody could read my lips, I said, "Was Clara telling the truth about the family just wanting privacy?"

"Heck if I know, Laurie Anne," Junior said. "I do know that the Todgers were originally mountain folk, and a lot of mountain folk keep to themselves, so that may be all there is to it. Then again, some people say they've got a cult in there, snake handlers or people speaking in tongues. Others claim there's a battered women's and children's shelter, or a retreat for ex-hippies to hide from the FBI. All I know is that an awful lot of food and supplies go in there."

"Weird," was all I could say. "I was surprised she was still protecting Seth's still, especially since she didn't like him."

"She wasn't," Junior said. "She was protecting Jake. Maybe David, too, but probably just Jake."

"What did I miss?"

"Clara won't give up anybody in the business. You remember how she talked about the delivery man but never mentioned his name, and he's been gone for twenty years. If I hadn't already known Seth was a moonshiner, and if he weren't dead to boot, Clara would never have admitted it."

"Really?"

"By the same token, she won't reveal the location of a working still, and you can bet she knows the location of every working still around here."

"So by her *not* telling you where Seth's still is, this tells you that it's currently in use, and since Jake worked with Seth, he's the one who'll be using it."

"Right. I wasn't really expecting to find out where the still is. I just wanted to know if Jake was going to stay in the business. Now I know."

I replayed the conversation in my head, trying to decide if I'd missed anything else. "Clara kind of talked in circles when you asked what Seth had been planning on doing. What do you think that means?"

"I'm not sure," she admitted, "but I was wondering about what your cousins said about that fight between Jake and Seth."

"Do you think Jake might have wanted Seth to start selling their stuff around here instead of shipping it up North?"

"Could be."

"That really puts Jake in the running as Seth's killer, doesn't it?" I said. "Because they'd been fighting, and because now Jake can run the business any way he wants."

"Right."

Then I thought of Jake's reaction when told Seth was dead. "I don't know, Junior, he really seemed to be upset about his daddy's death."

"What if he'd killed Seth accidentally?" Junior pointed out. "Say Seth said he was going to close down the still, which would leave Jake without a way to make a living. Jake could have tried to talk him out of it, and when that didn't work, he got carried away and hit him. He'd been working on sets, so he could have been holding a piece of wood when he went to talk to Seth."

I said, "Do you suppose he would have realized Seth was dead? Maybe he thought he was just knocked out, and hoped Seth wouldn't remember who'd hit him." I'd read that head trauma tends to play games with memory, especially the memories of how a person came to be knocked out.

"I think I'd have known right off," Junior

said, "but I've had more experience with dead bodies than Jake has."

"Unless bootlegging is a whole lot more dangerous than I thought." I went back over some of what Clara had told us. "You know, Clara is the first person I've run into that didn't like Seth."

"I know, and that bothers me."

"Why?"

"Because I liked him myself. Daddy liked him, even though Seth kept running circles around him. I don't know if you realize it, but cops sometimes do like the people we're going after. Sometimes it's a matter of respect for another professional."

"Like you and Clara?"

"Exactly. Daddy knew Seth was moonshining, and Seth knew Daddy knew, but that didn't stop them from being friendly when they ran into one another. When Seth's wife passed away, Daddy even sent flowers."

"Maybe Clara misjudged him. She said herself it was just because of that accident, and I can't blame her for that. It must have been awful."

"It might have made a decent motive, too, if it hadn't been so long ago."

"I suppose so." Then I thought of something. "You know, if Seth did cause that ac-

176

cident, then he's indirectly responsible for the Todgers getting out of moonshining. Could that be a motive? Maybe not for Clara, but somebody else in the family."

"Laurie Anne, do you remember how Clara said that if she'd wanted Seth dead, he'd have been gone long ago? That goes for her whole family."

"That's scary."

"You bet it is," Junior agreed. "I'm just glad they've never wanted anybody dead — that I know of, anyway."

I shivered. I'd run into people who'd killed for one reason or another, but each of them had killed for emotional reasons. Clara was the first person I'd ever met who I thought would kill calmly. And the funny thing was, I liked her.

"Well, we didn't get a whole lot out of the visit," I said, "though that stuff about organized crime could be promising. A sneak thief probably couldn't have snuck in on Seth, but a professional hit man could have."

"We still have the problem of how a hit man knew where Seth was going to be."

"What about my idea of them setting up a meeting?"

"They could have done that," Junior said, "but considering how careful Seth had been all his life, why would he have arranged something like that in the middle of a rehearsal? Where anybody from the town's biggest gossip to the chief of police could have walked in on him?"

"True. Umm . . . when you talk about the town's biggest gossip, you do mean Vasti, don't you?"

"Laurie Anne, I've never thought you were a gossip. Nosy, yes, but not a gossip."

"That makes me feel so much better."

She ignored me. "Besides, why would Seth have been a big enough threat to any Mafia types for them to kill him? According to Clara, he was either going to shut down or start distributing locally, which is exactly what they would have wanted him to do."

"You're right. It just sounded like a nice, neat answer. In fact, I'm surprised Mark hasn't jumped on it. He could still claim it was an outsider and not be expected to actually find the killer. Nobody would hold it against him if he couldn't track down a Mafia hit man. Of course, that assumes that he's heard about these guys being around. Does he know Clara?"

Junior shook her head. "I've never told anybody about the Todgers other than you, and Daddy never told anybody but me. But if the other moonshiners are as nervous as

Clara says they are, Mark could have picked up on the rumor easily enough."

"I wonder why he hasn't. Or do you think he's keeping it quiet?"

"I keep telling you, I don't know what Mark's thinking," she said sharply.

"Sorry," I said.

After a few minutes of strained silence, she said, "I'm sorry, too, Laurie Anne. This situation's got me on edge. I don't like not being in charge."

"That's all right." I patted my tummy. "With the little one here, I feel out of control myself. According to my aunts, once the baby arrives, I'm not going to be in control of much of anything for a long time to come."

CHAPTER FIFTEEN

We got back to the rehearsal just in time to stave off another tantrum — not from Richard, for a change, but from Kyle, one of Junior's nephews. Kyle was playing Tiny Tim and was refusing to use his crutch because he claimed it hurt him. He'd just thrown it down from the stage when we walked in, and Junior immediately took charge of him.

On stage, Richard was running his fingers through his hair as he watched the other young Cratchits indulge in a shoving match while their onstage parents tried not to laugh. "Could somebody please retrieve Tiny Tim's crutch?" he said in a tight voice.

"I'll get it," I said, and picked it up. I was surprised Kyle was putting up such a fuss. Up until then, he'd been delighted to have the plum child's role, and had practiced walking with a limp so much that I'd almost forgotten he wasn't crippled. The crutch's arm piece was padded with foam rubber, which was admittedly not authentic for the Victorian era but should have been fairly comfortable. Since I'm not exactly tall, Kyle wasn't much shorter than I was, so I tucked it under my arm for an experimental step. And yelped.

"Now what?" Richard snapped.

Instead of answering him immediately, I poked at the armrest. There was something sharp in there! "Richard, somebody stuck a pin or something into the crutch." I reached under my shirt to feel my arm pit, and brought my finger back with a drop of blood on it. "I'm bleeding."

"What!" Richard hopped down from the stage and took the crutch from me. "Idelle, will you bring me a pair of scissors?"

All three triplets came over and watched as Richard cut away the chamois cloth covering the armrest. My husband's not much of a cusser, but he cursed loudly when he saw what was under the material. Somebody had stuck a thin nail, like a carpet nail, right where it would prick whoever used the crutch. Without taking it out, he looked at it carefully. "I don't see any rust, but . . ."

"I had a tetanus booster last year, remember?" Then I called out, "Junior, has Kyle had a tetanus shot?"

"Does this have something to do with this gash under his arm?" she called back, and brought him in our direction. Kyle's eyes were red from crying, and he was holding his arm gingerly. Having felt that nail myself, I didn't blame him.

"It looks as if our prankster has struck again," Richard said, showing Junior the crutch.

"Is Kyle all right?" I asked.

"I think so," Junior said. "I was just going to put a Band-Aid on him, but I better check on his shots first." She pulled out her cell phone and stepped far enough away so that she could call her sister.

"Kyle," Richard said solemnly, "please accept my apologies. I had no idea that crutch was booby-trapped."

"That's all right," the boy said, red-faced at being the center of so much concern. "You didn't know."

"No, but I should have listened to you when you said it hurt you. What good is a director who doesn't trust his performers — especially one of the stars?"

Kyle's eyes glowed. "Me? A star?"

"Absolutely," Richard said. "Who do people think of when they hear the title *A Christmas Carol*? Scrooge and Tiny Tim.

Your role is key. I only hope you can forgive me and carry on."

"Yes, sir, I sure can." He wiggled his arm. "This ain't nothing but a scratch."

"Kyle had a shot the year before last," Junior announced. "He's in the clear, or will be as soon as I get him a Band-Aid."

"I don't need any Band-Aid," Kyle said loftily, his tears gone.

"No, let your aunt take care of it," Richard said. "An actor has to be in peak physical condition to give his best performance."

Junior looked at me, one eyebrow raised, but went off to get the supplies. Kyle stood by with a determinedly stiff upper lip when Junior doctored him; then he followed Richard back to the stage as if nothing had happened.

"I don't know what Richard said to him," Junior said to me, "but it sure did the trick."

"Just practicing to be a daddy," I said proudly. "Is your sister upset?"

"Some," Junior admitted. "I didn't tell her I wasn't here when it happened, but I think she guessed. So, if you don't mind, we better do our investigating here for the rest of the day."

"No problem." I looked at the crutch I was still holding. "I'd like to find out how this happened."

183

"Oh, we're going to find that out, I guarantee you. Whoever rigged this thing knew damned well that Kyle was the one who was going to be using this crutch. Running off with toilet paper is one thing, hurting my nephew is something else." From the look in Junior's eye, I wasn't about to get in her way.

Unfortunately, after talking to just about everybody, all we found out was that just about anybody could have put the nail in Kyle's crutch. Since the triplets were in charge of costumes, we went to them first to find out where the crutch was kept overnight. Only Odelle told me it wasn't part of Kyle's costume. It was a prop. So we tracked down Aunt Maggie, but she told us it wasn't the crutch that she'd dug up for Kyle to use, because hers had been modern and Vasti had said it didn't look right. We found Vasti, and she said that Jake had made the authentic-looking one out of scraps from building sets.

Jake was sitting backstage all alone, not even pretending to use the hammer in his hand, and I hated to interrupt what I was sure was mourning, but Junior asked him about the crutch anyway. It turned out that Jake hadn't kept up with the crutch after he made it — just handed it to Kyle during an earlier rehearsal. This led us back to Kyle, who admitted that he'd been in the habit of leaving it lying around when he left at night.

That meant that anybody could have sneaked away with it for long enough to stick in a nail.

We finally gave it up as a lost cause and retreated to chairs, where I could put my feet up and Junior could keep an eye on the kids. I had my usual ice water and tried not to envy Junior her can of Coke. "That was a waste of time," I said.

"Most police work is, when you come right down to it."

"Same with my nosing about." I rubbed my tummy idly. "What is it with these pranks? What's the point?"

"Why does anybody play practical jokes?" Junior said. "For the attention. To cause trouble. To embarrass people."

"Usually, I'd agree with you." An ex-boyfriend of mine had loved playing practical jokes, and in the long run, it had gotten him killed.[7] "It just seems like these tricks are for a reason."

"Don't tell me you think Vasti's right, and that Sally Hendon is trying to close down the play."

[7] *Country Comes to Town*

185

"I'm sure Sally would love to see Vasti fall flat on her face, but since Mark cleared her of leaving those costumes, she must be innocent. Though somebody else might want to shut things down."

"Why?"

"Let's look at the idea of practical joker as murderer again." I could tell Junior wanted to argue the point, but I waggled my finger at her. "Just listen for a minute. What if the earlier jokes were camouflage, just stirring things up until the killer got a chance to actually kill Seth? Maybe he'd planned to let it look as if Seth died as a result of a practical joke gone wrong if he got caught."

"As a fallback position?" Junior said.

"Exactly. But he got lucky and nobody caught him."

"So why didn't the jokes stop after Seth died?"

"He could be muddying the waters some more."

"Kind of risky, since every stunt he pulls increases his chances of being caught."

"True." I took a different approach. "Maybe he really is trying to shut down the play."

"Why?"

"Because of you and me. As long as rehearsals continue, we've got lots of access

186

to the witness and suspects. If the show were canceled, we'd have a harder time tracking people down. And I don't have to tell you how unreliable memories are. The minute people get out of here, they're going to start forgetting details, and it might be those details that will help us solve this thing."

"Except that nobody remembers any useful details."

"Not yet, but they might. Or maybe we've already heard something and it just didn't register." I looked at her, trying to read her expression. "What do you think?"

"It's interesting."

"Is that a punch line?" I said suspiciously. "Pardon?"

"Don't you remember that old joke? Two women who haven't seen each other in a while get together to catch up. The first one says her husband's a doctor and makes more money than God, and the second one says, 'That's interesting.' Next the first says her husband bought her a new Cadillac and a fur coat, and the second says, 'That's interesting.' Then the first says their house is huge and they've got umpteen servants, and the second says, 'That's interesting.' Finally the first one asks what the second one's been doing, and the second one says she went to charm school, and the first one wants to know what she learned. The second one says she learned to say 'That's interesting,' instead of 'Up yours, bitch!' "

Junior laughed so hard she blew Coke out of her nose. When she'd calmed down, and wiped her nose, she said, "No, Laurie Anne, that's not what I was thinking. But I still don't buy it. Seth's death didn't look premeditated to me. You see, head injuries are tough to predict. Just a light blow to the back of the head can cut off blood flow and kill a person, and other people survive massive wounds without any permanent damage. Now Seth was only hit once. Obviously it did kill him, but there was no way to know for sure that it would. If I'd gone to all the trouble to set things up so I could kill somebody, I'd have picked a method that would guarantee that he died."

"You're right," I admitted. "I just keep trying to link the murder to those silly tricks —" Remembering that Junior's nephew had gotten hurt through one of those tricks, I changed it to, "I mean, those nasty tricks. Maybe they really aren't connected."

"And maybe they are. We just don't know yet." She patted me on the arm. "But I do like the way your mind works. What next?"

I spotted Vasti greeting Aunt Nora at the

door. "In my unprofessional opinion, we should eat, because I smell fried chicken."

Aunt Nora had brought some of her fried chicken, which is so delectable that if Colonel Sanders were still alive, he'd have been beating the door down to find out how she did it. Not only had she cooked enough to feed everybody, she'd brought along all the fixings, too: mashed potatoes and gravy, green beans, biscuits, and double-butter Christmas cookies for dessert. With all that, she had the nerve to apologize for not having been able to find decent corn on the cob in December.

Needless to say, Richard put an immediate halt to the rehearsal. If he hadn't, he would have had a mutiny on his hands. Once our plates were filled, I dragged him into a corner so we could talk. Or rather, I talked, telling him what Junior and I had found out so far. Richard nodded, ate, and made encouraging noises in the appropriate places. When I finished, he said, "It sounds as if you two are making progress."

"You think so?" I said doubtfully. "We've been shooting down theories faster than we can come up with them."

"I have complete confidence in you, and having Junior around can only help."

Just then I looked up and saw Mark

watching us. "Has he been here all day?"

"In and out," Richard said. "I suppose he's investigating, but I haven't seen any progress from him."

"What's going on with him, anyway? He can't possibly be as stupid as he's been acting."

"Maybe he's trying to lull suspects into a false sense of security."

"If he's that good an actor, you should cast *him* as Scrooge."

"Don't even think of messing with my cast again," he warned me. "I've finally got the right Scrooge, but pulling this off is still going to be tough."

"Don't worry. You concentrate on the play and let Junior and me play detective."

"Have you two mapped out your next step?"

We hadn't, but he'd given me an idea. "I'm planning to question somebody who spent a lot of time with Seth recently, and who just happened to be nearby when he was killed."

"Great! He should be able to tell you a lot."

"I hope so." I looked at him expectantly.

A second or two later, he got it. "Oh, no, you don't! The deal was that you and Junior do your thing — I've got a play to direct."

"I'm not asking you to *do* anything. I just want to ask you some questions."

"Really?"

"Really."

"What if I don't cooperate?"

"I'll have to get tough."

"Whips? Chains?"

"Richard Fleming! This is a whole new side of your personality."

"We temperamental director types always live large."

"I can borrow Junior's handcuffs if you insist, but for now, how about bribery?"

"What did you have in mind?"

I tried for a husky whisper. "What about some cookies?"

"Aunt Nora brought cookies?"

After I brought him a plate-full, Richard was willing to tell me anything he knew. The problem was, he insisted that he didn't know anything that could help.

"Seth and I didn't discuss anything other than the play," Richard said in between mouthfuls. "I was working so hard to get him to stop being himself and start being Scrooge, I didn't want him to say anything personal. Even if he had been worried that somebody wanted to kill him, I wouldn't have given him a chance to talk about it."

"Rats," I said. "What about the rest of the cast?"

"The same goes for them. Half the time I don't even remember their real names. I just call them by their characters' names."

That made me think of something. "According to what Aunt Maggie said, Vasti pretty much let people pick their parts. Right?"

He nodded.

"Don't you think that the part a person picks says something about him?"

"Is this one of those pop psychology tests where you analyze people by finding out which Beatle they like best?"

"Probably, but play along anyway. After all, you did accept my bribe."

"So I did," he said, licking colored sugar off of his fingers. "Who first?"

"How about Tim Topper?"

"Bob Cratchit. Honest, and loyal to a fault. Loves his family. As far as I know, this also applies to Tim. None of which precludes his being a murderer, of course." He paused. "There is one thing. I don't think he liked Seth."

"Why do you say that?"

"As I said, Cratchit is loyal to Scrooge beyond reasonable expectations."

"I always figured he really needed the job."

"Partly, but Dickens created lots of characters who put up with cruelty because they're good. Most of them eventually get rewarded, at least in his early work, though in later —" He stopped himself. "Sorry, I get carried away."

"I understand." I'd known he was an English professor when I married him, so I could hardly blame him for acting like one.

"Anyway, Cratchit asks Scrooge for better treatment, but doesn't seem to resent it when Scrooge refuses."

"Right."

"Tim's performance didn't reflect that. His Bob seemed angry at Scrooge. Admittedly that's a more reasonable reaction, but it's not what the part calls for."

"Maybe Tim doesn't realize how it's supposed to be played."

"That's what I thought, and I was planning to address the problem when I got a chance, but after Big Bill took on the role, it wasn't necessary. Tim started playing it the way it was written."

"So either he really disliked Seth, or he really likes Big Bill," I speculated.

"Or maybe he reread his part," Richard said. "Who else?"

"Florence Murdstone. Now that I think about it, I'm surprised she didn't keep her

193

maiden name."

"Most women do still take the husband's name, even in these enlightened times. You did."

"I know, but there are other customs from less enlightened times. Around here, when women marry down, they generally either keep their maiden name or go by both names, like Florence Easterly Murdstone."

"Marry down? I shouldn't quote Dickens so much. The Victorian era is going to your head. Tell me, was our marriage considered marrying up or marrying down?"

"Up because of that Harvard ring of yours, but down because you're a Yankee. So it evens out."

"I'll accept that," he said. "What does Florence's choice tell us? Or rather, both of her choices, since she's playing Scrooge's old girlfriend Belle and Mrs. Cratchit."

I thought for a minute. "Start with Belle. She's trying to make Scrooge realize what's really important in life. From Aunt Maggie's gossip, Florence blew off her society friends to marry the man she loved. Right?"

"What about Mrs. Cratchit?"

"My take is that she had more common sense than her husband. She knew Scrooge was using Bob, but she couldn't do anything about it. If this represents Florence's relationship with Seth, it doesn't sound as if she liked him."

"Maybe all it means is that there are only two decent roles for women in the play."

I punched him gently. "Play nice. I'm carrying your baby, and look how swollen my ankles are."

"Put your feet up and I'll rub them."

"And?"

"And I'll play nice."

"Good." I allowed him to massage my feet for a few minutes before going on. "Next, David Murdstone as Scrooge's nephew Fred, who keeps trying to redeem Scrooge. Since there's no mention of Fred's father, can we assume that Scrooge is a father figure to Fred?"

"Nothing in the text says that," Richard said, "but nothing disputes it, either."

"Then isn't it indicative that Fred tries to change Scrooge? I heard that David didn't get along with his father."

"They did seem very different," Richard admitted. "Jake and Seth were much closer. Does that make David a more likely candidate for Seth's killer than Jake?"

"Not necessarily. Sometimes it's the people who are alike who fight the most."

"True, but there's a problem. David didn't pick the role of Fred. He only took it because Florence talked him into it. She wanted him to be in the play with her, and she thought he'd be good as Fred."

"Oh." I stopped. "Does this psychobabble make any sense, Richard?"

He didn't answer — just kept rubbing my feet.

"I get the hint. I'll hush up and enjoy the foot rub." I did hush, and I definitely enjoyed the foot rub, but I kept going over the suspects in my head. It was aggravating. I just couldn't come up with a reason compelling enough to commit murder over. Then I thought of newspaper articles about people being killed for nothing more than cutting off another driver in traffic. Maybe our murderer didn't have anything like what I would consider a good reason.

"Richard," I said, "what would it take to get you to commit murder?"

"Other than losing another cast member?"

"Seriously."

"Somebody threatening you or our child. Or me, of course."

"That would be self-defense, or wife and child defense, not murder. What else?"

"I don't think I'd kill for money, but if I were desperate enough, maybe I would. The same for revenge: I don't consider myself a vengeful person, but who can tell? I don't know, Laura. Quite honestly, I hope I never find out."

"Fair enough. I can't say that I've got a better answer." Like Richard, I wasn't sure I wanted to find out either. I looked around and noticed that people were finishing their lunches. "Looks like it's about time to get things rolling again."

"So it does. If you'll excuse me, I think I'll hit the men's room." He gave me a quick kiss and headed off.

Aunt Nora was starting to pack up her things, so I went to give her a hand.

"The chicken was wonderful," I said.

"I'm so glad you enjoyed it." She patted my tummy. "Did the baby get enough, too?"

"Lord, yes. I ate enough for me, the baby, and six or seven other people." Then I virtuously added, "I had lots of vegetables, too."

She beamed. There's nothing quite so satisfying to Aunt Nora as a bulging waistband. "So," she asked with studied nonchalance, "how's your project coming along?"

"Junior and I are still working on it. While you're here, let me pick your brain. Do you know of any reason why anybody would have killed Seth?"

Before she could answer, I heard Richard call out, "Would whoever it was who ran off with the soap dispenser from the men's room please return it?" There were a few snickers, but most people just looked irritated.

"Are y'all still having problems with practical jokes?" Aunt Nora asked.

I nodded. "At least this one is harmless." I told her about the nail on Tiny Tim's crutch.

"That's terrible," she said. "I like a good joke as much as the next person, but there's no excuse for hurting a child."

"You'll get no argument from me. But we're having even less luck catching the prankster than with catching Seth's killer."

"I don't know that I can help you with either, but I will tell you what I know about the Murdstones."

"Great." I sat down and got comfortable. Aunt Nora isn't known for fast talking.

"I didn't know Seth well, but I did know his wife. We were on a couple of church committees together. Of course, that was before she got sick and stopped leaving the house."

"She had cancer, didn't she?"

Aunt Nora nodded. "Liver cancer. She was already pretty far gone before they found it, so there wasn't a whole lot they could do to help her. Some of us up at the church would take meals and things by for her and the boys, and it about broke our

198

hearts. Her just wasting away, and poor David moping around, looking nearly as bad as she did, because he knew what was happening. Jake was younger, so it didn't hit him the same way."

"What about Seth? How did he take it?"

"He was worse off than David in a way. He didn't seem to believe that his wife was dying. Everybody in Byerly knew it was only a matter of time; she was so bad off she couldn't even go to the bathroom by herself. But he'd talk like she was going to get better and hop up off that bed."

"Maybe he was just trying to make her feel better."

"No, he was in denial."

I blinked. Even though they watch *Oprah* in Byerly just like everywhere else, it always surprises me when one of my aunts uses words like that. "What did he do when she died?"

"I've never seen a man take on so. What with him and the boys, it was the saddest funeral I'd ever been too. Seth fell apart, and David closed himself up, and Jake was mostly confused about what was going on. The other women at the church and I had to help them with just about everything: going through his wife's things, and cleaning the house, and making sure the boys got fed. Seth didn't pull himself out of it for months."

"He never remarried?"

"Everybody encouraged him to, since he had the boys to raise, but his heart was in the grave."

"I beg your pardon?"

"Don't you know that expression? It means he was still so much in love with his first wife that he couldn't bring himself to fall in love again. Which was a shame, because there were a couple of women who thought a whole lot of him." She nodded at somebody. "There's one of them right there."

I looked in that direction. "Mrs. Gamp?"

"Her husband died not long before Seth's wife, and since she didn't have any children of her own, she'd have been a good mother to his boys. Everybody thought sure he was going to marry her, but then he broke up with her and started going around with somebody else." She lowered her voice. "It was about then that she started talking about Mrs. Harris."

"Really?" I said. "He must have really hurt her." Of course, most scorned women act right away, not years later. "Did anybody else have a grudge against him? Maybe somebody else in the play?"

"Did you have anybody particular in mind?"

"What about the Christmas Spirits? Oliver, Sid, and Pete."

"Oliver?" She thought for a minute. "I don't know of any feud between Oliver and Seth, but it seems like there was something with Sid. You remember Tom Honeywell, don't you?"

"How could I forget?" Tom, a born troublemaker, had dated my cousin Ilene, and she was later accused of his murder.[8] Though Sid was a wonderful man, everybody in town pretty much thought Tom had gotten what he deserved.

"Tom worked for Seth for a while, but there was some kind of problem and Seth fired him. I think he said Tom stole from him, but I don't remember the details. I can't imagine he would have taken any of the chairs. It must have been tools or something like that."

Or maybe it had been moonshine. I was only surprised Tom hadn't blabbed what Seth was up to all over town, but then again, he couldn't have without admitting his own involvement.

"Sid was pretty hot at the time," Aunt

[8] *Trouble Looking for a Place to Happen*

Nora said. "He didn't want to believe his son would steal. Then Tom stole from him, too, and he realized Seth had been right after all. But that would have been more a reason for Seth to be angry at Sid than the other way around."

"If either of them held a grudge, I didn't see it," I said, "and since they had scenes together, I think I would have. What about Pete Fredericks?"

Aunt Nora giggled despite herself. "This is terrible, Laurie Anne, but all I can think of is that he might have done it to drum up business."

"I know, I've thought the same thing. Poor old Pete. I bet he's sorry he left the mill to become a mortician. He must have to put up with a lot."

"You know he does, but there aren't many places in Byerly where he could make as much money as he does at the funeral home. It's a shame, too, because he's got a degree in chemistry from NC State."

"I didn't know that." Could there be a connection there? Wouldn't a chemist have been helpful to a bootlegger, helping set up the distillations and testing the product for proof? Junior hadn't mentioned anything about Pete being involved, but there was a lot about Seth's operation she hadn't known. Then I pictured Pete delivering whiskey in his hearse, and started snickering again.

"What?" Aunt Nora wanted to know.

"Nothing," I said. "It was a silly thought."

She must have decided it was a pregnancy thing, because she let it slide. "Anybody else?"

"Only if you know about any other scores people might have wanted to settle." I looked around the room to see whom I hadn't asked about. "What about Big Bill?"

"Big Bill Walters with Seth Murdstone? Lord, Laurie Anne, I don't know that the two of them ever spoke until this play came up. They didn't exactly travel in the same circles, you know." She stopped herself. "No, wait. It seems like I heard recently that Big Bill wanted to buy Seth's house. Or at least the land. He's got a couple of acres."

"Was Seth going to sell?"

"That I don't know. But why would Big Bill kill somebody over a piece of property? He already owns most of the town."

"That's never stopped Big Bill. Besides, when you always get what you want, it must be all the more frustrating when you find something you can't have."

"I suppose. Do you think that's why he keeps chasing after Aunt Maggie?"

"You think he wants to buy the Burnette home place?"

"I'm not talking about real estate."

"Aunt Nora," I said in mock indignation, "you have a dirty mind!"

"I didn't say a word," she said, trying to look innocent.

"You've said enough that you ought to be ashamed of yourself."

She just laughed. As for me, I refused to speculate further. "If you can get your mind out of the gutter," I said, "is there anybody else who had a reason to kill Seth?"

She thought it over but finally shook her head. "I'm sorry, but I can't think of a thing."

"I appreciate you trying to help, anyway. Speaking of helping, can I help you carry the leftovers out to your car?"

"No, thanks. I'm leaving everything here in case any of y'all need a snack later on. I'll come back tomorrow to pick up what's left."

"Aunt Nora, I can personally guarantee that there won't be anything left tomorrow but fond memories."

Despite Aunt Nora's objecting that I didn't need to be toting boxes, I did help her carry leftovers into the kitchen before she left.

CHAPTER SIXTEEN

One of the few advantages of using the recreation center was having a kitchen available. Mrs. Gamp kept the coffeepot full and made sure there were cookies and other treats for every rehearsal. I'd been keeping bottles of water in the refrigerator, plus a bag of fruit. I was eyeing the leftover cookies, trying to decide if I had room for one more, when Florence came in. So I grabbed a cookie and leaned nonchalantly against the counter, figuring that calories consumed in the line of duty didn't count.

"Hey there, Laurie Anne," Florence said. "Won't you join me for a cup of tea?" She started pulling out the fixings.

"No, thanks. The doctor's got me staying away from caffeine for the duration."

"What with everything else going on, I haven't had a chance to congratulate you on the baby," she said. "You and Richard must be so excited."

"Absolutely. At least, when we're not in stark terror."

Florence smiled. "Don't you worry. Y'all are going to make wonderful parents."

"Thank you. And while we're congratulating, belated congratulations on your marriage." I winced. "I mean, best wishes."

"Don't apologize. I know you're not supposed to congratulate a new bride, but as long as it took me to get David to marry me, I think I deserve congratulations. Do you know I chased that man for ten years?"

"Really? Y'all are so clearly in love now."

"Oh, we were in love the whole time. He just didn't believe that I loved him as much as he loved me." She shook her head. "Men can be so silly. He had it in his head that there was no way that one of the Easterlys could be interested in plain old David Murdstone. As if I cared one bit that his father wasn't a banker or a lawyer. There isn't a thing wrong with making furniture."

I nodded, but I had to wonder if she would have been that understanding if she'd known what else her father-in-law made.

"Besides, it was David I married, not Seth, and he's as much a gentleman as any man I've ever known."

Darned if her eyes didn't glow when she said that, and I smiled, remembering the way I'd felt when Richard and I first got married. Come to think of it, I still felt that way.

She said, "Oh, I dated other men, and I've had my share of proposals, but I knew David was the man I wanted. And it's like my daddy says, once I've made up my mind, don't get in my way, or you'll have a Florence-sized hole in your middle."

"Then your family accepts David?"

"Absolutely. They know quality when they see it."

"How about David's family?"

"It did take some time to win Jake over," she admitted. "I think he figured I was too high and mighty to really be interested in David, and that I was toying with his brother's affections. But he came around. Even though Jake's rough around the edges, he's got a good heart."

"And Seth? He must have been delighted when David finally got married, at his age and all." Then I realized what I'd implied about Florence's age. "Not that David's old —"

Florence just laughed and patted my arm. "That's all right, Laurie Anne, I know I'm not the usual blushing bride. Goodness knows my family has reminded me of that fact more than once. Seth did seem happy that David was settling down. In fact, he joked that if David hadn't married me, he'd have proposed himself. I'm glad that we married in time for him to see it. Their family — my family now — has seen so much sadness. David's mother, and then Jake's little boy, and now Seth."

The Murdstones had lost a lot, and I suddenly felt ashamed of grilling Florence. "David must be so glad he has you to help him through this."

"No more so than I am to be here for him. He's everything to me, Laurie Anne. I'm sure you know what I mean." She finished her tea. "If you'll excuse me, I think I'm going to visit the little girls' room."

"That sounds like a good idea to me, too." I stopped long enough to cover up the cookies so they wouldn't go stale, but I couldn't have been more than half a minute behind her. That put me right at the bathroom door when I heard Florence shriek, and then a loud thump.

I yanked open the door, saw Florence on her back, and started inside, but she said, "Don't come in! You'll fall!"

Looking down, I saw that the floor was coated with pale pink liquid, and I realized that I'd found the soap that had been stolen from the men's room.

CHAPTER SEVENTEEN

David came running when he heard that Florence had fallen, and it was he who made his way cautiously across the slippery tiles to check his wife for broken bones before lifting her into his arms. Only when he was sure that she was all right, other than a few bruises, did he let his fury show.

"I demand to know who is responsible for this!" he roared.

Nobody spoke, which wasn't surprising. Had I spilled that soap, I would have been afraid to admit it in the face of so much anger.

"You heard the man!" Richard added. "Who the hell is playing these damned games?"

I blinked, surprised by my husband's reaction. Then he took my hand, and I understood. If I'd gone in first instead of Florence, I would have been the one to fall instead of her, and in my condition, I might have suffered more than a few bruises. I could have lost the baby. Suddenly, all I wanted to do was wrap my arms around my tummy and hide.

"Are you all right?" he asked.

"I'm fine," I said in as strong a voice as I could manage.

"Let me take a look in there," Junior said, and strode past us. She stayed in only a minute or two, then came back with an empty soap dispenser in her hand. "Nothing fancy. Whoever it was just spilled the soap on the floor. No way to tell who."

"What's wrong now?" somebody said. Mark Pope was pushing his way in.

"Another prank," Junior said.

"One hell of a prank," David snapped. "Florence could have been seriously hurt. Something has to be done."

"Damned right!" Richard said. He told Mark what had happened to Florence, and finished with, "This is on top of what happened to Kyle this morning."

"Did anybody see anything?" Mark asked. "Who was the last one to go in there?"

It took a bit of sorting, but we finally figured out that the triplets had taken Junior's two nieces in there at ten-thirty for a costume fitting, and that they'd been in there at least half an hour. Jake had gone to the men's room during that time, and the soap dispenser was still intact then. Richard had discovered the missing soap right before one o'clock, so the trap had been set some time during those two hours.

Once again, pretty much anybody could have done it, because everybody had been busy during that time.

"It had to have been a woman," Oliver insisted. "Somebody would have noticed a man going into the ladies' room."

"No more so than a woman going into the men's room to get the soap," Aunt Maggie shot back.

"Maybe nobody went in," Junior drawled.

"What do you mean by that?" Mark asked sharply.

"The bathroom window is open, there's no screen, and there's a splash pattern around the spot where I found the dispenser. I'm guessing that whoever it was went outside and threw the dispenser in. Otherwise they would have left tracks in the soap." She pointed to the path David had left when carrying out Florence, and lifted one foot to show the soap smeared on the bottom of her boots.

Mark said, "Then there's absolutely no way of knowing who it was. People, I'm sorry, but I don't have time to babysit you

211

in the middle of a murder investigation."

"You could have fooled me," Aunt Maggie said. "I can't see that you've done a thing all day."

Mark ignored her. "I've half a mind to close down this show just to make sure nothing else happens."

"You can't!" Vasti said. "There's — I've got — you can't!"

"I understand how you feel, Mrs. Bumgarner, but in the interest of public safety . . ."

"In the interest of public safety, you had better find out who is doing this!" a voice boomed. Big Bill was standing in front of Mark. I'd gotten so used to him being one of the gang that I'd almost forgotten that he was Big Bill Walters. Apparently, so had Mark.

"But Mr. Walters, surely you don't want to risk —"

"Deputy Pope, it's your job to investigate *all* crimes in Byerly, not just the ones that make the newspaper. If you can't handle the job, then perhaps Junior would be willing —"

"No, sir, I can handle it." He took a deep breath. "Don't worry, sir, I'll take care of it."

"Good. Then I suggest you get to work. I

assume that's why you're here."

"Actually, I came to let the Murdstones know that the coroner has released Mr. Murdstone's remains so they can make the necessary arrangements."

"Thank you, Deputy Pope," Florence said. Then she said, "Mr. Fredericks? How long would it take to prepare the services we discussed?"

"I can have everything in place by as soon as tomorrow evening," Pete said.

"That'll do fine."

"I'll have your father-in-law picked up immediately." I was glad Pete wasn't wearing his Spirit of Christmas Yet to Come costume. It would have been too creepy for words.

"Thank you." Florence raised her voice. "While everybody is here, I want to let you know that the visitation for my father-in-law will be at Giles Funeral Home at seven-thirty tomorrow evening, with the funeral there at ten the next morning." To Richard she added, "I'm sure you realize that David, Jake, and I will miss rehearsal."

"I'm canceling rehearsals for both those times," Richard assured her.

"Thank you. Then let's take advantage of the time we've got."

"I think I should take you home, darling,"

David said.

"I don't think that's necessary," Florence said. "My big scene is coming up."

"But —"

"You are the sweetest man to be concerned, but if you'll let me stand up, I'll show you that no harm was done."

Sure enough, she wasn't even limping once she got on her feet again.

"Are you sure?" he asked.

"Absolutely. Though I'll feel so much better if you stay by my side."

"Of course," he said happily.

I heard Mrs. Gamp say, "Aren't they the sweetest couple?" at about the same time Aunt Maggie snorted.

Then Richard said, "Laura, don't you want to go back to Aunt Maggie's house? To take a nap or something?"

"Aren't you the sweetest thing?" I cooed.

"All right, I get the message. I just don't want you or the baby getting hurt."

"And I don't want *you* getting hurt. The next prank could just as easily be set for you."

"You're right. I'll be careful if you are."

"It's a deal." I kissed him and then pushed him toward the stage. "Now get to work." Not that I wasn't nervous, but I was even more angry. Whether the trickster had anything to do with Seth's murder or not, now I was bound and determined to find him.

I said as much to Junior a few minutes later.

"Then we're on the same page. I thought I'd wander around and make sure nothing else goes wrong."

"Do you think he would try anything else today? He's got to know that you and David will string him up if we catch him. If Richard doesn't get to him first, that is."

"Whatever else he may be, he's been pretty gutsy up until now. So I'll see if I can fade into the background a while."

"I'll come with you."

She didn't say anything. She just looked down at my tummy.

"I guess I'm not in any condition to fade, am I?"

"Maybe you should keep on talking to people instead," she suggested tactfully.

I didn't like it, but she was right. So while Junior lurked, I looked around to see who I might talk to. Tim Topper was sitting by himself, drinking coffee, and I remembered what Richard had said about him not liking Seth. Since I had nothing better to do, I figured I might as well find out why.

"Hey, Tim," I said, taking the chair next to him.

Tim was a big man, around my age, with caramel-colored skin, hazel eyes, and untamed eyebrows. "Hey, Laurie Anne," he said. "How's the little mama?" He reached out toward my tummy, then stopped himself with an embarrassed grin.

"Go ahead," I said. "Everybody else in town has already patted us. I don't want you to feel left out."

He laughed, but he patted. "Have you decided on names yet?"

"Richard and I are still negotiating. He's thinking Portia for a girl or Mercutio for a boy, but I'm partial to Scarlett or Rhett."

He nodded but didn't say anything.

"Tim! I'm kidding!"

"Whew!" he said with a loud sigh of relief. "I didn't know how long I was going to be able to keep a straight face."

"You know us better than that. Scarlett?" I shuddered, especially knowing that Vasti had put that one on her short list for Bitsy.

"People do get creative with their children's names. I'm mighty grateful my mama went with something simple like Tim. And Laurie Anne is a real pretty name."

Actually, my mother always called me Laura, but the rest of the South was stuck on Laurie Anne, and I'd given up on changing their minds. So I just said, "Thank you." Then, wanting to edge the conversation toward something more useful, I said, "Are you enjoying your acting debut?"

"I'm having a great time. You know I've got a weak spot for Dickens."

I looked up on the stage, where Big Bill was practicing the jig Scrooge dances upon realizing that he hasn't missed Christmas. "Big Bill seems to be having fun, too. Maybe I shouldn't say so, but I think he's a lot better in the part than Seth Murdstone was."

"A whole lot better," Tim said emphatically.

"It is terrible what happened to Seth. Did you know him well?"

"Never met him until we started on the play, and even if he hadn't been killed, I don't expect I'd ever have spoken to him again afterward."

"Really? Did you not —"

Tim downed the rest of his coffee. "Excuse me, Laurie Anne, but I better head on up to the stage. Richard's going to be calling for me any minute."

He was gone before I could point out that Richard had just backed up a couple of scenes, meaning that Tim wasn't going to be needed for a while yet. I frowned, not happy with the implications. Not only had Tim not liked Seth, but he wasn't even willing to talk about the man. I hated to be suspicious of him, but it looked as if I had to be.

CHAPTER EIGHTEEN

I must have been looking as nonplussed by Tim's reaction as I felt, because Mrs. Gamp appeared at my elbow and asked, "Are you all right, dear?"

"I'm fine."

"Are you sure? Mrs. Harris says you shouldn't be too careful when you're in the family way."

"She's probably right." Then, recognizing an opportunity, I said, "How are you doing? I mean, after the upset of finding Seth and all."

She shook her head back and forth. "That poor man. It's a terrible thing to be murdered to death that way. Mrs. Harris hasn't been able to sleep a wink since it happened."

"Bless her heart," I said sympathetically, though I wondered if Mrs. Gamp had stayed awake with Mrs. Harris. She was looking a bit worn around the edges. "It must have been a shock for you. Somebody told me that y'all used to date."

"Is that what they call it now?" Mrs. Gamp giggled. "We used to call it sex."

I blinked, not sure if I'd heard that right.

"We were both lonely, don't you know," Mrs. Gamp said. "His wife had passed over, and Mr. Gamp was gone. So Seth and I had sex for a while, just to pass the time."

"Oh." It was an inadequate response, but I couldn't imagine what would have been a better one.

"We eventually broke it off. Seth wanted people to think it was his idea, but I'm the one who wanted to stop. He wasn't very nice."

"Really?" I said, thinking I'd found somebody else who didn't approve of Seth. "Most everybody I've spoken to liked him."

"Oh, I don't mean he wasn't a nice man. I mean he wasn't nice in bed. Not much of a lover."

I gave up on words and just nodded a few times.

"Too much in a hurry, if you take my meaning. Not like my Mr. Gamp. He knew how to satisfy a woman."

I nodded some more.

"How's your husband?"

"I beg your pardon?" I squeaked.

220

"Sorry, dear, was I mumbling? Mrs. Harris says I'm always mincing up my words." In a louder voice, she said, "How's your husband? Is he enjoying working on the play?"

"Oh, yes, very much," I said, happy to change the subject. "He's always wanted to direct."

"That's nice. I do enjoy seeing you two together. So much in love. Just like Mr. Gamp and I were." She sighed. "He's been gone such a long time."

"I'm sorry," I said. "Was he ill?"

"No, dear, and that's a blessing. Mrs. Harris says being sick takes such a toll on a person's health. Mr. Gamp was making a delivery on wet roads and lost control of the car."

"I'm sorry," I said again. "My parents died in a car crash, too."

"It's hard to lose somebody suddenly, don't you think? Though at least it's quick. Not like some of the poor souls I see at the hospital. Lingering for weeks or even days before passing on."

"At least they get a chance to say good-bye to their families."

"Yes, and that's something I wish I could have had from my dear husband, but not if it meant he had to suffer. Like poor Barnaby Murdstone."

"I heard he lived quite a while after the accident."

"Over a week. Burns are so painful, but Barnaby truly believed that he'd get better, and that can make all the difference. The doctor had told him there was a chance he'd be home for Christmas, and Barnaby was hoping for that. He wouldn't admit it, but I think he was afraid that Santa Claus wouldn't find him if he was in the hospital." She smiled. "You don't often find a boy his age who still believes. I even helped him write a letter to Santa."

"That's sweet," I said, but I couldn't help but feel badly for the boy that Santa would never find.

"Now, now, dear," Mrs. Gamp said, "don't mourn for Barnaby. He's in a better place, just as Mr. Gamp and your parents are. I truly believe that."

"I do, too," I said, "but I still miss them."

"Just try to remember the good times. Every time I'm feeling lonely, I think about Mr. Gamp's last gift to me."

"What was that?"

"The dear man had signed up for a life insurance policy just before the accident, almost as if he'd known something was going to happen. I've been living off of the proceeds ever since."

"Really? That must have been some policy."

"With the baby coming, I'm sure you understand what a blessing security is. In fact, when Mr. Gamp passed away . . ." She stopped. "Anyway, it was such a relief when Miss Todger told me about it."

"Miss Todger?" I said. "Clara Todger?"

"Do you know her? My husband worked for the Todger family, and the policy was arranged through work. Every month the insurance company sends them a check, and then they send me one."

I nodded, but I couldn't believe that Mrs. Gamp was that naive. Didn't she know what the Todger family did, or where that money really came from? Though I didn't know much about bootlegging, I was fairly sure they didn't have group insurance plans. Besides, the payoff for life insurance was typically a lump sum, not monthly payments. While the settlement from my parents' death had paid most of my way through college, it had run out years before.

"You should be looking into insurance, too, for your little one. You never know what could happen, so you have to plan for it." She patted my arm and said, "I have to get back to work now. Mrs. Harris says idle hands are the devil's work."

It was just as well that she left — I needed a few minutes to catch my breath. First, she'd given me far too much information about her relationship with Seth, but at least I was reasonably sure that she hadn't been a woman scorned after all. Then she turned around and gave me a much better motive for her to want Seth dead. Her husband must have been the Todger deliveryman who'd died. Not only had Mrs. Gamp been left a widow, but she'd lost her baby, too.

The question was, did Mrs. Gamp realize that Seth had been the cause of it all?

Chapter Nineteen

After all that, I needed a drink, even if it couldn't be anything stronger than water. I found Junior at the kitchen sink, elbow deep in soap suds.

"What are you doing?" I asked her.

"What does it look like I'm doing?"

It looked like she was washing dishes, which was completely out of character, but I didn't know if she'd appreciate my mentioning it. I reached into the refrigerator to get a bottle of water.

"Is that bottle sealed?" she asked before I could open it.

"I think so." I checked the plastic screw-top to be sure. "Why? What happened?"

"Nothing, but something almost did. I came in to get a cup of coffee, and was about to take a swallow when I noticed that it smelled funny."

"Poison?"

"I don't know about that, but there was

something in there that wasn't supposed to be. It smelled like dishwasher soap."

"Is that dangerous?"

"Heck if I know, and even if it is, I don't imagine people would have drunk more than a swallow, but I'm taking no chances." She reached into the soapy water for the coffeemaker's glass pot and carefully rinsed it. "I'm going to warn people to be careful of what they leave open; I'm not eating or drinking anything that's been left unattended unless it's sealed."

I checked the screw top again, just to be sure, then opened it to take a drink. "This is crazy," I said.

"It's not the only thing I found while I was lurking. Jake's got a workshop backstage to put sets together, and I got to thinking that tools can be dangerous at the best of times. So I took a look and noticed that the guard on his circular saw was so loose it was just barely staying on."

"You lost me, Junior." In fact, she'd probably have lost me if she'd mentioned any tool other than hammer, pliers, or screwdriver.

"You know what a circular saw looks like?"

"Sort of."

"The guard is the round metal piece that covers up the blade until you start cutting.

It's supposed to help you guide the saw and protect you from pieces flying up. If the guard fell off while you were using the saw, you'd probably ruin whatever it was you were working on, not to mention what it could do to your hand."

"Jesus, that's scary."

"Not as scary as knowing that there might be other traps that I haven't found yet." She finished washing up and dried off her hands. "I sure hope you've found something that will tell us who killed Seth."

"No such luck. All I've got is more maybes."

"Can't you come up with a yes or no once in a while?"

"How many definite answers have you come up with?"

"Only that I definitely hate practical jokes. What have you got?"

I told her about Tim first, ending with, "I know it's not much, but other than Clara Todger, he's the only one we've found who didn't like Seth."

"The only one who admits it, anyway," Junior pointed out. "Chances are that the killer wouldn't come out and say he hated the man."

"Granted. But I wish I knew what Tim had against Seth."

"We'll see what we can do about that," Junior said. "Who else?"

"Would you believe Mrs. Gamp?"

"At this point, I'd believe Mrs. Harris."

I told her what Aunt Nora had told me about Mrs. Gamp and Seth dating, then repeated what Mrs. Gamp had said about it.

"You are kidding me!" Junior said.

"I wouldn't have believed it myself if I hadn't heard it, but that's what she said."

Junior scratched her head. "Just when I think I've heard everything . . . Anyway, if she's the one who dumped Seth, doesn't that let her out of the running? Unless you think she was lying about it."

"I don't think she was. It was what she told me next that I'm thinking about." I explained how I'd figured out that Mrs. Gamp's late husband must have been Clara Todger's delivery man. "So she had a whopping big motive to kill Seth."

"Maybe," Junior said doubtfully.

"You don't think a hit-and-run makes a good motive? Not to mention the miscarriage."

"Sure, either of them could lead to payback when the emotions are running hot. But not this many years down the road."

"Revenge is a dish best served cold."

Junior raised an eyebrow.

"All right, it's hard to imagine Mrs. Gamp carrying a grudge all this time and not doing something about it."

"Not to mention the fact that she'd hardly have slept with the man if she'd known he killed her husband. So we've got no reason to believe Mrs. Gamp knew it was Seth who caused the accident. She didn't even know her husband was carting moonshine."

"It doesn't sound reasonable to me either, but you've got to admit that a grown woman with an imaginary friend might do unreasonable things now and then."

"There's crazy and then there's *crazy.*"

"Is that something Mrs. Harris says?"

Junior didn't answer. "What else have you got?"

I ran through the other gossip I'd gotten from Aunt Nora, but without much enthusiasm.

Junior wasn't enthusiastic either. "Either Sid hit him for being absolutely right about his son a long time ago, or Big Bill got tired of trying to buy his property. Yeah, either one of those would drive me to kill a man."

"I'm doing the best I can," I said, irritated. "How did you think I work?"

"I didn't know, but I didn't expect you to come up with silly ideas like these."

"Why don't you go see what *you* can find out?" I snapped. I shouldn't have, but my feet were swelling and I was hungry again.

"Don't be that way, Laurie Anne," Junior said. "If this is the way you work, then that's the way we'll do it."

I didn't say anything.

"You want me to get you something to drink?"

"That might be nice," I allowed.

She fetched a bottle of cold water for me, a Coke for herself, and some cookies for us to share. "Do you feel better?" she asked once I'd eaten more than half of the cookies.

"Yes, thank you," I said sheepishly. "I'm sorry for snapping. Blame it on the hormones."

"That's all right. I'm sorry for calling your ideas silly."

"They were silly," I said. "At least, this batch was. Most of my theories are pretty outlandish. But when I dig into something, eventually something starts to make sense."

"And that'll be the answer?"

"Of course not. The sensible one is never the answer. It's always something even more ridiculous, which makes me feel like a complete idiot for not seeing it in the first place."

"This is something you do for fun?" Junior asked. "Why do you keep doing this, Laurie Anne?"

"Why do you?" I countered.

"It's my job."

"You could get another job."

"I suppose I could, but I like being a cop. The thing is, I like the whole job, not just solving murders. I don't think you're interested in the rest of what I do."

"You mean making traffic stops and breaking up bar fights and all?"

She nodded.

"No, I'm not interested in that."

"You do like being a programmer, don't you?"

"Absolutely. It's fun in a geeky way I won't even try to explain."

"So why do you keep getting tangled up in murder?"

I could have told her that I only did it because people asked me to. But that wouldn't have been honest. My family wouldn't have kept asking me if I'd told them not to. Well, maybe Vasti would have, but even she would have given up eventually. There was more to it than that. "You know what I think it is, Junior? The fact is, I'm a good programmer, but I'll never be a great programmer. There are fourteen-year-olds who can write more elegant code than I can, and they can write it faster, too."

"Are you serious?"

"Absolutely. The great programmers seem to be born to it, just like with other artists. I met some real-life geniuses in college, and that's when I realized that I just wasn't that good. Don't get me wrong. I do solid work, and I make my deadlines, and I can supervise projects. That's all important. But I'm not ever going to be anything *special* at work. The only time I feel like I'm special, that I'm doing something other people can't do, is when I'm trying to solve a murder."

"But other people do solve murders. Other than cops, I mean. I was talking to cops from other parts of the state one time, and they told me there's an older lady in Asheville who's a peach of a crime solver, and a judge near Raleigh. Charlotte's got a realtor and an antiques dealer."

"There are people other than Larry Bird who play basketball, but I bet he still feels special."

"You've got a point," she admitted, then paused for a minute. "Laurie Anne, you know I'm not sentimental and I'm not good with words. Heck, if it weren't for Hallmark, I wouldn't be able to wish my own mama happy Mother's Day. But I want to tell you something. You are special. Not just because of finding killers or programming or anything like that — it's because of who you are. The way you dropped everything to come down here so Richard could direct this play, and the way you help out your family when they need you, and the way you put yourself out for your friends. I think that's mighty special."

My eyes teared up, and it wasn't the hormones that time. "I don't know what to say."

"Good," she said firmly. "Because I sure as heck don't want to hear that you've repeated this to anybody else." She swigged down the last of her Coke. "Now let's get back to work."

"Can I hug your neck?" I asked.

"Lord, no." Then she relented. "All right, but don't expect a Christmas present from me!"

CHAPTER TWENTY

Once Junior had endured my hug, I was ready and raring to go. All I needed was a direction. "Any suggestions?" I asked Junior.

"We've still got the Murdstone brothers to talk to."

"I've been avoiding them," I said, wrinkling my nose. "I've questioned bereaved parents, siblings, and spouses without blinking, but I have a problem with the recently orphaned. It's probably because I wonder how I'd have felt if somebody had bothered me right after my parents died."

"I understand, but if we're going to do this . . ."

"I know, we've got to talk to David and Jake. Wouldn't it be better for you to talk to them solo? Having the two of us approach them might make them suspicious."

"Laurie Anne, do you think there's anybody in this building who doesn't know what we're up to?"

"All right, which one first?"

"Since David's onstage, and I don't think your husband would appreciate our taking him away, let's try Jake."

We found Jake in the workshop backstage. There was a board laid across two sawhorses to use as a table, and around it were scattered bits of wood and cloth and a miscellany of tools. Jake was carefully painting a freestanding fake fireplace.

"Hey, Jake," I said cheerily.

He turned our way briefly and said, "Hey," before turning back to his work.

I asked, "Is that Scrooge's fireplace?"

"Yep," he said, not looking up.

"It's very convincing. If somebody didn't know better, he'd try to set a real fire in there." Then I remembered how his son had died, and hastily added, "All the sets look great."

"Thanks."

A minute passed. I said, "Can I help you any?"

"You could hand me that rag on the table."

"Sure," I said, and did so. "Anything else?"

"Not a thing."

Junior and I stood there while Jake continued to paint. When I started to feel my feet swelling, I nudged Junior. She was the professional. Let her interrogate the man's back.

"Jake, I imagine you know Laurie Anne and I have been asking questions about your father's death," she said.

"That's what I hear. Mark Pope said I don't have to talk to you if I didn't want to."

"No, I suppose you don't," Junior said, "but why wouldn't you want to?"

"You wouldn't want to talk about it either if you were in my place," he said, his voice catching. "But your daddy's alive."

"Mine's not," I said softly. "We can't bring Seth back no matter what we do, but if it were my father, I'd do everything I could to find out what happened to him."

He stopped painting — stopped moving at all for a few seconds. Then he put his brush down, wiped his hands on the rag, and turned around. "All right. What can I tell you?"

Junior said, "Do you know why somebody would have wanted to kill your father?"

"Everybody liked Daddy."

"What about in his business?"

"You mean the chairs?" Jake asked, and I thought I heard sarcasm. Of course he must have known that Junior had wanted to arrest Seth for moonshining.

"In any of his business dealings," Junior said evenly.

"Daddy wasn't the kind of man to make enemies."

"Is that right? I hear he and your brother didn't always see eye to eye."

Jake flushed angrily. "That doesn't mean David would kill him!"

"You know I had to ask," Junior said.

He took a deep breath and said, "I guess you did."

"What about Florence?"

"Daddy wasn't against the marriage, if that's what you're asking. Even if he had been, that wouldn't have stopped them two. Daddy's only regret was that at their age they weren't likely to give him any more grandchildren." He paused. "Anything else?"

Junior looked at me.

I said, "I heard that Big Bill Walters was interested in buying your house, but that your father didn't want to sell."

"That's right, but there wasn't enough money involved to kill over."

"Are you going to sell the house now?"

He flushed again but answered me. "I haven't decided yet. I haven't decided much of anything."

"What about your father's business? I as-

237

sume you inherit it."

"I get the business and the house, and David gets Daddy's insurance," he said tersely, "which comes out about even."

"Are you going to keep the business going?"

Jake looked me in the eye, as if trying to decide how much I knew about his business. "I expect I will. I don't know anything else. Just making chairs."

I mentally ran through our other suspects, but I couldn't think of anybody Jake would be able to tell us about. Apparently, Junior couldn't either.

"I guess that's it, then," she said. "Thank you for talking to us."

He didn't answer — just went back to his painting. I wanted to say something comforting to him, but there wasn't anything I could say.

Junior and I came out from backstage and found ourselves in the middle of a three-way argument involving Vasti, Aunt Maggie, and Carlelle.

"Why haven't you been keeping up with it?" Vasti was asking.

"I only volunteered to be in charge of props, and it's not a prop," Aunt Maggie said. "Scrooge's cane is part of his costume."

Vasti turned to Carlelle. "Then you should be keeping up with it."

"Maybe I should be, but I haven't been," she retorted. "I didn't make it, so I didn't store it."

"Don't tell me somebody booby-trapped Scrooge's cane, too," I said.

"How would I know?" Vasti snapped. "We don't even know where the foolish thing is."

"When was the last time anybody saw it?" Junior asked sharply.

"Big Bill says he never saw it, so Seth must have — I mean, it must have gotten misplaced in all the confusion. I could ask Jake to make another one, but . . ." Even Vasti must have realized how awkward that would be.

Aunt Maggie said, "I think I've got one Big Bill can borrow for the show. It won't be authentic, but —"

"I'm sure it will be fine," Vasti said. "Just make sure this one doesn't get lost."

The three of them went in separate directions, and I noticed Junior was looking speculative.

"Junior?" I said. "What did I miss?"

"I was just wondering about that cane."

"It sounds like the practical joker struck again."

"Maybe. But don't you remember Seth

239

carrying that thing around all the time, practicing with it?" Then she answered herself. "No, of course not. You and Richard weren't here when Jake made it for him."

"What's your point?"

"I'm just wondering if Seth had it in his hand when he went for that last cigarette break. Because now that I think of it, that cane was just about the right thickness to make that dent in his skull."

"Lord, I bet you're right." I thought about it. "Then the murder must have been a spur-of-the-moment thing. Otherwise the killer would have brought something along to do the job."

"Not necessarily. The killer might have had something else in mind, but when he saw the cane, he decided to use it instead." Before I could object, she said, "But I think you're right. I've thought all along that this killing felt unplanned, and the cane as murder weapon just reinforces that. I just wish we could find the thing so we'd know for sure."

Junior wanted to talk to David after that, but there was no chance of that. Since all three Murdstones were going to be missing rehearsal the next day to get ready for Seth's visitation and funeral, Richard was making the most of Florence's and David's time by working on their scenes. Even when David wasn't onstage, he was staying close by Florence, obviously making sure she came to no harm.

With opening night just two days away, everybody else was working at a fevered pitch, too, so we decided to call it quits for the day. Junior did lurk some more, both to defuse any other practical jokes and to search for Scrooge's cane, but I spent the evening hemming a black robe for the Spirit of Christmas Yet to Be.

It was far too late when Richard finally shut things down for the night. I tried to bounce our ideas off him, which might have worked had he not been trying to bounce ideas for blocking off me. We finally decided that we both needed distraction, and went to bed to provide the best distraction we knew. We fell asleep immediately afterward.

CHAPTER
TWENTY-ONE

At least the next morning started out well. I think the Murdstones' absence improved the mood. I always feel kind of guilty having a good time when there are people in mourning nearby, and maybe others felt the same, because up until mid-morning, people were more enthusiastic than they'd been since we got into town.

Then Vasti showed up and things went downhill quickly. She started out griping because the program page proofs weren't ready yet, and she was sure Sally Hendon was behind the delay. Since she couldn't do anything about that, she laid into the triplets for not having the costumes ready, refusing to remember that rearranging the cast had slowed them down. Then she went after Aunt Maggie, because we still needed a coal scuttle and an artificial turkey, but Aunt Maggie gave her a look that shut her up pretty quickly.

Before she could find another target, Vasti's in-laws showed up. They were supposed to be watching Bitsy, but she was coming down with a cold and was refusing to take a bottle. So Vasti had to take her, and though I felt sorry for both mother and daughter, their combined whining started to get on everybody's nerves.

"She's got good lungs, hasn't she?" Junior said, talking loudly to be heard over the caterwauling.

"Do you mean Bitsy or Vasti?"

"Both, now that you mention it," she said.

If all that weren't enough, Sally Hendon picked that moment to sail in, immaculately clad in pink as always. Bitsy had spit up on Vasti twice, had thoroughly wrinkled her blouse by hanging on to her and crying into her shoulder, and had yanked on Vasti's hair so much that every bit of curl had fallen out. It was not Vasti's proudest moment; Sally smiled broadly when she saw her.

"Oh, bless your heart," she cooed. "Is the baby not feeling well?"

Vasti glared at her. "What do you want?"

"Vasti, don't you think you should take that little darling home? She needs her rest, and it looks like you could use a little down time yourself."

Bitsy picked that moment to sneeze, messily, on Sally, which improved Vasti's spirits. "Actually, Bitsy loves being around people," she said with a smile. "Don't you want to hold her?"

Bitsy sneezed again and Sally hastily stepped back.

"I better not," she said. "I was wondering if you'd received any more packages from Morris Costumes."

"Why would we?" Vasti asked suspiciously. "We already got what we ordered. In fact, I've been meaning to ask you about that —"

"Shoot!" Sally said, cutting Vasti off. "I was hoping they'd delivered them here by mistake. Let me call my stage manager again." She pulled a cell phone — pink, of course — out of her pocketbook, and dialed a number. "Lil? This is Sally."

Vasti glowered, both because Sally had ignored her question and because Lil was another Junior League member who could have helped vote Vasti in.

Sally said, "Has that box shown up? The one with the musicians' costumes? . . . It has? All of them? . . . Are you sure they're going to fit? You know what a big man Roger Bailey is. . . . Wonderful. I'll be back over there in two shakes. Bye, now." She put the phone back in her purse and said, "Silly me.

244

The costumes were there all along. I'm so sorry to have interrupted you when I know how far behind y'all must be."

"Why do you have costumes for the Ramblers?" Vasti asked.

"Haven't you heard? They're going to be playing in the Follies."

Vasti's face turned bright red. Roger's Ramblers was Byerly's only group of professional musicians, and they were a big draw at any local event. Roger was also our uncle, so for him to be playing in Sally's show was adding insult to injury.

"Aunt Ruby Lee said they were booked all month!" Vasti said.

"I guess they had a cancelation," said Sally, smiling so much like the cat who ate the canary that I was surprised there weren't feathers between her teeth. "I've been meaning to ask you, Vasti. What kind of music are you having for your show?"

"It's a play, not a musical," Vasti snapped. "We don't need music."

"That's funny. The version of the script I looked at said there was supposed to be music before and after the show."

"What?" Vasti shot a look at Richard onstage.

Richard said, "Traditionally, there is music while the audience is seated, and sometimes

245

Scrooge leads the audience in a carol at the end, but it's not necessary."

"I suppose you can use a tape," Sally said sweetly. "That would be almost as good as real music."

"We're having live music, too," Vasti declared.

"Really? If you like, maybe I can help you find somebody."

"I can find somebody myself. In fact, I've already got somebody in mind."

"Who?" Sally wanted to know.

Vasti assumed an air of mystery. "It's a surprise."

Sally hesitated, probably trying to decide if Vasti was bluffing, but finally said, "I can't wait to hear who you get."

"Buy a ticket," Vasti said ungraciously, "and you can find out."

"Oh, I'll be here, ready to help out with any last-minute problems you have come opening night."

"There won't be —" But I guess Vasti realized that she might be tempting fate. "You go tend to your own show." Then she looked around for a handy victim. "Odelle, would you walk Sally to her car? I don't want any more practical jokes."

"Whatever do you mean?" Sally said, but Vasti grabbed her cell phone and started dialing. Realizing she'd lost her audience, Sally let Odelle accompany her to her car.

As soon as she was gone, Vasti put down the phone and said, "All right, who around here can sing or play an instrument?"

"Vasti," Richard said, "the play really doesn't need music. Or maybe we can use a Victrola — that's what one version of the play calls for."

"I *said* we're having live music," Vasti said in a tone that brooked no argument.

"If that's what you want," Richard said, sounding exasperated, "but you'll have to handle that part yourself. I've got my hands full already."

"Fine," Vasti snapped. With Bitsy on one shoulder, she got out her address book and started thumbing through it furiously while Richard went back to his scene.

Junior came over, looking alarmed. "We better get out of here."

"What's the matter?"

"Your cousin is on a rampage. Five will get you ten that in a few minutes she'll be dragging people together to make them sing. I'm a terrible singer, Laurie Anne."

"You can't be that bad," I said.

"Have you ever heard someone run their nails down a blackboard?"

I nodded.

"I'm worse."

"Then don't worry. Vasti won't try to force you."

"Are you sure about that? She's got that same look Daddy gets on Christmas Eve when he hasn't found a present for Mama."

I looked at my cousin, and sure enough, she was already asking Mrs. Gamp if she knew the words to "God Rest Ye Merry, Gentlemen." "Where do you want to go?"

"Anywhere but here."

I grabbed my pocketbook and coat, waved to get Richard's attention, and mouthed the words *we're going out.* Vasti called my name as we headed for the door, but I pretended I hadn't heard. We didn't stop until we were out of the parking lot.

"We weren't doing any good in there, anyway," I said. "The one we really need to talk to is David."

"He's probably at home," Junior pointed out. "We could go pay him a visit."

"We can't just barge in and start questioning him. Especially not today. They're burying his father tomorrow."

"In this line of work, I can't always afford to be sensitive."

"You're a cop. Nobody expects you to be sensitive."

"Thanks."

"Sorry. What I mean is that people will forgive you if you bypass the niceties. If I do, I'll get grief for the next umpteen years." Five years earlier, I'd worn black to a wedding, and even though people did it all the time in Boston, it wasn't done in Byerly, and I still heard about it every time anybody planned a wedding. "Of course, it is acceptable to go calling if we bring food."

Junior looked at me sideways. "We don't have to cook it ourselves, do we? My cooking is as bad as my singing."

"I think we could get away with buying something." I wasn't a bad cook, but I wasn't interested in spending a lot of time in the kitchen. "They've always got nice fruit baskets at the grocery store this time of year. Let's go get one of them."

It was still early in the day, so the store wasn't crowded, and it didn't take us but a few minutes to find what we wanted.

As we walked back to the car, I saw a familiar face. "Looks like your deputy is on foot patrol," I said to Junior.

She looked over to where Mark Pope was leaned up against a car, drinking a cup of coffee. "The criminals of Byerly must be shaking in their boots," she said in disgust. "Not that we've done a whole lot of good ourselves."

"The day is young," I said, determined to be cheerful. "Come to think of it," I said, "the day's a bit young to go to David's house, don't you think?"

She checked her watch. "You're right. I don't think it would be polite to go over there until ten, eleven o'clock. Any suggestions?"

"Nothing to do with the case," I admitted, "but how would you like to go to the mall in Hickory?"

"Laurie Anne, please don't make me go to the mall during Christmas season."

"Come on, Junior, it'll be fun. How crowded can it be on a Wednesday morning?"

At least, that was what I thought. As we circled the parking lot at the Valley Hills Mall, trying to find a reasonably close spot, I admitted that I might have been overly optimistic. But I still needed to get some stocking stuffers for Richard, and unlike Junior, I enjoy Christmas shopping. So I sweet-talked her into continuing to look for a space, with promises of a treat from Charleston Cookie Company.

On the third or fourth circuit, I said, "Junior, look!"

"Is somebody pulling out?"

"No, but look over there. Isn't that Mark

again? In that green Saturn."

She peered through parked cars. "Yes, it is. What's he doing here?"

"Shopping?"

She shook her head. "Trey has a dentist appointment today and won't be on duty until six. Mark's on his own, which means he shouldn't be outside the city limits, let alone in Hickory — and he's not even in the squad car."

It suddenly dawned on me. "Junior, he's following us."

"I think you're right."

"He's sure going to be disappointed when he figures out we're just shopping. Unless you want to borrow a camcorder so we can videotape him neglecting his duty and show it to the city council."

"It's tempting, but he'd come up with some excuse or another." Then she grinned. "Want to have some fun?"

"I'd love to."

The parking place gods must have approved, because just that second, a station wagon pulled out in front of us. Junior parked, but we stayed in the car long enough to plan, and to give Mark a chance to find a place to leave his car.

Then, with much ostentatious looking around and whispers, we headed inside the mall. Mark walked down the next row, hunched over as if that would keep us from seeing him over the roofs of the parked cars. The funny thing was, if he'd just walked normally, we probably wouldn't have noticed him, but walking like that made him painfully obvious.

Once inside, Junior and I led the poor fellow on the wildest goose chase we could manage. We synchronized our watches, shared significant looks, and exchanged hand signals. We'd stop suddenly at window displays, and just as suddenly take off again. I made a point of asking half a dozen people for the time, trying to make it seem as if something more meaningful were being said. Junior made two or three cell phone calls, then switched to pay phones, as if she were trying to avoid being traced. Then we split up, just to see which one he'd follow.

Mark looked terribly confused, but he finally decided to take off after Junior. That gave me time to do what I'd wanted to do in the first place, which was shop.

I quite enjoyed myself despite the crowds. The mall was festooned with garlands and lights, with a very credible Santa Claus holding court in the middle of the mall. I imagined Richard and me in another year, taking our baby to get a picture taken on

Santa's lap, and had a hard time resisting the impulse to buy something made of velvet and ruffles to put on a baby that hadn't even been born yet.

It was also a relief to get my thoughts away from Seth's murder. What with the last-minute trip and the play, Richard and I hadn't had much time to savor the holiday season, and it did me good to remember the message the three Spirits had brought to Scrooge.

An hour and a half later, I went to meet Junior and found her in the food court, sipping a Coke and looking mighty satisfied.

"Didn't you buy anything?" I asked her.

"Just this Coke and a bottle of water for you. It looks like you bought enough for both of us." She took my shopping bags so I could sit down. "Is all of this for Richard?"

"Most of it," I said sheepishly.

She looked into one bag, pulled out my new pocketbook, and raised one eyebrow. "I didn't realize that the men in Boston were carrying pocketbooks."

"That's for me. Belk had a sale on them — it's a D'Arcy Designs. It cost less than half what it would in Boston."

"And this?" she said, pulling out a music CD.

"It's Christmas music," I said defensively. "Richard likes Kathé Ward's songs, too."

"I'm sure he does." She reached for the bag from Tamsin's Toy Chest, but I took it from her before she could open it. "That's a surprise. So where's our tail? Or did he give up?"

"Nope, he's over there by that planter. He looked so worn out, I sat down early so he could catch his breath."

"Where have the two of you been?" I asked.

"Where haven't we been?" she said. "I think we must have walked every foot of this mall, not to mention three rides on the merry-go-round."

"He followed you onto the merry-go-round?"

"He wanted to, but he settled for finding a column he could duck behind every time I came around." She shook her head. "I bet that now he thinks he should have followed you instead." She checked her watch. "Are you about ready to head back to Byerly? I think we've tormented him enough."

I finished up the bottle of water. "Just let me take a quick pit stop." Darned if Mark didn't follow me to the ladies' room. In fact, he was so busy watching me instead of looking where he was going, that he almost came inside.

Junior and a semi-hidden Mark were waiting when I came out, and we all headed for the door. There was a bench right next to it, and I nonchalantly dropped the bag from the toy store on it and kept going.

"I thought that was my Christmas present," Junior said.

"It is, in a way." As I'd expected, Mark saw me leave the bag and couldn't wait to grab it. I started snickering on the way back to the car.

"What's so funny?" Junior wanted to know. "What's in that bag?"

"An official junior detective kit," I said. "I figured Mark could use all the help he can get."

Junior burst out laughing, and then we drove by Mark's car. He was in the front seat with the detective kit in his hand, and the expression on his face started us laughing all over again.

"Laurie Anne," Junior said, "we have got to go shopping together more often."

CHAPTER
TWENTY-TWO

Though we kept a sharp eye out on the drive back to Byerly, apparently Mark had quit following us, so we went to David and Florence's house.

I wasn't sure what David did, but whatever it was, it paid well. Or maybe Florence's law practice brought in the money. They had a large, white shingle house in the nicest part of town, just two doors down from the Walters estate, which was the benchmark for society in Byerly.

There were a couple of cars already in the circular driveway, but Junior thought the BMW was David's and the MG was Florence's — meaning that we'd caught them at home and alone, which was what we wanted.

After we rang the door chime, I looked doubtfully at the grocery store fruit basket I was carrying. "Are you sure this is nice enough, Junior?"

"Social niceties are your department, re-member?"

Florence opened the door then, and her smile of delight reassured me. Though I didn't quite believe her when she said it was the prettiest fruit basket she'd ever seen, at least I could be sure that she hadn't been insulted by our offering.

"Y'all come right on in," she said, taking the basket from us. "David was just saying he could use a break, and I know he's going to dig right into one of these lovely tanger-ines."

"I hope we're not interrupting anything," I said.

"Not at all. We've just been checking e-mail and voice mail. I'm afraid we've been so distracted by all that's been going on, that we've neglected our businesses ter-ribly."

"I'm sure everybody understands that."

"Of course they do, but one does like to live up to one's obligations."

As we spoke, Florence led us down the entry hall with its sparkling chandelier and mirror-polished black and white tiles, through a living room that was far too big to be as cozy as it was, and into a kitchen that was as large as the Todger family's but far more modern.

"You go ahead into the sun room and let me get y'all something to drink," Florence said. "Iced tea? Maybe a Coca-cola? Or would coffee be better on a cold day like this?"

"A Coke would be great," Junior said.

"I don't suppose your iced tea is decaffeinated, is it?" I asked wistfully.

"I've got both kinds. Y'all go have a seat and tell David to shut down his computer for a minute or two."

David must have heard his wife, because he was already rising to greet us when we came into what Florence had called the sun room. It was another spacious room, with two desks and accompanying office furniture in one half, and a wicker love seat and chairs in the other half. Both sides were lined with hanging baskets of plants and flowers, including poinsettias and a blooming Christmas cactus.

"Junior, Laurie Anne. How nice of you two to come by. Did I hear Florence say you'd brought us something?"

"Just a little fruit basket," I said. "So you'd have something to snack on."

"It was so kind of you to think of us. Please, come sit down and visit for a while."

The two of them were so gracious, I almost felt guilty. But my rational side reminded me that if either of them had killed Seth, I had nothing to feel guilty about. And if not, surely they'd want his murderer found, so I still had nothing to feel guilty about.

When Junior took one of the chairs, I sat in the other to leave the love seat for David and Florence. Sure enough, after Florence brought us our drinks, she promptly cuddled up next to him.

"How are things back at rehearsal?" Florence asked.

"A little rocky," I admitted, and explained how Vasti was trying to find somebody to play or sing as part of the play.

"Goodness," Florence said, "your cousin is so energetic."

"That's Vasti, all right," I said wryly. "She never gives up when she really wants something."

"That must be a family trait," Florence said, a twinkle in her eye. "I think we all know this isn't just a condolence call."

"No, it's not," I said. "I know y'all realize that Junior and I are looking into Seth's death."

"That's what Florence told me," David said, "but I have to admit that I'm not comfortable with the idea. I can understand your interest, Junior — it must be frustrating to be sidelined during an investigation. But Laurie Anne . . ." He shook his head, as if disappointed in me. "I can't say how much the thought of making my father's death into some sort of game pains me."

I flushed, half in anger and half in shame that he might be right, but before I could say anything in my own defense, Junior spoke.

"That's where you're wrong," she said. "Laurie Anne doesn't think Seth's death was anything other than what it was: murder. Now there are people in this world who could see a man drowning and not jump in to save him, or see an old lady fall and not stop to help her up. Not Laurie Anne. She knows that somebody killed your daddy, and that Mark might not be able to find out who it is. So she's not going to sit by and let a murderer go free. Here she is five months pregnant, but instead of knitting booties, she's spending every minute trying to get a murderer off the streets. Maybe you call that playing a game, but I don't!"

I don't know who was more astonished by Junior's outburst, David or me. He stammered, "I had no idea that — I mean, I thought that —" Finally he gathered himself together. "I beg your pardon, Laurie Anne. Please forgive me."

"That's all right. I know my snooping around is kind of weird, but —"

"No, not at all. Now that I can appreciate what you're trying to do, please tell me what I can do to help."

"Me, too," Florence chimed in.

They gave me their full attention, and it made me downright nervous. After Junior's build-up, I was sure they expected a brilliant bunch of questions, and mine were bound to disappoint them. "My first question is the obvious one. Why would anybody have wanted to kill your father?"

"I just don't know," David said. "My father had no enemies. I can't even think of anybody who didn't like him."

"That fits in with what I've heard elsewhere, with only one exception." Actually, there were two, but I didn't think Junior would want me to bring Clara Todger into the conversation. "Tim Topper didn't care for him."

"Really?" David sounded sincerely surprised. "I didn't think Tim had ever met Dad before we started rehearsals, and they seemed to get along. They even went out together one night."

"Maybe I misunderstood," I said, though I didn't think so. Tim was one of those folks who let their feelings show, and the feelings he'd shown about Seth hadn't been friendly ones.

"In fact," David said, "I'd be a more likely candidate than Tim. Not that I wanted Dad dead," he quickly added, "but it's no secret that we didn't agree about everything."

Florence chuckled. "You didn't agree about anything."

"I'm afraid not. Even though we were both in town, we didn't see each other all that often. I regret it, but the best explanation I can give is that my father and I were very different men, and we wanted different things in life."

"Do you mean in terms of Seth's business?" I said carefully.

For the first time, David wouldn't meet my eyes. "That was an old argument. Dad had always assumed that once I finished school, I'd go into business with him and Jake. Unfortunately, I had no interest in . . . in furniture."

"Or in moonshine," Florence said.

"Dear Lord!" David's face turned white. "How did you . . . ?" Then, "Not in front of —"

"Pish," Florence said, waving her hand airily. "Junior already knows, and I'd be very much surprised if Laurie Anne didn't, too. So why pussyfoot around?"

"But . . ." Words failed him.

"Poor darling, I didn't mean to spring it on you this way, but I've known for ages that your father wasn't supporting himself making lawn furniture. I've sat in his chairs. There's no way he could have raised a dog on them, let alone two boys. But don't worry. It's still a closely guarded secret. My source is completely discreet, and I'm sure these ladies are, too."

"You knew before the wedding?"

"Of course."

"And you married me anyway?"

"David Murdstone, I'd have married you if your father were General Sherman come back from the grave to burn down Byerly."

"Oh Florence . . . I'm so sorry I didn't tell you, but I was afraid. Not just because of your place in society —"

"Pish to that!" Florence said.

"But you're an officer of the court. I didn't want to compromise your position."

"I thought as much, which is why I don't blame you for keeping your secret." She waggled her finger. "As long as you don't keep any more secrets from me."

"Never," he said, catching her hand to bring it to his lips.

While still holding his wife's gaze, David said, "I'm sorry, Laurie Anne, but I don't think there's anything else I can tell you."

"I hear Big Bill Walters wanted to buy your father's land," I said.

"He did, but my father told him he wasn't interested in selling for a few years, and Big Bill was willing to wait."

"Didn't your father have an argument with Sid Honeywell?"

"That was years ago. Dad bought gas at Sid's station every week."

"What about Mrs. Gamp?"

"What about her?"

"Never mind." I looked at Junior, who shrugged. "I guess there's nothing else we need to ask you. Unless either of y'all know of anything."

"No," they said in unison.

"We'll let ourselves out," Junior said, and neither Florence nor David argued the point. They were still looking deeply into one another's eyes when we left the room, and we got out of the house as quickly as we could.

"I wonder if that love seat folds out into a bed," Junior said once we were back in the car. "Not that that would stop them."

"Junior Norton, you ought to be ashamed."

"Ashamed! Hell, I'm jealous. You might be, too, if you didn't have Richard."

"I didn't realize you were in the market for a husband."

"Do you think I want to stay single my whole life? I'm not in a hurry, but it'd be nice to have somebody to come home to."

"Kids, too?"

"Sure, why not?"

I couldn't help but picture a pregnant Junior with a gun belt stretched across her maternity smock. Then I thought about her under the sway of hormones, which was scary. My own mood swings were terrifying enough, and unlike Junior, I didn't carry a gun.

Junior must have misinterpreted my silence, because she said, "You're not going to start fixing me up, are you? My sisters keep dragging single men over to meet me, and it's worrying me to death."

"Of course not. Though I do know a guy —"

"Laurie Anne, you've got the right to be silent, and I advise you to take advantage of it."

I didn't push it any further. After all, Junior was well equipped to track down a man for herself. Instead I said, "I appreciate what you said in there."

"Daddy always told me to say whatever it takes to get a suspect talking."

"Oh," I said, disappointed. "Does that mean you don't —"

"Of course," Junior said, interrupting me, "this time all I had to say was God's honest truth."

"Thank you, Junior."

"You're welcome. But no hugs!"

CHAPTER
TWENTY-THREE

Junior was still worried that Vasti was going to try to get her to sing, so instead of heading straight for the recreation center, she talked me into having lunch with her at Birmingham Bill's Burritos. Though Alabama isn't known for authentic Mexican food, the burritos were excellent and, unfortunately for Junior's anxiety, quite fast.

We needn't have worried. By the time we got back, Vasti had arranged for the First Baptist Church children's choir to sing at all three performances of the play. Not only were we going to have the live music, but this guaranteed that every one of those children's parents, grandparents, and other relations would buy a ticket to the play just to see their little ones singing in their holiday finest.

The cast and crew were eating lunch when we arrived, so I dragged Richard away long enough to tell him what Junior and I had been up to. He was as surprised as we'd been to find out that Florence knew about the moonshining, and he nearly fell off his chair when I told him what we'd done to Mark.

Once he caught his breath, he said, "Are you sure it was wise to make an enemy of him that way? As Dickens said, 'Never be mean in anything; never be false; never be cruel.' *David Copperfield,* Chapter Fifteen."

"Copperfield never had to deal with Mark Pope. Has he been around today?"

"I don't think so — at least, he hasn't interrupted anything."

"How's the rehearsal going?"

He looked pleased. "I probably shouldn't say this, but I think we're actually going to pull it off. We're still rough on a couple of scenes, and the blocking isn't quite right at Fezziwig's party, but we just might make it."

"Hey, what are you worrying about? You've got two more days."

"Easy for you to say. I'm the one stuck cracking the whip over these people. I doubt any of them will want to talk to me by the time this is done."

"I bet they're grateful you're making them look good." Oliver Jarndyce picked that moment to walk by, glaring at Richard. "Most

268

of them, anyway. I'm sorry I haven't been here to lend support."

"That's all right. I just wish I'd been able to help you out. Though it looks as if you and Junior make a good team."

That last part sounded wistful. "It's okay," I said, "but not nearly as much fun as working with you. She doesn't quote anybody except her daddy, and she won't let me hug her, and —"

"Does this mean I get to play Doctor Watson next time?"

"Honey, you can play doctor with me anytime," I said, fluttering my eyelashes.

Once rehearsal started up again, Junior decided to have another lurk, just in case our practical joker had struck again. I wasn't convinced that the jokes had anything to do with Seth's murder, but I was sure I was tired of them. I still couldn't lurk, of course, so I wandered around.

With opening night coming closer, people had begun to overcome their reluctance to go down the hall where Seth had died, and the triplets were working in the dressing rooms. I saw Carlelle working furiously at her sewing machine in the women's dressing room while Idelle added flounces to a bonnet, so I decided not to disturb them. When I passed by the men's dressing room,

Odelle saw me and said, "Hey, Laurie Anne, can you give me a hand?"

Odelle had Tim Topper in front of a makeup mirror and was applying a heavy coat of foundation. "What do you think of this color?" she asked me.

I took a look. "The color's fine, but isn't the makeup kind of thick?"

"It has to be," she explained. "Stage lights are so bright that he'll get washed out if I don't put it on like that."

"Right," I said, remembering how long it took Richard to clean up after a performance. "In that case, he looks good." I wasn't sure if Tim had already given his opinion, or if he even got to voice one. "How's it going, Tim?"

"Fine. Though after this, I've got a whole new appreciation for what you ladies go through with your makeup."

I looked at the table in front of him, which was covered with a rainbow of greasepaint, brushes of all sizes, triangle sponges, false eyelashes, spirit gum, crepe hair, and a big cake of powder. "Tim," I said, "I've never worn this much makeup in my entire life."

He started to smile, but Odelle said, "Don't move your face!"

"Sorry," he said, through unmoving lips.

Odelle smudged pinky-brown greasepaint

under Tim's cheeks and then smoothed it into his skin. "How's that? Do you think it gives his face more shape?"

"Absolutely. It looks great."

"It does, doesn't it? I better change it."

"Why?"

"Because this makeup is for the first scene, when he's about to freeze to death while working in Scrooge's office. He shouldn't look this good. But I can use these colors for Bob's happy scenes, like during Christmas dinner and when Scrooge gives him a raise."

"I had no idea makeup was so complicated," I said, impressed by the level of detail.

"Oh, it's not that bad," she said modestly. "I love fooling around with makeup. If a woman really knows what she's doing, she'll never need a facelift."

"Really?" I looked at my own face in the mirror, wondering if Odelle would have time to give me a pointer or two once the play was over.

"Could you get me that notebook over there?"

"Sure." The notebook was a thick three-ring binder that was bristling with dividers. "What is it?"

"It's our makeup bible. We write down

what colors each person takes for foundation and blush and all, so that we'll be able to do it in a hurry for the performance. Take a look."

I thumbed through it and was impressed again. Not only was every character's makeup described, but Odelle had even pasted in photos of each person before and after makeup, along with notes like "Add bags under the eyes," and "Bring out eyes." For the actors playing more than one role, like Florence and David, both sets of makeup were in the book. I said, "This must have taken forever to do."

"Not as much time as it would take to recreate everything later on. Could you write some notes down on Tim's page? My hands are covered in makeup, and I don't want to get the book dirty."

"Sure." I found the page for Tim and dutifully printed the color names Odelle read out to me. Then she told me how to use the instant camera so I could add a photo of Tim's "happy" makeup to the book.

While I took care of that, Odelle wiped Tim's face clean with healthy amounts of cold cream and started all over again with makeup designed to make him look miserable.

I hung around, both because I thought

Odelle might need me to take more notes and because it really was interesting. I looked at the pictures in the notebook, amazed by how much difference a color choice or a drawn line could make in a person's appearance.

The actors were in order of appearance, naturally enough, so I looked at the page for Scrooge first. If Odelle had worked up makeup for Seth, she'd already taken it out of the book, because only Big Bill was included. I was amused to see that they hadn't had to do much to change his appearance.

Next was Tim, and then three pictures of David: as himself, as Scrooge's nephew Fred, and as the young Scrooge. At first glance, it looked like three different men. Of course, there were plenty of characteristics that couldn't be changed, so I had no doubt that it was all David.

It was while looking at Tim's and David's pictures that I noticed something. The two men looked a whole lot more alike than I'd realized before. Though Tim's face was fuller, probably from sampling his own barbecue, both men's cheekbones had that slant that usually means American Indian blood. Their noses were almost the same shape, and their eyes were the same shade of hazel. Even their eyebrows were shaped alike. The longer I looked at the pictures, the more I noticed how much the two men favored one another. In fact, if I hadn't known better, I'd have said . . .

I stopped the thought and went from just looking at the pictures to flat-out staring at Tim, mentally cataloging David's features. It was while I was comparing the shape of their earlobes that Tim caught my eye. Despite Odelle's complaints, he turned around in his seat until he could see the page of the notebook I was looking at, and I could tell that he knew exactly what I was thinking.

Odelle turned him back around long enough to add one more puff of powder and announced, "Tim, that's how we're going to do you for the first scene. All I need to do is take another picture and you're done."

I don't think Odelle noticed that Tim didn't say a word while she finished up with him, but she did look surprised when he said she didn't need to wash the makeup off. He left the room with it still on, and I excused myself to follow him.

He was walking away quickly, and I nearly had to run to catch up with him. "Tim, can we talk for a minute?"

"What about?" he said.

I just looked at him and he nodded. Nobody was in the room Aunt Maggie was using to store props, so we went in there.

Once the door was safely shut behind us, I said, "How long have you known?"

"Known what?"

"How long have you known that Seth Murdstone was your father?"

CHAPTER TWENTY-FOUR

Tim leaned up against the Cratchits' dining room table and shook his head ruefully. "I should have known you'd figure it out."

"It took me long enough." In fact, I was embarrassed by how long it had taken. For years I'd bragged to Richard about how good I was at spotting family resemblances, but I'd missed it completely with those two, and I knew that if David hadn't been white and Tim black, I'd have caught it right off. Talk about being color-blind! "How did you find out?"

"He told me — Seth, I mean. You'll excuse me if I don't call him 'Daddy.' " He looked disgusted at the thought. "It was right after we started rehearsing the play. I was a little worried when Vasti gave me the part — a lot of people wouldn't want a black man playing a white role. But Seth was real nice and seemed interested in talking to me. Then he asked me out for a drink after the second night of rehearsal. I thought he'd bring his boys along — at least Jake — but it was just the two of us. We met over at Dusty's — you know Dusty's, don't you?"

I nodded. It was a hole in the wall, but since it was just outside the gates to the mill, it was the favorite place to get a beer after shift's end.

Tim said, "There weren't many people in there at that time of night, and Seth got us a booth in the back. He'd said he just wanted to talk about the play and relax, but I could tell he had something on his mind. He was kind of agitated, and drank down the first beer like it was water. He was working on his second when he started asking me questions about Mama and what it was like growing up without a father."

"Didn't you think that was kind of odd?"

"Naturally, and after I'd talked a little, I asked him if he'd known Mama."

"What did he say?"

Tim's mouth turned down as if he'd tasted a bad batch of barbecue sauce. "He said he'd known her real well, and that there was something he wanted to tell me. That's when he said it: 'I'm your father, Tim.' Like it was something to be proud of."

"What did you do? What did you say?"

"I didn't say anything. Hell, Laurie Anne,

277

I didn't know what to say. He told me how he and Mama had done business together, and how one thing had led to another late one night. I think it was just the one time. He said he didn't even find out she'd gotten pregnant until after I was born."

"Did you believe him?"

"I wasn't sure."

"Did he ever try to see you? Or to do the right thing by you and your mother?"

"A white man marry a pregnant black girl? Back then?" He snorted. "Hell, I don't know many who'd do it now."

"I suppose not," I agreed sadly.

"Besides, he was married at the time and already had the two boys."

"Still, he could have done something. Sent y'all money, at least."

"He said he waited for Mama to contact him, and when she didn't, he figured she didn't want anything from him."

"Right," I said, rubbing my belly. I couldn't imagine Richard just waiting around for somebody to ask him to bear responsibility for his child. He'd do it no matter what. Nor could I imagine an unmarried black girl crossing over to the white side of town to beg for what was due her and her child. "What a weasel."

"He hinted that he wasn't sure he was the

father, but I stopped that talk right then and there. I don't have any idea that Mama was a saint, but she wasn't a tramp, either."

"I've never heard one word against your mother," I said firmly. "He had no right to imply that."

"To give him credit, he did apologize. He said he'd been immature and that he'd been worried about what people would do if they found out. His wife was sick, and he was afraid of what knowing about me would do to her. Besides, he had his sons — his other sons — to think of. I could understand that."

"He's had plenty of time to come up with excuses," I said cynically.

"Maybe so. Anyway, he said that he wanted to make up for his mistake by us getting to know one another."

"Did you want that?"

"I wasn't sure, Laurie Anne. I've wanted a father my whole life. I had Uncle Eb, of course, but I always knew he wasn't my real daddy. Maybe Seth wasn't the kind of daddy I'd dreamed of, but I could look at him and see part of myself. He was blood, and I thought that meant something."

I nodded. Goodness knows, I'd put up with a lot from my own relatives for no better reason than our blood connection.

Tim said, "I told him I needed to think about it, and he said he understood. When I got up to leave, I think he wanted to hug me, but all I could manage was a handshake." He shook his head. "If I'd known the truth, I wouldn't even have done that."

"What do you mean?"

"The next morning, I talked to Uncle Eb and Aunt Fezzie. They'd always said that they didn't know who my father was, and even though I believed them, I've always felt like they knew more than they would say. So I didn't let up on them until they told me everything." He looked down. "Then I almost wished I hadn't asked."

I didn't know what to say to that, so I waited for him to go on.

"They had told me the truth, Laurie Anne. They didn't know who my father was. But they did know what happened to Mama."

"I don't understand."

"Part of what Seth told me was true. The night it happened, Mama told Uncle Ed and Aunt Fezzie that she was going to meet with somebody about buying something for the bar. They thought it was liquor, but once they knew it was Seth, they realized that he must have wanted to sell her some furniture."

Actually, they'd probably been right the first time, but I didn't say anything. Maybe I'd eventually tell Tim about Seth being a moonshiner, but it wasn't the right time yet.

"Mama and Seth met after the bar was closed," Tim said, "and had a few drinks. Then they had a few more. I always wondered why Mama was so down on drinking when she ran a bar, and now I know. She took one drink too many that night, and the next thing she remembered, she was waking up with her clothes all over the place while Seth got dressed."

"Did he rape her?" I asked softly.

"I don't know if you would call it rape or not. What Aunt Fezzie said was that he took advantage of her. Mama wasn't exactly sure herself how it happened. She might have gone along with it, her being drunk and all. I don't know for sure that he forced her."

"Still, the best you could say for him was that he was a married man who got a single woman drunk and seduced her."

Tim nodded. "Mama was pretty much sober by the time he left, and he kissed her goodbye and said he'd call her."

"Did he?"

"What do you think? The next time she heard anything out of him was the Fourth of July picnic a few weeks later. She saw

281

him at the park and then went in his direction. By then she had a pretty good idea she was pregnant, and she wanted to tell him about it. But she felt funny going up to him, him being married and white, so she was hanging back, waiting for him to see her. But before he did, she heard him talking. About her."

"Oh, Lord," I said, sickened. Though I knew comparing notches in the belt was considered normal male behavior in some circles, I'd never understood it.

"Not by name," Tim said, "and in a way, that made it worse. Seth was talking about the 'brown sugar' he'd had, and how he was going to get himself some more that night if the 'bitch' hadn't gone off with somebody else."

"Your poor mother," I said. "What did she do?"

"What could she do? She couldn't confront a white man in public, not without everybody finding out what she'd done. So she went back home and cried it out of her system."

"Bless her heart."

"Aunt Fezzie said Mama promised herself she'd never let it happen again. I don't think it would have made much difference to her life if it hadn't been for me."

"She never told him about you?"

"After hearing him talk about her that way, the last thing she wanted was to have him as part of her life or mine. Besides, she figured he'd just deny that he was the father. She couldn't afford a lawyer, so she just decided to raise me on her own, and that's what she did."

"She must have been one strong woman. I can't imagine having a baby all alone." I patted my tummy absently. "I can just barely imagine doing it with Richard."

"You're going to be a fine mama, and I know Richard is going to be a good daddy," Tim assured me, "but Seth wasn't any kind of daddy, leastways, not to me. At the next rehearsal, he came looking for me, wanting to know if I'd thought about what he'd said. I told him I'd found out what really happened with Mama, and that I didn't want anything more to do with him. After that, I don't think I spoke another word to him other than the lines Dickens wrote."

"I'm surprised that you didn't quit the show."

"I thought about it, but I didn't want to let Seth take anything away from me." Then he half-smiled. "I was enjoying myself too much. I'd always wanted to try out for community theater, but with the restaurant and taking classes at night, I've never been able to. I wouldn't have done it this time if your cousin hadn't talked me into it. I sure didn't want to let her down by backing out at the last minute."

"I know Vasti appreciates it. And Richard has been raving about what a good job you've been doing."

"Is that a fact?" he said, smiling more broadly. "Now that Big Bill is playing Scrooge, I think we're going to have ourselves a pretty good show." Then, as if remembering why we'd gotten a new Scrooge, he got serious again. "Anyway, now you know why I didn't have any use for Seth Murdstone."

"I don't blame you, Tim, not one bit."

"I realize that this all sounds like a good reason for me to kill the man, so I've got to ask. Do you think I killed him? Because I didn't. I hated what he'd done to Mama, but Mama's been gone a long time. Killing him wouldn't have done her any good. Hell, Laurie Anne, he wasn't worth the trouble it would have taken to kill him. Even if I had wanted him dead, I'd never have done that to Jake and David."

"I didn't know you were friends with them."

"We're not exactly friends, but they are

284

my brothers. Half-brothers, anyway."

"Do they know?"

"They haven't shown any signs of it. I guess that when I didn't welcome Seth with open arms, he decided not to tell them. Still, I've been trying to get to know them, and I like them both. At first I thought Jake was too much like his daddy, but he's not sneaky like Seth was. If he tells you something, you know it's true."

"Are you going to tell them?"

"I don't think so. Even if I could prove it, they'd probably think I was just after their inheritance."

"You are entitled to it."

"I don't want nothing that belonged to Seth Murdstone."

I wasn't about to argue with the tone in Tim's voice.

"Anyway, whatever else he was, Seth was David and Jake's father. I spent my whole life with no daddy — the last thing I'd have wanted to do was to take theirs away from them."

"It's hard losing a father," I said. I'd been through it when I was fifteen, and then again when my grandfather died. "No matter how old you are."

"Do you think I killed him, Laurie Anne?"

I didn't think Junior would have considered it proper procedure, but I said, "No, Tim, I don't. I just don't think you're a killer."

His smile came back in full force. "That means a lot to me." Then he asked, "Do you think this is going to have to come out? About Seth being my father?"

"I don't see why. Like Mark keeps reminding us, Junior and I have no official standing, so we don't have to file any reports. I will tell Richard, if that's all right, and probably Junior. But you know you can trust the two of them to keep quiet."

"That's fine," he said. Then Mrs. Gamp came looking for Tim to get him out on stage. I went back into the auditorium to get a bottle of water, then watched Tim and Florence run through the scene of the possible future where the Cratchits were mourning the loss of their son. I realized I was starting to cry.

It wasn't because of the play, though Tim and the others did a wonderful job. It just seemed so sad to me that Tim had waited his whole life to find his father, and when he found him he wasn't even worth killing, let alone keeping.

CHAPTER
TWENTY-FIVE

"You probably think I'm silly for believing him," I said to Junior after telling her Tim's story, "but —"

"Not really," Junior said. "You've known Tim Topper quite a while. Making a judgment call on somebody you've known that long isn't exactly jumping to conclusions."

"Really?"

"Still, going into a room alone with a suspect wasn't the brightest thing to do. Especially not in —"

"Don't you dare say, 'in your condition'!"

Junior went on as if I hadn't spoken. "What if he had been the killer?"

"Odelle saw us go off together," I said. "He'd have to have been nuts to try anything."

"Don't forget the killer attacked Seth in a hallway that anybody could have walked down at any time."

"Good point. I'll be more careful."

"I'd appreciate it. If I let you get hurt, the entire Burnette family would come after me."

"Then the Nortons would come after them. . . ."

"And we'd end up with a feud that would make the Hatfields and the McCoys look like best buddies."

I shuddered at the thought. "Anyway, even if Tim wasn't the killer, he could have provided a motive."

"How's that?"

"What if Tim's wrong, and David and Jake do know he's their half-brother? They might not want anybody else to find out." Though I'd never seen signs of either brother being particularly racist, it might not show when they were dealing with another white person. "Having a moonshiner in the family could be romantic, but having a black, illegitimate half-brother is something else. I know it's better in Byerly than it used to be, but racial stuff goes pretty deep."

"Especially with somebody like Florence Easterly in the family," Junior said. "She could have done it to keep her name unbesmirched."

"Or if David knew and she didn't, he could have done it to keep her from finding out. Jake might have done it because he was ashamed."

"Or either David or Jake could have done the math and realized that Seth cheated on their mama while she was dying of cancer."

"Right! Though the timing seems funny. Do we still agree that the killing looks un-premeditated?"

"We could be wrong about that, but I've got a hunch —"

"Say no more. I'm not arguing with one of your hunches. So if the killing wasn't premeditated, that implies that Seth had just told either David or Jake about Tim, and whichever brother it was reacted immediately by killing him." I shook my head. "I don't think that works."

"Go back to the scandal, then," Junior said.

"If they were trying to avoid scandal, killing Seth was the absolute wrong thing to do. There's nothing like a murder to get tongues wagging and people prying into secrets."

Junior nodded. "It would have made more sense to kill Tim than Seth. Considering how long Seth had kept the secret, I don't think he'd have come forward if Tim were dead."

"And there's no way to guarantee that Tim won't come forward now," I added.

"Though with both Tim's mother and Seth gone, he couldn't prove it."

"Sure he could. DNA testing. They could exhume Seth's body, or even just compare Tim's DNA to Jake's or David's, the way they compared samples from Sally Hemmings' descendants to Thomas Jefferson's to find out they're related."

"Wouldn't they have to get permission?"

"That's right. If any of the Murdstones killed to avoid a scandal, they sure as heck wouldn't allow it."

Remembering something Tim had mentioned, I said, "What about the money? Tim said he didn't want Jake and David to think he was after Seth's inheritance. Maybe they didn't want him to get it, either. Jake said he and David are splitting everything, and half is a whole lot more than a third. Florence could be involved, too, because she'll have access to David's share." Then I had to add, "Of course, it doesn't sound as if Seth had a whole lot."

"We could find out. The will's probably gone into probate."

"This soon?"

"Florence is a lawyer," Junior reminded me. "With Jake living in the house, they'd want to get the title clear as quickly as possible."

"That makes sense. Though you realize that the will might not tell the whole story. I bet it doesn't include the money Seth made from moonshining."

"You may be right. Most moonshiners only deal in cash, and then hide it in a jar or under a mattress. Daddy and I have both taken peeks at Seth's finances, and we never saw anything that wasn't accounted for legitimately. Which is probably why he kept the furniture business going — to cover his tracks."

"So there might be a lot of money involved after all."

"Of course," Junior said, "all this hinges on whether or not Jake or David or Florence knows about Tim, which we have no way of knowing other than asking them."

"We can't do that without breaking my promise to Tim, and they wouldn't necessarily tell us the truth anyway." I thought some more. "Even if they didn't know about Tim, one of them might have been after the money. In fact, I feel like an idiot for not thinking about Seth's money before now. Isn't 'Who benefits?' one of the classic questions a real investigator asks?"

"Don't beat yourself up over it, Laurie Anne. I thought about the money even before I asked you to help."

"You don't think Seth's ill-gotten gains are involved?"

"Not really. When people kill for money, it's usually from greed or desperation. If either of the Murdstone brothers were that greedy, they'd have left Byerly years ago. There are a whole lot better places to make a living. I don't think either of them is desperate, either. Jake gets the house and the business, but he already lived in the house and made a decent living off the business, so he's not gained that much. David gets the insurance money, but from looking at his house, he's not exactly short on cash. And if either of them are in debt, I've never heard anything about it."

"What about Jake's son? The hospital bills must have been high."

"They were pretty steep, but Jake had insurance to cover part of it and the community has been helping with the rest. That's why we're doing this play, remember?"

"I almost forgot," I admitted.

"Anyway, I don't think money was the issue, but it's not a hunch, so you can argue with it if you want to."

"No thanks. What you said makes too much sense." I thought for a minute. "One other thing. Why did Seth pick now to tell

Tim the truth?"

"Maybe because he was handy, what with the two of them working together. Does it matter?"

"It might. David said Seth had been diagnosed with a bad heart, and we know he was thinking about retiring. Those two combined could make a man start thinking about coming to the end of his life."

"Which he did," Junior said, "though a bit sooner than he expected."

"It reminds me of Richard's Uncle Claude. When he found out he had cancer, he started cleaning up all kinds of loose ends. He wrote his will, and gave away all the stuff he said he wouldn't need anymore, and made up with people he'd been feuding with. He wanted to die with a clear conscience."

"That must have been comforting at the end."

"Actually, he didn't die. The chemotherapy worked, and he's healthier than ever. The point is that maybe Seth was trying to clean up unfinished business. That's why he told Tim."

"I still don't know why it matters."

"What if he confessed to others, too? Maybe he finally told Mrs. Gamp that he's the one who caused her husband's death."

"Meaning that she has a motive after all?" she said.

"Right. I couldn't see her holding a grudge against Seth all these years, but if she'd just found out, that's another story. The timing would have been tight, but I think she had enough time to kill him. Remember how bad off she was when we got to her? Maybe that's when she realized what she'd done."

"Or maybe she'd just found an ex-lover dead. That would throw most people for a loop."

"So would killing somebody. It seems to me that a grown woman with an imaginary friend might not be the most stable person in the world."

"I don't know, Laurie Anne. She's never shown any sign of violence. Being eccentric doesn't make somebody a killer."

"But —"

"Do you want examples from your own family?"

"Never mind," I said. "I get your point. But I still think we should keep Mrs. Gamp on the list."

"Fair enough, but I sure as heck wish we could take *somebody* off of that list."

Right then, Richard announced that he was shutting down rehearsal so that people could get home in time to dress for Seth's visitation.

"Are you going, Junior?"

She shook her head. "Mama invited some of her cousins over for dinner. You?"

"I imagine so. Richard said he thought he should go."

"Then keep your eyes and ears open. Not that I've ever known a killer to break down and confess at one of these things, but you never know." She left to gather up her nieces and nephews, and I went to find Richard.

CHAPTER
TWENTY-SIX

"Do these shoes look ridiculous?" I asked Richard as he helped me out of the car. I'd quit wearing high heels after having my feet swell during an early holiday party, and even my flats weren't comfortable anymore, so the only shoes I'd brought to Byerly were sneakers. I just didn't feel properly dressed.

"Don't worry," Richard said. "You look fine, and anybody should be able to figure out why a pregnant woman isn't in stilettos."

"I guess," I said doubtfully. At least the outfit I'd borrowed from Vasti was suitable. I'd been trying not to spend a lot of money on maternity clothes and didn't have anything appropriate with me, but my cousin had an entire wardrobe of maternity dresses, including the navy blue one I was wearing.

The sign inside the funeral home directed us to the Magnolia Room. "Florence must have set this up," I told Richard. "That's the nicest room in town. I've heard that deathly ill society types will hang on for just another week to make sure they get it."

"You're making this up."

"I am not," I insisted. "Byerly's Junior League set takes these things just as seriously as the Boston Brahmins would."

"If you say so."

Thinking about the rules of society led me to think about Florence marrying David Murdstone. As crazy as it sounded to me, women were frequently judged on their husband's lineage and bankbook. Of course, Florence was an Easterly, and the Easterlys were thoroughly entrenched in local society. So I didn't think anybody would dare snub Florence, especially not with David being so well dressed and such a successful businessman. But what if they found out what Seth had done for a living?

Admittedly, I'd considered bootleggers romantic figures, at least until I found out about Seth and Clara Todger, but the Junior League members might not have those same fantasies. I was willing to bet that they wouldn't accept a real, live bootlegger in their midst. Easterly or not, Florence would have been cut dead. The question was, would she have minded? She said she didn't care what people thought, but then again, she'd booked the Magnolia Room.

I was relieved to see that the Murdstones had opted for a closed casket. Though I can certainly understand wanting to see a loved one one last time, I've never felt comfortable making small talk with that loved one's face in sight. To me, the casket covered with flowers was more than enough of a reminder of why we were there.

David, Florence, and Jake were receiving people as they entered, and Richard and I joined the line to greet them. After Junior's and my earlier conversation with Florence and David, I felt a little awkward, so I relied on the standby line my mother had taught me. "I'm so sorry for your loss."

"Thank you, Laurie Anne," David said. "I appreciate your coming, and everything you're trying to do for us." To Richard, he said, "My father was so pleased to have a part in the play, and he'd be glad you were here."

Though David was holding up well, Jake looked terrible. His clothes were fine, probably thanks to David or Florence, but his hair was a mess and his hand must have been shaking like a leaf when he shaved to have left so many nicks.

"I'm sorry about your father," I said helplessly. Jake just nodded and swallowed hard.

Florence gave me a quick hug and, with a tiny grin, said, "Sorry we didn't see you out properly this afternoon."

"That's all right. I was a newlywed once myself."

"It's wonderful, isn't it?" she said. "Now don't stay on your feet too long. There are some comfortable chairs right over there."

Richard and I moved on to let the next group of people come through. I imagine that a real investigator wouldn't have hesitated to hang around the receiving line to eavesdrop, but I couldn't do it. Especially not with swelling feet. Instead, I found the chairs Florence had pointed out and took advantage of them.

"Are you feeling all right?" Richard said. "Do you want anything?"

"I'm fine," I said, trying to calculate how many more times I'd have to tell him that before the baby was born.

I saw Tim Topper going through the receiving line and wondered what he was feeling. He'd just found his father, and even though he'd had no reason to like him, surely the man's death had meant something to him. He shook hands with his two half-brothers just as Richard had, when by rights he should have been receiving guests with them.

Big Bill Walters came through the line next, dressed elegantly in a black pinstripe suit. He was widely known as a tough businessman, but I honestly couldn't imagine him killing Seth over a piece of land. Which was a relief, considering his obvious feelings for Aunt Maggie.

"Laura," Richard said, "do you mind if I go see Big Bill? I've got an idea for the last act I'd like to discuss with him."

"Go ahead," I said. "I'll keep on people-watching."

He gave me a quick peck on the cheek and joined Big Bill just as he made it through the receiving line.

It was actually an interesting group of folks to watch. There were some rough types who looked as if they didn't come to town often, and I suspected that some of them were Seth's moonshining colleagues. Then there were society types, paying their respects to Florence. Or maybe, I thought cynically, scoping out the family she'd married into. And naturally, there were quite a few people from the play.

I hadn't been by myself long when Oliver Jarndyce came over.

"Hey there, Oliver," I said.

"How're you doing?" he asked.

"I'm doing all right. I think it's nice that

so many of us from the play came. Or did you know Seth before then?" It wasn't the smoothest opening gambit, but since conversation at a visitation is always awkward, I figured Oliver wouldn't notice.

"I didn't know Seth well," he said, "but I had done some business with him. At least, I tried to."

"Is that right?"

"He and I went to see some land late last summer, but he decided it wasn't what he was looking for."

"Maybe he was thinking about moving," I said idly, "since Big Bill wanted to buy his property."

"Big Bill Walters is in the market?" Oliver said eagerly, his ears all but pricking up.

"I don't know that for sure," I said, not wanting to steer him the wrong way. "It's just something I heard."

"Still, it won't hurt to inquire. Now that I think about it, Jake will almost certainly want to move now. That house is far too big for just one man, especially considering the tragedy that happened there." He looked over at where the Murdstones were still greeting people, and straightened his tie. "If you'll excuse me, Laurie Anne, I should pay my respects to the family."

"Of course," I said. There's nothing quite

301

so determined as a real estate agent who smells a commission, even if it did mean talking business at a visitation.

Then again, there were those for whom a visitation was business. Pete Fredericks wafted toward me, carrying a tray with a glass of ice water.

"Mrs. Murdstone was concerned that you might be overexerting yourself," he said, "and asked me to bring this to you."

"Thanks, Pete," I said, taking it from him. "Thank Florence for me, too." I lifted it to my lips and then hesitated ever so slightly. After all, Pete was still a murder suspect, and I didn't know for sure that Florence had asked him to bring me anything. Then I went ahead and sipped. It tasted fine, of course. Pete would have had to be a fool to try anything in public, in his own place of business. Besides, I didn't even have a motive for him. Not yet, anyway.

I said, "You've done an excellent job pulling this all together so quickly."

He nodded in acknowledgment and said, "Our services are usually performed expeditiously. Even with advanced planning, there are always last-minute details to attend to."

"I suppose so." He looked as if he was about to leave, so I quickly added, "Does it ever bother you, working with a client you know?"

Pete smiled as if he'd heard the question before. "In simpler times, the women of a family would prepare the departed for his final farewell. They saw it as their duty to tend to the remains with care and respect, all the more so because they'd known the person. I regard my work the same way."

I'd always thought of a mortician's job as fairly grisly, but Pete made it sound like a noble calling. Thinking of how hard it must be to deal constantly with bereaved families, I was glad there were some compensations for the job. "Were you and Seth good friends?" I asked.

"No, we only met in connection with the play, but I knew of him through David, who I met through the chamber of commerce. Since I left the mill, I've lost touch with many of my old friends and have had difficulty cultivating new ones. You may not realize this, but many people are reluctant to socialize with a man in my line of work."

"Is that right?" I said, trying to sound shocked even though I'd have been just as reluctant as anybody else.

"It's ironic, actually," he said. "David encouraged me to talk to Vasti about a part in the play because he thought it might help if people saw me in another aspect than as a funeral director. My assisting with Mr. Murdstone's final arrangements has only reminded the community of what it is I do."

"I hadn't thought of that," I said sympathetically. "Don't worry, Pete. People will figure it out eventually. Maybe you can try out for another play." Though if he really wanted to change people's assumptions about him, he might do better than playing Jacob Marley's ghost and the spectral Spirit of Christmas Yet to Come.

"I hope you're right. Now if you'll excuse me, I should check in with the Murdstones."

Richard came back then. "Hi, love. Are you all right?"

"I'm still fine, Richard," I said in exasperation.

"What's wrong?"

"Nothing. I'm just aggravated. Finding out who killed Seth should be simple. It *was* simple — somebody hit him upside the head, and there aren't that many people it could have been. Why can't Junior and I figure out which one? Maybe being pregnant kills brain cells."

He patted my leg. "Come on, Laura. It has nothing to do with being pregnant. You always come to a point where nothing makes any sense and you start grasping at straws."

"Thanks," I said sarcastically.

"Then you figure it all out. Just be patient."

"Patience is not my strong point."

"You'll forgive me if I don't respond to that."

I looked back over at Oliver, now deep in conversation with Jake. "Maybe Oliver killed Seth so he could play Scrooge."

"But he didn't get the part."

"I know, but he thought he was going to. Remember how shocked he was when you picked Big Bill instead of him? Maybe he'll go after Big Bill next."

"I told you not to joke about my cast."

"Sorry." I looked around the room and saw that the crowd was thinning. "Do you suppose we can get away with leaving now?"

"I'm sure we can," Richard replied. "Did you have another avenue to investigate?"

"All I'm interested in investigating is dinner. I've got a craving for a hamburger and french fries."

"Hardee's or McDonald's?"

"McDonald's," I said, my mouth watering. I knew I was supposed to be eating good, healthy meals, but ever since I'd been pregnant, nothing had satisfied me quite so much as junk food. "Wait a minute! Is it all right to eat at McDonald's?"

"Why wouldn't it be?"

"If it's bad luck to quote the Scottish play, it must be bad luck to eat at a Scottish restaurant."

"What Scottish restaurant?"

"Isn't McDonald's a Scottish restaurant?"

CHAPTER TWENTY-SEVEN

I got up the next morning fully intending to go to Seth's funeral, both to pay my respects and to snoop. But it was drizzling, and my feet hurt from being on them so much the day before, and I was still sleepy. I knew the Murdstones had planned the funeral for early in the day to keep from interfering with rehearsal, but that didn't make it any easier for me to get moving.

Still, I managed to get into the shower, but when I pulled on the second loaner dress from Vasti, I looked at myself in the mirror and said loudly, "For pity's sake!"

"What's the matter?" asked Richard, who was already dressed.

"Look at this." I held my arms out so he could see how the dress fit, which was much the same way that a circus tent fits the center pole. "It's huge!"

"It is kind of loose, isn't it."

"Richard, there's enough room for you in

here. I wouldn't fit in this if I was having quintuplets. Does Vasti think I look this big?"

"I'm sure she doesn't, but if she does, obviously she's wrong."

"I can't wear this!"

"Then wear the dress you wore last night."

"People have already seen me in it."

"Then wear a scarf or something — my mother says you can wear the same outfit a dozen times if you accessorize properly."

"I didn't bring any accessories with me. Besides which, I spilled ketchup down the front of it last night."

"Then keep your coat on. Or wear your regular clothes."

"I can't dress that way for a funeral."

"Then —" He stopped. "You don't want to go to the funeral, do you?"

"Not really," I admitted. "I know I should . . ."

"Why? You barely knew Seth."

"Then for the investigation."

"Laura, how often do people really say anything meaningful at a funeral? They're coming to bury him, not to confess to killing him."

That sounded suspiciously like Shakespeare, at least in paraphrase, but I didn't think it was *Macbeth* so I didn't point it out.

"I know, but —"

"Junior is going to be there, and so am I. You go back to bed, and we'll tell you if you miss anything important."

I looked at the bed, cozy with the fluffy quilt my grandmother had made. "Are you sure?"

"Go to bed. I'll pick you up on the way to rehearsal."

"I'll go you one better. I'll get a ride to the recreation center and meet you over there."

"It's a deal." Then he got me a drink and put me to bed. I should have felt bad about it, but I didn't have enough time before I fell asleep.

An hour and a half later, I was much better rested. I called around to see who was available and caught Aunt Nora on her way out the door. She said she'd be glad to drop me off, and even brought me a hefty breakfast of eggs with fruit salad on the side. Being Aunt Nora, she also had fresh biscuits handy.

The funeral must have still been going on, because the parking lot was empty when we got to the recreation center. Vasti had made a production out of keeping the doors locked in a vain attempt to prevent practical jokes, so I couldn't go inside, but it was such a balmy day for December that I didn't mind. Aunt Nora volunteered to stay with me, but I knew she was meeting Aunt Edna so they could plan what we Burnettes were having for Christmas dinner. I had a vested interest in their doing a good job and didn't want to hold them up, so I sat down on the stone wall and pulled out the latest issue of the *Byerly Gazette*.

Byerly not being a hotbed of news activity, it didn't take me long to read the *Gazette* from cover to cover. I was surprised people hadn't shown up by then, but I figured the Murdstones must have laid out a good spread back at their house after the funeral. Or maybe the killer had confessed after all, I fantasized, and Junior was busy taking his or her statement.

It was about then that I heard something, a kind of rhythmic sound. More restless than curious, I wandered toward the building, trying to figure out what it was and where it was coming from. I got to the front door and decided it was definitely coming from inside. Now that I was closer, it sounded like someone sawing wood.

The front door was at the far end of the building, with the stage all the way at the other end. With the lights out I could just barely make out motion at the back of the stage. Somebody was sawing something.

My first thought was to knock on the door, so whoever it was would let me in, but I changed my mind. What was that person doing in there, anyway, and why hadn't he or she turned the lights on? I thought Vasti was the only one with a key. Besides which, almost everybody in the cast and crew was at the funeral.

There was only one reason I could think of for somebody to be inside. Our practical joker was setting up another prank.

My first thought was to run along the side of the building until I found a window closer to the stage so I could see who it was. I probably would have, too, but the baby started kicking, reminding me that I needed to look before I leaped. Though Junior and I didn't think the practical joker was Seth's murderer, I sure as heck didn't want to be proven wrong by making him come after me. Even if he wasn't the killer, he'd been working hard to hide his tracks. I didn't know how he would react if I caught him red-handed.

Before I could decide what to do, the sawing stopped. I ducked down and crept to the nearest bush that was big enough to hide behind. I was hoping the prankster would come out the front door so I could see him in the daylight, but eventually I heard the distant sound of a car door shutting and realized that he must have been parked in the back parking lot.

I quickly moved to the other side of the bush, where I couldn't be seen by the driver of the car that appeared and drove out the exit. It was moving too fast for me to read the license plate, but I didn't need to. I knew that car, and I knew who was driving it. But why would he be playing practical jokes? It didn't make sense, and I decided not to say anything until I was sure I'd seen what I thought I'd seen. There had to be another explanation, even if I couldn't begin to figure out what it could be.

Only when the car was long gone did I get out from behind the bush and go back to my seat on the fence. This time I was too nervous to read the newspaper or to do anything other than keep watch in all directions. I was mighty relieved when Vasti's red Cadillac pulled into the parking lot, followed closely by Richard in our rental car. The rest of the cast and crew were close behind.

"Hey, love," Richard said, giving me a hug. "I hope you haven't been waiting long."

"Not too long," I said. "How was the funeral?"

Richard shrugged. "Very nice. Tasteful. About what you'd expect a funeral to be."

"I hope you gave the Murdstones my regrets."

"They didn't mind your not coming, if that's what you mean. They'll be here later. In the meantime, Florence sent you a box of food from the post-funeral gathering."

"That's nice."

Vasti had the door open by then, and we followed her inside.

"Is anything wrong?" Richard said.

"Why do you ask?"

"You look pale, and you didn't ask what food Florence sent."

I managed a smile. "I'm fine, but —"

"Richard!" Vasti yelled. "Have you proofread the program yet? It's got to go to the printer right away or it won't be ready in time."

"Sorry," he said to me. "Do you mind?"

"Of course not," I said. I wanted to know more, even before I told Richard what I was thinking. "You go ahead."

He went to see what Vasti needed, and I stared at the stage, trying to remember where the prankster had been.

Everything was laid out for the scene where Scrooge spies on the Cratchits' Christmas dinner. There was a dining room table with chairs stage left, with the fireplace Jake had made in the center, and Tiny Tim's chair stage right. The scenery flats were painted to create the illusion of a plain house, just this side of poverty-stricken, with faded wallpaper and a framed needlepoint sampler.

I headed toward the stage, walking carefully to make sure I didn't set anything off. I decided that the prankster had been standing stage right, near the door into the set, and sure enough, there was sawdust on the floor all around there. But what had he been sawing?

Gingerly, I reached over and touched one of the flats. It wobbled, but just a little. Then I touched the one next to it, the one with the door through it. It wobbled a lot. I jumped back, watching it rock back and forth, and only breathed again when it stopped moving.

"Richard!" I called out, surprised at how shrill my voice sounded.

"Just a minute!" he called back.

"I need you now!"

He came at a dead run. "What's the matter?"

"Something's wrong with that flat," I said, pointing. "When I touched it, it nearly fell on top of me."

"Are you sure? I know Jake braced them." He reached out.

"Don't touch it!" I yelped. "I'm serious, Richard. I think it's about to fall."

"It's okay," he said soothingly, then yelled, "Can somebody flip on the spotlights?" A few seconds later, someone complied.

"There's sawdust on the floor," I offered, and though Richard looked confused, he realized the implication and started looking up and down the wooden frame of the flat. "Jesus!" he breathed.

"What is it?"

He stepped completely out of range, and in a tight voice said, "Somebody sawed through the frame on both sides. One little push, and the damn thing would fall right over."

"But it's just boards and canvas, right?" I said. "It wouldn't hurt anybody, would it?"

"Most of them wouldn't, unless you got hit by the frame itself," he said, "but this one is heavier than the others so it can support the door. If it hit you, you could get a concussion, or a broken arm, or . . ." He didn't bother to finish. "Get off the stage."

"But —"

"Now. Please."

I got off the stage.

Richard looked around at the gathering

315

cast and crew, who were watching us with more than a little curiosity. "Folks, our practical joker has been busy again, and this one is nasty. He's rigged one of the flats, and we've got to get it down before it falls down. Martin, Sid, and Big Bill, I could use a hand."

I suppose I should have been offended that he only called for the menfolk to do the heavy work, but I was too shaken to think about it. I just stepped out of the way while they carefully took hold of the flat and brought it down. Even though I was watching them, I jumped when they let it fall the final foot or so. As much noise as it made, I didn't want to think about what would have happened if it had hit one of the cast. Had the prankster recognized the set? Had he realized that Big Bill, Sid, Florence, and David would have been on stage, along with all of Junior's nieces and nephews? Or did he care who it was he could have hurt?

On stage, Richard and the others were checking the other flats and starting to talk about repairing the damaged one. Everybody else had gone back to their various jobs, and I was sure they didn't know how bad it could have been.

Except Junior. She was staring at the stage, and from the look on her face, I could

tell she realized what might have happened.
"How did you catch it?" she asked.
"I saw him doing it."
"What? Who?"
"It was Mark Pope."

CHAPTER
TWENTY-EIGHT

Junior swore fluently under her breath for a full minute, then said, "What did you see?"

I explained getting there early and hunting down the source of the noise I heard. "I recognized Mark's car when he drove off. It was the same one he was in at the mall yesterday."

"Did he see you?"

"I don't think so." Then, a little embarrassed, I said, "I was hiding."

"Good!"

"Has he been playing all of the jokes?"

"It's possible," she said in an odd tone of voice.

"Did you know Mark was setting these things up? Is that why you didn't want to spend any time tracking down the jokester?"

"I didn't know for sure," she said carefully.

"Junior! You've been holding out on me!"

She looked around quickly. "Keep your

voice down."

"You knew!" I said angrily.

"I didn't *know* anything," she said. "I only suspected."

"Yeah, right."

"I mean it, Laurie Anne. It's just that I saw him outside not long before Florence slipped on the soap that day. And I thought it was interesting that there weren't any jokes set yesterday, the one day he didn't show up."

"I've told you everything I suspected," I reminded her. "I haven't held anything back."

"I know, and I'm sorry."

"Do you know why he's been doing it, or are you keeping that a secret, too?"

"The fact is, I've been watching Mark pretty closely ever since this started."

"Why?"

"Because of something he did the day Seth was killed."

"I don't understand. What did he do?"

"It was right after he got here that day. I'd expected him to be pissed that I was at the murder scene ahead of him, knowing that he wanted to make a big show for the city council. And I was willing to let him run the investigation as long as he didn't mess it up too badly. The way I figured it, if him solving one case was enough to make them want to replace me, they could go ahead and do it."

"But you love your job."

"Of course I do," she said, "but not enough to kiss anybody's butt to keep it. Anyway, I was planning to tell Mark that I'd stay out of his way, but he started throwing his weight around before I could. Reminding me I wasn't in charge, threatening to tell my mama I was working during my vacation. I'd known for a while that he was after my job, but he'd been fairly subtle up until then. All of a sudden it was out in the open, as if the stakes were higher than they'd been before."

"I can see where that might have gotten you thinking."

"There's more. Since Mark was being so high and mighty, I decided he could do all the scut work himself, and I let him think I hadn't done anything while waiting for him except stand over Seth's body. Then I watched him do all the looking around I'd already done; I was kind of hoping he'd miss something so I could rub it in."

"Did he?"

"Yes and no. His initial examination was fine. At least, he hit everything I would have. But when the medical examiner came, Mark tried to get him to say that it could have been an accident, that maybe Seth fell and hit himself."

"On what?"

"Exactly. It took you two minutes to see it wasn't an accident. Mark should have seen it faster than that. Of course, the medical examiner set Mark straight, and I could have let that pass. But then I heard Mark and some of the state troopers talking about who was going to take statements from which witnesses. One of them was planning to talk to Jake, and she asked Mark if there was anything special about him she ought to know. That's when Mark should have told her about Seth and Jake being moonshiners. Criminal connections are *always* of interest in a murder investigation. But all Mark told her was family background: stuff about Jake's son recently dying and him being in the furniture business with Seth."

"Did you tell her about the moonshining?"

"I should have, but that's when Mark chased me off, and that didn't sit too well, so I thought I'd let him make a fool of himself. Then I could step in and solve the case, which would have ended any talk about Mark getting my job once and for all."

I must have looked disapproving, because Junior said, "I know, it wasn't a mature thing to do. Here I've been maligning Mark for playing politics instead of getting the job done, and I'd done the same thing myself. I don't think I'd have let it go on for much longer, but while I was waiting to be interviewed, I started thinking. How on earth had Mark made a mistake like that? Two mistakes, if you count him thinking that Seth could have died by accident."

"People do make mistakes."

"Laurie Anne, Mark has been my deputy ever since I've been chief of police, and I have never known him to make a mistake like that. Maybe he's not brilliant, but he's always been thorough and he's always been competent."

"Dead bodies tend to make people nervous."

"Mark's seen people shot, knifed, and so torn up by car accidents that you couldn't tell which parts belonged to which person. As bodies go, Seth's was darned mild."

"Still, he was in charge this time."

But Junior shook her head. "Mark's been in charge before. I do go on vacations sometimes, no matter what my mama thinks, and so did Daddy."

"Then what did you think?"

"Nothing specific, but I knew something was going on. First he didn't want it to be a murder at all, and when that didn't work, he withheld information that could have led to the murderer. So I decided to let him run things his way so I could see what he'd do."

"Giving him enough rope to hang himself?"

"Which he did by the way he handled the investigation. Everybody knows that the first place you look for a killer is the family, but he didn't do much with any of the Murdstones. Failing that, he should have done something with the moonshining connection, but instead he came up with that fairy tale about a thief sneaking into the building. Then he dreamed up the idea that the practical joker was the killer, only now we find out he was setting up those pranks himself. It's been like he's been working as hard as he can to keep from catching the killer. Which is why I wanted to work with you, so I could keep an eye on him."

I nodded, remembering all the things Mark had been doing that I had thought were just bone stupid. Of course, I was feeling pretty darned stupid myself because of how Junior had been using me. I didn't need any hormones to make me furious.

"Junior, I thought we were working to-gether. If all you want to do is play games, you can do it by yourself."

"Hey, I didn't mean to get you mad."

"What *did* you mean to do? Make a fool out of me?"

"Come on, now, Laurie Anne. Give me a chance to explain."

I might have walked out on her, but I could see where Richard and the others were still trying to fix up the damaged flat, and I remembered that what we were doing was more important than my ego. Still, I wasn't happy with Junior. "You could have told me what you were really up to. After all we've gone through together, I'd think you'd trust me."

"I do trust you."

"Then why did you tell me all that stuff about wanting to see how I work?"

"I really did want to see how you work. I'm learning a lot."

"Sure," I said, not believing her.

"I mean it."

"Thanks, but that doesn't make up for not telling me the truth."

"I'm sorry, Laurie Anne, I really am, but I had my reasons."

"I'm listening."

She took a deep breath. "Look, I was hoping I was wrong about Mark, and I didn't want to ruin his reputation without knowing for sure what's going on." She held up one hand to stop me before I could object. "I know you wouldn't have told anybody but Richard, but I didn't want even y'all distrusting Mark without a good reason."

"I can understand that," I said.

"And I wasn't all that sure of my own motives, what with the way he's been treating me. I was afraid I was making something out of nothing."

"You wouldn't do that, not with something this serious."

"I'm glad you think so, but other folks might not see it that way."

I nodded, knowing that there were people in town who'd think that she'd framed Mark to protect her job.

"One other thing," she said. "I felt like I owed Mark a chance to do the right thing. I thought that once he knew I was working with you, he'd come clean because he'd know I wasn't going to just go away. The fact that he hasn't — that he's following us and setting up pranks to distract us — that worries me, Laurie Anne. But I've still got to know exactly what's going on before I make a move."

"You don't think he . . ."

"Go ahead and say it," she said wearily. "You think he may have killed Seth himself."

CHAPTER
TWENTY-NINE

Neither of us said anything for a long time after that. I don't know about Junior, but I was picturing a murderer riding around with a gun and a badge. It wasn't the first time I'd heard of police corruption, of course — the *Boston Globe* was filled with articles about cops stealing valuable evidence, and FBI agents letting informants get away with terrible crimes — but it wasn't something I'd ever expected to see in Byerly.

The front door opened, and I said, "Speak of the devil. Mark just walked in."

"Remember, Laurie Anne, I don't want him to know we suspect anything."

"I'll do my best," I said, but I wasn't feeling confident. Not only am I a lousy liar, but I've got an awful poker face.

Mark came right to us. "Junior, Mrs. Fleming."

"Deputy Pope," I said.

He looked at all the frantic activity on the stage. "What's the problem now?"

"The practical joker rigged one of the flats to fall over," I said, watching his face for some sign of guilt or remorse.

"Was anybody hurt?"

Before Junior or I could answer, Aunt Maggie stomped over. "It's about time you showed up. When are you going to do something about all the foolishness going on around here? You see that piece of scenery? Somebody could have gotten hurt if that thing had fallen!"

"I thought it did fall," Mark said.

"Lucky for us, Laurie Anne found it before it went down."

"Is that right?" Mark said, looking at me.

"Don't even think it," Aunt Maggie snapped. "Laurie Anne didn't do it, even if she was here before the rest of us. She was waiting for us outside the whole time. Right, Laurie Anne?"

"Yes, ma'am," I said, trying not to sound as nervous as I felt. Though I appreciated Aunt Maggie leaping to my defense, I sure wished she hadn't given Mark so much information.

"You've got a job to do, deputy," Aunt Maggie said, "and I expect you to get off your duff and do it. Is that understood?" It

328

didn't really call for an answer, which was just as well, because Aunt Maggie was gone before he could say anything.

"Then you weren't at the funeral?" Mark said to me.

"Nope, I was too tired from running around the mall," I said, trying to sound nonchalant. "So, did you get much shopping done yesterday?"

Mark didn't answer, but his face turned bright red, and he marched off.

"Laurie Anne . . ." Junior started to say.

"I wasn't teasing him just for the sake of teasing him, Junior. I just wanted to make him mad enough to leave before I gave anything away."

"You made him mad, all right."

"Better mad than suspicious, but he's probably both now, thanks to Aunt Maggie." Just knowing that was an uncomfortable feeling, and I resolved not to spend any time alone until this thing was finished. "Do you know why Mark would have killed Seth?"

"I've got an idea."

"Do I get to hear it?"

"I've already apologized once."

"You're right. I'll behave."

"Anyway, I was trying to figure out why Mark was avoiding the moonshine angle.

After all, it would have been quite a coup if he'd been able to prove Seth was a moonshiner when neither Daddy nor I ever could. It might even have helped him convince more council members that he ought to be chief of police. Then I wondered if maybe that's what he was after all along."

"You lost me."

"What if Mark decided to go after Seth while I was out of the picture? Even though he doesn't know Clara Todger, he could have heard from other sources that Seth was thinking about retiring. If that happened, Mark would never have had another chance at him. Daddy and I have never been big on harassing suspects, but suppose Mark decided that was the only thing left to try. Suppose he confronted Seth that day, trying to get him to admit he was making moonshine. When Seth wouldn't, Mark lost his temper and hit him. His night stick would have been just about right for that dent in Seth's head. But he hit Seth harder than he meant to and killed him. So he hightailed it and waited for the call to come through."

"That's not bad," I said, "but was Mark even here that day? And did he know about that door?"

"I don't know for sure, but I do know he'd been here other days. Vasti got him over here

330

at least once so she could complain about the first batch of practical jokes. As for the door, I saw him go out that way to talk with Big Bill when Big Bill was smoking one of his cigars."

"Then it really could be him," I said. "How do we prove it?"

"Hold your horses," Junior said, holding up one hand. "We've still got other suspects."

"I didn't see any of them setting a flat to fall."

"Oh, Mark's up to something, but it may not be murder."

"Then what?"

"He could be trying to distract us from the murder so he'll be able to solve it himself."

"If he's been setting up all the pranks, he hasn't had time to solve a murder."

"Then maybe he already knows who it is and is covering for him."

"Who? Why would he do that?"

"I don't know, Laurie Anne!" she snapped. "Maybe he thinks it was Florence, but he's got a secret passion for her and doesn't want to see her in jail. Maybe he hated Seth so much he thinks the killer should get a medal instead of a jail term. Maybe he really thinks it was an accident. All I know is that we've got other suspects." She took a deep breath. "Sure, Mark is still on the list. Maybe he's even at the top of the list. But he's not the entire list."

I opened my mouth to argue but closed it when I realized what Junior's problem was. I'd been in a similar position myself the summer before, when my cousin Linwood was the main suspect in a series of arson fires.[9] Even though I wasn't all that fond of Linwood, and even though I wasn't sure he was innocent, I'd defended him because he was family. Though Mark wasn't exactly a member of Junior's family, they'd worked together a long time, and before that, he'd worked with her father. On top of that, they were both cops, which was another powerful bond. So even though he wasn't related by blood, in a way Mark was part of Junior's family. Even though I would have loved to pin it on him, if for no other reason than to keep Junior's job safe, I couldn't push her on it.

I said, "Okay, who's after Mark?"

"David, for one," Junior said.

"To hide the moonshining and/or Tim from his society wife," I said.

"Florence."

[9] *Death of a Damn Yankee*

"To hide the moonshining and/or Tim from her society friends."

"Jake."

"To keep the moonshine flowing, or to keep Tim away from Seth's money."

"Mrs. Gamp."

"If she found out that Seth was the one to kill her husband."

"Tim Topper."

"Revenge for his mother, or to get an inheritance."

"On the not-very-likely end of the list, we've got Oliver, Sid, and the Todger family."

"Don't forget the Mafia," I added.

"I hadn't forgotten. They're smack dab at the bottom of the list."

I started to count them up but then decided I didn't want to. "That's scary. Everybody liked Seth, but here there are this many people with reasons to kill him."

"If everybody had liked him," Junior pointed out, "he wouldn't be dead."

"It still doesn't seem right. Of course, I didn't really know Seth."

"Me neither. Under the circumstances, it would have been difficult for me to socialize with him. I wish I had known him better. It's easier for me to work a case when I know the victim."

"I almost always know the people involved, myself," I said. "How do you get a feel for a victim you didn't know?"

"I talk to the spouses and family and friends — just like we've been doing. And at some point, I check out the victim's house."

"Does that help?" I asked.

"Sometimes. Most murders don't come out of the blue, you know, and there's usually something in a person's house to show that trouble has been brewing. Angry letters from an ex-wife, or new locks on the door if the person's been running scared, or all kinds of things. I never know what I'm going to find."

"Has Mark searched Seth's place?"

Junior looked irritated, so I left that alone.

"There must be a way to get inside that house," I said. "Maybe Jake left a window or a door unlocked."

"No breaking and entering," Junior said sternly. "I am still chief of police, you know. Besides, we wouldn't be able to use anything we found in court."

"How's this? We went to see David and Florence, but we haven't paid a condolence call on Jake. We can take him a fruit basket, and while you keep him busy, I'll tell him I have to go to the bathroom and go snooping instead."

"You wouldn't have enough time to find anything. What if you pretended to go into labor on Jake's front lawn, and when he carried you in, you sent him off to boil hot water while you tossed the place."

"Hey, you're the one who wanted a look around Seth's house."

"Sorry," she said, unable to hide a grin. "Any other ideas?"

"Just one." I don't know if Junior thought it was a good idea or not, but at least she kept a straight face when I told her about it and made the phone calls necessary to set it up.

CHAPTER THIRTY

It took a while to get the ball rolling, but that was just as well. We had to wait for Jake to get to rehearsal anyway, which he didn't do until after lunch. A little while after that, Aunt Nora showed up with Aunt Edna and Aunt Nellie in tow.

They looked in my direction just long enough to make sure I saw them, then went to where Jake was repairing the damaged flat. "Jake, have you got a minute?" I heard Aunt Nora say, and they spent a little while talking before he handed her a set of keys. I'd expected him to be reluctant, but he seemed grateful, which made me feel guilty about what I had in mind.

Aunt Nora came my way next, saying brightly, "Hey there, Laurie Anne. Are you busy this afternoon?"

"Nope, just taking up space," I said, trying to sound natural. "Why do you ask?"

"Are you up for some housecleaning?"

"Housecleaning?" I repeated, thinking that it was a good thing I wasn't in the play, because my performance would have given Richard conniptions.

"I was talking to Edna," Aunt Nora said, "and we realized that the church hadn't done a thing to help poor Jake during his troubles, so we volunteered to go clean his house. If you're not busy, we could use another set of hands."

"Sure," I said. "Just let me get my coat."

Junior was watching us play-act, and Aunt Nora said, "What about you, Junior?"

"I can't," she said. "I'm keeping up with the kids." Actually, she refused because we'd decided that her being directly involved would taint anything I found. Besides, she hated housecleaning nearly as much as I did.

We kept our fake smiles in place until we were in Aunt Nora's car. Then Aunt Nora excitedly asked, "Did we fool everybody?"

"I think so," I said, watching the recreation center door until we pulled out of the parking lot. "Nobody is following us."

"Thank goodness. I was so nervous I was afraid I'd forget what I was supposed to say."

"You did fine, Nora," Aunt Nellie assured her. "Laurie Anne, do you really think there's anything important in Seth's house?"

"I don't know, but there might be." I hadn't told them who Junior and I suspected, only that we hoped to find something that would point us in the right direction.

The Murdstone house was an old farmhouse, painted brick red with dark-gray shutters. It was surrounded by a couple of acres of land, most of it wooded, and the place was a good distance off the road, with no neighbors in sight. It reminded me of the Todger compound, and I figured Seth had liked his privacy for the same reason they did. Though he hadn't run his still out of his home, he still wouldn't have wanted people to know about his comings and goings.

Aunt Nora unlocked the front door with Jake's keys and waved me inside. "You go ahead. We'll get the cleaning things out of the car and get to work."

"Thanks, Aunt Nora. I really appreciate this."

"Don't be silly. We're all glad to pitch in for your last time."

I resented the "last time" part, but decided it was no time to be picky. After one look inside the front door, I was glad I hadn't argued with her. My aunts were getting more than they'd bargained for.

338

The place was a pigsty. The hardwood floor was muddy, there were newspapers and empty bottles scattered around, and every ash tray was filled with cigarette butts. Of course, I reminded myself, Jake had lost his son and then his father in the space of a few months. I didn't think my place would be any cleaner under those circumstances.

The triplets had told me that Seth lived on the second floor, while Jake and his son had lived on the first, so I headed up the stairs, turning on lights as I went.

It wasn't as bad up there. A bit dusty, and since Seth had been a smoker, the smell lingered, but I didn't think anybody had done much in there since Seth died. That was all the better as far as I was concerned.

Knowing the age of the house and the usual layout for places like it, I could tell that there'd been a lot of modifications made to the place. I'd have expected a bathroom and three or four bedrooms. Instead, there was a den, a compact kitchen, a larger than usual bathroom, and a roomy bedroom. I wondered if Seth and Jake had done the work themselves, because if they were that good, they should have gotten out of moonshining and into construction.

There were a desk and a filing cabinet in one corner of Seth's bedroom, and I started there. I found a ledger book right off, and I went through it first, hoping that I'd find some solid evidence of Seth's moonshining. Unfortunately, it only had records of the household expenses, and listings for buying supplies and selling furniture. The rest of the desk drawers held the usual stuff people accumulate: unpaid bills and giveaway pens and tape and a postcard reminding Seth to make a dentist's appointment. The filing cabinet looked promising at first with its neatly labeled folders, but though I glanced through every folder, I didn't find any threatening letters or panic-stricken journal entries.

It didn't take long to search the rest of the bedroom, but unless I counted the three well-thumbed copies of *Penthouse,* there was nothing suspicious. Then I hit the living room, then the kitchen, and even the bathroom. Nothing. At least, nothing that pointed to Seth's murderer.

There were a few paperback men's adventure novels scattered about and a couple of woodworking magazines, but apparently Seth hadn't been a big reader. There were some videos on the shelf under the TV and VCR, but all store-bought ones. Seth had liked *Top Gun* and *Benny Hill.* Plus, there were photo albums, and the memorabilia any parent or grandparent collects: graduation programs, homemade cards of construction paper, school book reports, and crayon drawings. But I didn't find anything out of the ordinary.

Knowing that Seth and Jake were carpenters, I tapped around on the walls and furniture, looking for secret compartments. All I got were sore knuckles.

I even tried to get mystical. I sat down on the end of the couch that showed the most wear, figuring it must have been where Seth liked to sit, and closed my eyes, trying to sense what the dead man had been like. Why had he spent his life breaking the law, and what had he done when he wasn't making moonshine? Why had he slept with Tim's mother and only admitted it recently? Why had he never remarried after his wife died? Who in the heck was Seth Murdstone?

I opened my eyes. Maybe the strangest thing I found was nothing. Despite the obvious signs that Seth had lived there and kept his belongings there, there was almost no personality in those rooms. It was as if Seth had hidden himself as carefully as he'd hidden his still. Maybe Junior or a psychologist could have gotten to know Seth Murdstone by looking at his home, but I couldn't.

I finally decided I might as well go help

my aunts, but halfway down the stairs, I stopped and stared in amazement. If I hadn't known better, I'd have thought I was in a different house. Every surface either shone or gleamed, as appropriate, and every newspaper, cigarette butt, and beer bottle was gone. I wouldn't have to worry about leaving fingerprints while searching that house — my aunts would polish them right off again.

"Hello?" I called out.

"We're in the kitchen," one of them replied, and I followed the voice through the newly immaculate living room. They'd just gotten started in the kitchen, so I could see what a mess the room had been, but the smell of Pine-Sol promised that any germs were on their way out. Aunt Nellie had her head in the refrigerator and was pitching styrofoam containers into a green garbage bag while Aunt Edna sprayed glass cleaner and Aunt Nora loaded plates into the dishwasher.

"Did you find anything?" Aunt Edna asked eagerly.

"Not a thing," I said. "I thought I'd look around down here."

Aunt Nora said, "Go right ahead. We've got plenty to keep us busy."

In fact, they had enough to keep me busy

for a month, but I suspected they would be done in an hour or two.

The downstairs part of the house was bigger than the upper floor because of a long room along one side that had probably started out life as a porch. There was the living room and kitchen I'd already seen, a half bathroom off the front hall, and a full bathroom with doors to both bedrooms. The former porch had been set up as a combination den and playroom, although from the number of toys scattered around, I suspected the playroom function had taken over.

Even though my aunts hadn't cleaned in there yet, and despite the toys, it was probably the neatest room downstairs, and I wondered why. Then I saw the scorched patch of carpet and realized that was where Barnaby must have gotten burned. I was surprised it wasn't worse, considering how badly Barnaby had been hurt. Even thinking about the boy's injuries made my stomach roll, and though it was the wrong time of the day for morning sickness, I decided I needed some fresh air.

There was a door leading outside from the playroom, and I called out, "I'm going out back," before stepping through.

The yard wasn't much to see. The grass

had been mowed and the weeds kept under control, but it didn't look as if Jake or Seth had spent any time planting flowers or bushes. There was a large-ish wooden building out there, too big for a playhouse, and when I checked the door, it was unlocked.

Inside was a home handyman's dream, with all the woodworking tools anybody could want. Not that I knew what most of them were, but they looked impressive. There was also plenty of lumber waiting to be made into furniture, and a few completed pieces. Even though their real business lay elsewhere, clearly Seth and Jake had spent a lot of time in the workshop. There was a little refrigerator, a coffeemaker, and even a telephone.

One of Seth's signature chairs was sitting in the middle of the room, and after making sure the varnish had dried, I took a seat. Florence was right; it wasn't as comfortable as the average church pew. While sitting there, I saw a mangled pile of metal on one of the worktables. It took a closer look and some imagination to picture what it must have been, but once I did, my stomach turned again. It was the remains of a space heater.

I nearly ran out of the little building, and went back inside the house. My aunts had finished up in the kitchen, and I offered to tackle Jake's bedroom. Then I looked inside and started to regret it. It was strewn with the same kinds of trash as in the rest of the house, but with dirty clothes thrown in for good measure.

"Aunt Nora," I called out, "did y'all bring any spare rubber gloves?"

Once my hands were protected, I brought myself to start searching, but other than learning that Jake was a briefs man, I didn't know a bit more than I had before. Aunt Nora came in while I was gingerly picking my way through. She said, "Throw the dirties into the hall, and I'll put them in the washer later."

"You're a braver man than I, Gunga Din," I said.

"Lord, Laurie Anne, after washing up after Buddy, Augustus, Thaddeous, and Willis all these years, this is nothing!"

"Do kids make that big a mess?" I said, worried for the future.

"Not until they start walking," she said cheerfully. "Unless they spit up a lot, of course."

"Maybe I should hire a cleaning service."

She just laughed. "You start over there, and I'll start over here, and we'll meet in the middle."

Actually, we met when I was only one-third done, and she'd already gotten two-thirds of the way through. She might have gotten farther along than that if she hadn't stopped at Jake's chest of drawers. A minute later, I realized she was crying.

"Aunt Nora?" I said. "What's wrong?"

She waved a piece of paper at me. "Oh, Laurie Anne, this breaks my heart."

"What?"

"Read it," she said, handing it to me as she looked for a tissue to blow her nose.

It was a letter, hand printed on notebook paper and dated December 1.

Dear Santa,

How are you? I am fine. Only I'm in the hospital, but the doctor says I might get to go home for Christmas. If not, you can find me here.

I have tried to be a good boy this year. I did lie once, but Grandpaw says it's okay to lie if it's for a good reason. So I hope it doesn't count.

I would really like the new PlayStation if you can get one. Daddy says they are hard to find, but I figure you can make one yourself. And games for it, too.

I would also like you to bring my Daddy a CD player for his car. I broke

346

the old one, and have been trying to earn money to buy a new one, but I got hurt before I got enough. If you'll bring him one, I promise to spend the money I have saved on CDs for him. Or on Play-Station games so you don't have to bring me so many.

I hope Mrs. Claus is good, and that the reindeer are, too. Especially Rudolph, if he's real.

Love,
Barnaby Murdstone

PS: If you can't find a PlayStation, that's OK, but don't forget the CD player for Daddy.

I started crying, too, and Aunt Nora handed me the box of tissues she'd found. Aunt Nellie and Aunt Edna must have heard us, because they showed up, wondering what was going on. Both of them read the letter and reached for the tissues.

"I've never read anything so sad in my whole life," Aunt Nora sniffed. "Asking for a present for his daddy when he was in the hospital dying. Can you imagine?"

I shook my head. I'd never been that sweet in my Christmas letters. After a perfunctory inquiry into Santa's health, I'd methodically listed a page's worth of stuff I wanted.

"He had such pretty handwriting, too," Aunt Nellie said.

"He didn't write that," Aunt Edna said. "Mrs. Gamp told me she did it for him. He died not long after he wrote this, and she never got around to mailing it, so when she found it in her pocketbook the other day, she gave it to Jake. It must have torn the poor man up. She should have just thrown it out."

Aunt Nora said, "No, she did the right thing. Now Jake knows what a wonderful boy he had."

That made us start crying all over again, and we had to stop working long enough for Aunt Nora to brew some iced tea for us to drink. For once I didn't pay attention to the caffeine or the amount of sugar she added. I had to have something to loosen my throat.

After we pulled ourselves together, we started cleaning as if our lives depended on it. There was no way we could comfort Jake for the loss of that little boy — we couldn't even admit we'd read such a private letter. What we could do was get that house so spic and span that you could have eaten off any floor in the place.

I knew I was going to have to tell Junior that I hadn't seen anything that would lead us to Seth's killer, but I didn't regret having spent the time out there. Making Jake's house fit to live in was the least we could do for him.

CHAPTER
THIRTY-ONE

It didn't take long to report to Junior what I'd found at Seth's house, once Aunt Nora dropped me off at rehearsal, because there wasn't much to tell. So we hashed over what we knew, and we rehashed it, and then we made goulash out of it. None of it did any good. All it did was make me hungry.

Richard kept everybody but the kids late that night, trying to make up for the time lost because of Seth's services. But finally he admitted that we'd accomplished as much as we were going to. The next day was the technical rehearsal and the dress rehearsal, with our first performance the night after that, so he warned everybody to get plenty of sleep because come tomorrow, he wasn't going to let anybody go until everything was perfect. People were out of there in record time.

As soon as we got into the car, I said, "Richard, I can tell you're worn out, but we've got to talk."

"Are you feeling all right?"

"I'm fine; the baby's fine. It's about Seth's murderer." I launched into a report of everything Junior and I had done over the past couple of days, which lasted through the ride home and into our preparations for the night. Only when we were in bed, with Richard's arm around me, did I tell him about what I'd seen Mark doing.

"Jesus, Laura!" Richard said. "Why didn't you say something before?"

"I didn't get a chance," I said, "and I was so horrified, I didn't want to. It was like when I was a little kid. If something bad happened, I thought that if I didn't say anything, nobody would find out, and it wouldn't be real. Telling somebody would have made it true. I know that doesn't make much sense —"

"No, I think I understand."

"Once we saw the flat was broken, you were busy trying to make sure nobody got hurt. I told Junior because he's her deputy. She and I decided not to tell anybody else."

"Why not?"

"There's no proof. It would be his word against mine."

"Don't you think people would believe you over him?"

"I don't know. The point is that it wouldn't do any good to tell people now. We need to find out what's going on, and we can do that better if he doesn't know we're onto him."

"Are you sure he doesn't already know?"

I thought about how he'd acted after talking to Aunt Maggie. "He might suspect, but he can't know for sure."

"Laura, if this is true, Mark's got to be getting desperate, and he's got a gun. I'm worried." He gently rubbed my tummy. "About both of you."

"I'm worried, too," I said, "but I'm going to be careful. I won't go anywhere without somebody with me — preferably you or Junior — and I'm going to stay as far away from Mark as humanly possible."

"Good," he said firmly. "Otherwise I'd be tempted to get us onto the next plane out of here."

"We can't do that! The play is the day after tomorrow, and everybody is depending on you. And Junior is depending on me."

"Do you think any of that would make a difference to me if I thought you were in danger? Would it mean anything to you if I were in danger?"

"No, I guess not. But I don't think I'm in danger."

"Then we'll stick around. But if there's the first sign that Mark, or anybody else, might hurt you —"

"We head for the airport. Got it."

"Good. You get some rest," he said. "I love you."

"I love you, too."

Despite everything, Richard was asleep in minutes. It took me a little longer. I was thinking about what Richard had said about Mark getting desperate. He was right, and that explained why the so-called practical jokes had been getting nastier. The question was, how much more desperate was Mark going to get?

CHAPTER
THIRTY-TWO

Thanks to my taking so long to get to sleep, Richard and I were late getting to rehearsal the next day, and when we arrived, people were milling around and looking a lot more upset than they should have been over missing five minutes of rehearsal. I snagged Mrs. Gamp as she rushed by, and said, "What's going on?"

"Haven't you heard?" she asked. "The most terrible thing happened last night. At least, it almost happened. Though of course it would have been much more terrible if it had happened. But like Mrs. Harris always says, to have something almost happen is nearly as bad as it actually happening. Don't you think?"

I just blinked at her, wishing mightily that there really was a Mrs. Harris, because surely she'd be able to explain things better than Mrs. Gamp did.

Fortunately, Junior came over then. "It's

about time y'all got here. People are kind of stirred up."

"So we see," Richard said. "What has Mar —" Junior looked at him sharply, and he changed it to, "What has our practical joker done now?"

"No joke. Jake Murdstone nearly died last night from gas fumes."

Mrs. Gamp said, "He's going to be fine, but if he'd been in there much longer . . ." She wagged her head. "Thank goodness for his brother. Because poor Jake was feeling no pain, if you know what I mean."

Actually, I had no idea what Mrs. Gamp meant, so I looked to Junior for a more coherent explanation.

"David went over to the Murdstone house last night," Junior said obligingly. "Jake's car was there, but Jake didn't answer the door, and when David went inside, he smelled gas. Jake was passed out at the kitchen table, so David dragged him outside and called for help. By the time the ambulance showed up, Jake was already coming round. He was sick as a dog, but he's going to be all right."

"Good Lord," I breathed. "How did it happen?"

"These things do happen," Mrs. Gamp intoned. "Especially when liquor is involved.

Mr. Gamp went that way. Only he was driving a truck, not using a stove, and of course he would never have taken a drop when he was driving, but it happened just the same. You just never know."

"Mrs. Gamp," Junior said, "did Vasti find you? I think she wanted you to help her fold programs."

"Did she? I better get right over there." She trotted away.

"Did Vasti really ask for her help?" I asked Junior.

"No, but I knew I'd never get the whole story out if we didn't get her out of here. Anyway, when the fire department got there, they found one of the eyes of the stove had been turned on full blast and the pilot light was out. Jake is just lucky his brother picked last night to bring him something to eat."

" 'Accidents will occur in the best-regulated families,' " Richard said. "*David Copperfield,* Chapter Twenty-eight."

"How did that eye get turned on?" I wanted to know.

"Ask Jake yourself. He just came in the door."

Pretty much everybody in the room looked in Jake's direction as he walked past. Jake's face colored and he refused to meet anybody's eyes.

David stepped toward him. "Jake, what are you doing here? The doctor said you need to take it easy for a few days."

"I feel fine," Jake said, but I don't imagine anybody believed him. Other than the angry flush on his cheeks, he looked as pale as could be. "I've got things to do before the play opens."

Richard said, "Jake, nobody appreciates your devotion more than I do, but there's no reason to make yourself sick."

"I'm fine," Jake insisted. "I had a little accident, that's all. Just let me get back to work."

"Jake, be reasonable," David said. "Go back to the house and lay down."

"I'm not going to sit out there all day!" Jake snapped.

David looked at his brother for a long time, then nodded. "All right, if you think you can handle it —"

Jake laughed, but it was a bitter sound, not a happy one. "This isn't the part I'm having problems handling." He walked past David and went backstage.

Richard, Junior, and I went over to David. "Is he really fit to work?" Richard asked.

"You heard what he said," David said helplessly. "It probably is better for him than sitting around the house by himself. I'll keep an eye on him."

"Okay, but let me know if you need me to order him out of here." Then, to me Richard said, "Are you going to be sticking around here today?"

"As far as I know. I'll let you know if anything changes."

"Good." He gave me a kiss on the cheek and headed for the stage.

"What happened?" I asked David. "Was it really an accident?"

"Of course it was an accident! What else would it have been?" He glared at me briefly before stalking off.

"Sounds as if you hit a nerve," Junior said.

"Apparently so. Look, I don't know about you, but I need to sit down."

"Lead the way."

Finding a quiet corner was getting harder to do the closer we got to opening night, but we finally settled in the back of the auditorium.

"What I want to know," I said, "is whether or not it was really an accident."

"That's what Jake says. In fact, I was talking to a friend of mine at the hospital, and she says that when he was being treated, Jake put the blame on your aunts."

"What?"

"He thinks one of them accidentally turned on the eye when y'all were out there cleaning."

"They did no such thing!" I said heatedly. "Besides which, if they had, it would have stunk up the house. If we hadn't smelled it when we left, Jake would have noticed as soon as he came in the door."

"He claims all he could smell was Pine-Sol."

"They did use a lot of it, but —"

"You don't have to convince me. I don't have any idea that that's what happened."

"Well, I don't see how Jake could have done it himself. If the kind of mess left around is any indication, he hasn't cooked anything in a while. All I saw were takeout bags and the trays from some microwave meals. Nothing that would require him firing up the stove."

"He was drunk," Junior pointed out.

"I'm not surprised. I can't tell you how many empties we carted out of there." I thought about it. "Do you think Jake tried to kill himself?"

"David says he didn't find a suicide note."

"Do all suicides leave notes?" I asked.

"Nope, plenty of them don't. Some don't want people knowing it was suicide, so they try to make it look like an accident."

"Goodness knows Jake has had more excuses than most to want to give up. His son dying, and now his father being murdered." I paused. "Maybe guilt, too."

"You mean over killing his father?" Junior said. "I thought about that, but I've never known a killer to commit suicide because of remorse. At least, not one who's gotten away with it. Once they get caught, sometimes they'll take the easy way out, but not before. I'm not saying it never happens, but if I ever ran across a case that looked like it, I'd be mighty suspicious.

"So it could have been an accident, but it doesn't seem likely, or it could have been attempted suicide, but we don't have any proof of that, or . . ."

She finished for me. "Or somebody tried to kill Jake. Probably the person who killed his father."

"Jesus, Junior, Jake could have been murdered while we run around playing cops and robbers."

"I *am* a cop! How do you think I feel?"

"Sorry. This just throws me for a loop."

"Do you want to bow out? I'd understand if you did."

"You know me better than that!" I said. "If that so-and-so thinks he can get away with killing more people, he's got another

360

think coming!"

"That's what I wanted to hear," Junior said.

"Let me put this together. If it really was an accident, then it doesn't mean anything to our investigation."

"Right. If it was attempted suicide, it might mean that Jake is off our list because murderers almost never kill themselves. So if he did try, then he wasn't the killer."

"This is starting to sound like one of those logic puzzles," I said. "If somebody tried to kill him, it should also get him off our list. Unless there are two killers running around."

"Possible," Junior admitted, "but I'd rather assume that Seth's killer went after Jake. So why did somebody want Jake dead?"

"Maybe Jake knows who killed Seth," I suggested. Then I had to add, "But if he did, why wouldn't he have come forward?"

"What if he's protecting the killer?"

"Then it would have to be David, because I can't imagine who else Jake would protect, when it's his own father who was killed. Since David is the one who saved him from the gas last night, he can't be the one who tried to kill him."

"Right. What other motive have we got?"

Junior said.

"What if Seth was killed to shut down the still, and once the killer realized that Jake was going to keep it going, he went after him, too?"

"Why? We ruled out the idea of anybody in organized crime caring about the still, and all that leaves is David trying to keep Florence from finding out about it. But she already knows, and he knows that."

I thought for a minute. "Let's go back to the two-killer theory. What if Jake killed Seth, and somebody found out and tried to kill him for revenge?"

"That gets us back to David," Junior said. "Those two are the only kin Seth had."

"Could David have intended to kill Jake and then changed his mind? After all, David is the most reasonable choice for being able to get in the house and set it up. How do we know he really just wanted to bring Jake something to eat? Did anybody actually see any food?"

"That's a point."

"Come to think of it, could Jake have faked the attempt to draw attention away from himself?"

"Nice idea, but my friend at the hospital saw how sick Jake was last night — he wasn't faking that. Not to mention the fact that he was lucky that the gas didn't ignite. More people die from gas fires than gas poisoning. All it would have taken was one little spark and the place would have gone up. Jake's not the sharpest knife in the drawer, but I don't think he's that dumb."

"You're probably right," I had to agree. "Maybe the killer is going after all the Murdstones. Seth was just the first, and Jake was supposed to be next. Heck, even Florence slipping in the bathroom could have been part of his plan — she's a Murdstone by marriage."

"Except that anybody could have slipped in the soap. Any female, at least."

"Then ignore the soap spill. Somebody could still be trying to take out the Murdstones."

"Why?"

"Maybe Seth really does have moonshining money hidden away, and some relative is planning to step forward and inherit once all the Murdstones are gone."

"Who?" Junior said skeptically. "I told you, they didn't have any other family. Unless you think Seth had a secret twin living out in the woods somewhere."

"Don't make fun unless you have a better idea."

"Sorry. It's just that I'm used to dealing

with likely solutions. That one was getting pretty far out there."

"If there were a likely solution, don't you think we'd have been able to figure it out by now?"

"All right, keep speculating," Junior said.

"Thank you. You know, there might be a reason somebody would want all the Murdstones dead. Aunt Nora said Big Bill wanted to buy their house but Seth wouldn't sell."

"Laurie Anne, please don't make me interrogate Big Bill Walters."

"I'm not saying it was Big Bill. I'm just wondering why he wanted it. Is there going to be a factory built there or something that would make the land worth a lot?"

"Sorry to burst your bubble. Big Bill wants the land because it's next to a piece he already owns, but he doesn't have any specific plans for it that I've heard of."

"Then I guess that leaves us with . . . Shoot, Junior, what does that leave us with?"

"Heck if I know," she said in disgust. "Other than the fact that somebody killed Seth and maybe that same somebody tried to kill Jake, and damned if he hasn't gotten away with it."

"Not yet he hasn't," I said firmly. "We are going to catch this killer if it takes us until next Christmas!"

CHAPTER THIRTY-THREE

I'd thought regular rehearsals were boring, but that was before I watched a technical rehearsal. As Richard explained it, we had to go through every lighting cue and special effect and make sure they were perfect. Unfortunately, we didn't actually have anybody in charge of lighting and effects, thanks to Sally Hendon making off with all the experienced people. Instead, everybody pitched in between other jobs and their lines on stage, meaning that it was darned confusing and provided endless opportunities for mistakes. Every time somebody messed up, Richard would make them go through things over and over again until they got it right.

As Junior whispered to me, the worst part of it was that Richard was keeping his temper through all of it, so we didn't even have a good tantrum to break the monotony.

Junior and I would gladly have gone

somewhere — anywhere — to try to make sense of Seth's death and the attack on Jake, but neither of us could come up with anyplace useful to go. Junior indulged me by listening to my most whimsical flights of fancy, but even that didn't lead to anything that we could actually do. So we sat and brooded.

Richard didn't want to interrupt the tech rehearsal, which meant he wouldn't even let us break for lunch until it was done. By the time he was satisfied, we had an auditorium filled with cranky, hungry people. Including me.

Fortunately, Richard ordered in pizzas for lunch and announced that we'd have an extra long lunch break so that everybody could rest. Otherwise we might have had another murder.

Since Richard was too agitated to eat and I didn't want to sit with Junior and her ravening horde of nieces and nephews, I ended up at a table with the three Spirits of Christmas.

"Are you three about ready for tomorrow night?" I asked them over a bite of pepperoni pizza.

Sid and Pete only nodded, but Oliver said, "I can't wait! Of course, having two roles is particularly challenging, but I assure you that I'm up to it."

I caught the other two men rolling their eyes, and hid a grin.

Just to make conversation, I said, "I hope all these rehearsals haven't kept you too long from your work, not to mention getting ready for Christmas. Richard's so used to college vacations that he forgets everybody isn't so lucky."

"I don't mind," Sid said. "I like to take time off at the holidays, anyway. I've got a college boy who's tickled to death to earn some extra money for Christmas shopping, and he's taking good care of the station."

"My uncle has been handling everything for me," Pete said. "I only stepped in to assist with Mr. Murdstone's arrangements as a favor to the family, and they really took very little of my time."

"Then they sure don't take after Seth," Oliver said with a little laugh. "He made a habit of taking up people's time."

"Oh?" I said.

"Laurie Anne, do you remember how I told you I'd shown Seth some land a while back, but that he'd decided not to buy it?"

I nodded.

"Well, when I was at the realty board's Christmas party last night, I found out I was only the last in a long string of realtors that he'd gone to. He's been looking at land for years. We couldn't even count all the parcels he's looked at, let alone the amount of time the realtors around here have wasted sending him listings and taking him out to see plots."

"I know a woman like that," I said. "She goes to every open house she sees, even though she's not in the market for a new house. She says it's for decorating ideas, but I think she just likes snooping around houses."

"I've seen that, too," Oliver said, "and those people are easy to pick out, but Seth only looked at undeveloped property."

"Why would he do that?" Sid asked. "Was he planning to build a new house?"

Oliver said, "Beats me. I'm just glad I found out before he wasted too much of my time." Then he looked abashed and added, "May he rest in peace."

The conversation wandered elsewhere after that, but I wasn't really paying attention. I was mulling over an idea, and as soon as I could do so politely, I excused myself and headed for Junior. Fortunately, the kids were fast eaters and had already run off to play with their Gameboys, so I could explain what Oliver had told me without interruption.

When I was done, she said, "You think looking at real estate had something to do with Seth's murder? Maybe the realtors got together and decided to do away with him to keep him from bothering them?"

"No," I said, exasperated. "What I think is that now we know where Seth's still is."

"You lost me."

"You said that Seth never put a still on his own land, and that he kept moving it places where neither you or your father could find it. So how did he find places that were safe? I bet he kept going to realtors so he could find out which places were empty. Once the land sold, or if he decided things were getting hot, he'd go to another realtor and find out another piece of land to use. Rent free, I might add."

"Slick," Junior said admiringly.

"Seth or me?"

"Both."

"Thank you," I said, but I had to add, "Of course, it's too late to catch Seth now."

"But not Jake. When did you say Oliver showed Seth that piece of land?"

"Late in the summer. Why?"

"I bet that's the last time Seth relocated. It's a pain to move a still, because you have to set up another place and get everything moved without being seen in either spot, so

I don't see how Jake could have had time to move it since Seth died. Richard's been keeping everybody at rehearsal every waking moment."

"Then all we have to do is find out from Oliver where the land is."

"There's no time like the present. Where is the Spirit of Christmas Present anyway?"

"Why the hurry? Do you think there's some evidence about Seth's murder out there?"

"Who cares? Laurie Anne, I have been hunting for Seth Murdstone's still ever since I became chief of police. Do you really think I'm going to pass up a chance to finally find it?"

"Not to mention how badly you want to beat Mark to the punch."

"That, too. And maybe there will be something related to the murder out there."

"Then let's go get Oliver."

We found him reading his script, mumbling his lines out loud.

"Oliver," I said, "can we talk to you for a minute?"

"Certainly. What can I do for you two ladies?"

Junior said, "We want to talk to you about the land you showed to Seth Murdstone."

"Why is that?"

I left the explanation to Junior. Since we weren't planning to mention Seth's moonshine operation, I wanted to see just how she was going to finesse the information out of Oliver. I should have realized that Junior doesn't need finesse.

"It's police business, Oliver," she said bluntly. "I need to know the location of the plot you showed to Seth, and I don't have time to mess around."

He blinked but didn't argue. "I've got the listing in my car."

"Then fetch it in here."

Darned if he didn't rush to do as he was told.

While he was gone, I said, "Do you think you can teach me how to do that? It sure would come in handy with the baby."

"Sorry, Laurie Anne, I think you have to be born with it."

By then, Oliver was back, leather portfolio in hand. He unzipped the case, licked one finger, and started turning pages. "It's been several months, so I'm not sure what it could have to do with the murder investigation."

"Who said it had anything to do with a murder investigation?" Junior said.

"I thought — or rather, I assumed —"

"Just show it to us."

He pulled out a page. "Here we go. A three-acre site on the north side of town."

"Three acres," I said, thinking about how long it would take to search that big an area.

"It's a lovely piece," Oliver said, "though a bit isolated. The nearest paved road is a ways off, though there is a well-cleared dirt track."

"Where's the track?" Junior demanded.

He pointed to a plot plan. "Here, in red."

That would help. Surely Seth and Jake wouldn't have wanted to lug their equipment and product too far over ground. Unfortunately the track went right through the middle of the plot, and the still could have been anywhere along it. We'd be able to find it eventually, but not without an extended search.

"What's this here?" I said, pointing to a blue blotch on the plan. "Water?"

"There's a small pond," Oliver said. "Seth was particularly interested in that because the plot isn't on the water system."

"Mud!" I nearly shouted. "Junior, there were muddy tracks on Jake's floor, and it hasn't rained the entire time I've been here. His clothes were muddy, too."

"And the pond isn't far from the track," she said.

We looked at each other and smiled.

Maybe it wasn't an engraved invitation to the still, but it was close enough.

"Can we borrow this?" Junior said, taking the piece of paper away from Oliver.

"Of course, but —"

"Thank you, you've been a big help. Now I want you to forget we've had this conversation."

"But —"

She just looked at him.

"It's forgotten," he said.

"Good. I owe you one."

He brightened at that. Having Junior owe you a favor was no small thing in Byerly. "I'll just go practice my lines."

"You do that," Junior said. Once he was far enough away, she said, "Are you in the mood for a walk in the woods?"

"I might be." Then I saw the front door open. "Rats! Look who just came in."

"Tell me it's not Mark."

"I would if I could." He looked our way, and though he headed for the stage, I could see he was still looking. "He'll know something's up if we leave in the middle of dress rehearsal."

"He'll probably try to follow us, too. We need a distraction."

I thought for a minute. "I've got an idea. You go wait by the door."

She did so, and I went and found Richard, who was settling up front in preparation for the start of dress rehearsal.

"How's that blocking during Fezziwigg's ball working out?" I said for the benefit of Mark, who was listening.

Richard lifted one eyebrow, then saw Mark. "Much better," he said heartily. "I think that if we get people to move in a counterclockwise reel pattern rather than in a waltz configuration, that should solve the line-of-sight problems and give more weight to the motion as a metaphor for the change in Scrooge in the past and in the present."

I didn't have the slightest idea what he was talking about, and I wasn't sure Richard did either. The important thing was that Mark walked away.

I leaned in closer and whispered, "Thanks. You scared him off."

"What's the problem?"

I quickly explained what was going on and added, "Junior and I need a distraction to make sure Mark doesn't see us leave. It won't take time away from the rehearsal. Not more than a few minutes, anyway."

"What do you have in mind?"

"Could you throw a tantrum?"

"Hey, I haven't lost my temper in days."

"I know, but if you throw one now, nobody

will notice us sneaking out."

"You'll be careful? And you'll stay with Junior?"

"Yes on both counts."

"Now that you mention it, Bob Cratchit has been a bit distracted today. Maybe a tantrum would do him good. When do you need it?"

"In ten minutes. No, make that twenty. I've got to go to the bathroom."

"Good hunting!"

"Thanks, love. Break a leg, or whatever it is I'm supposed to say." I quickly smooched him, and took a bathroom break. By the time I got out, Richard had started rehearsing, and as unobtrusively as possible, I ambled toward Junior. She and I were pretending to talk when I heard Richard yell, "Stop, stop, *Stop!*"

"Right on time," I said.

We watched for a minute or so as Richard blasted poor Tim for not looking cold enough. Then I nudged Junior. Mark had his back to us and was watching Richard stomp in front of the stage and wave his arms around.

Junior said, "I hate to miss this. He's got a real head of steam up this time."

"If you like, he can throw you a tantrum for your very own for Christmas. Let's go."

We got out the door as quickly as possible, and I kept watch while Junior drove out of the parking lot. Then I announced, "We're clear!"

CHAPTER THIRTY-FOUR

Just to be sure Mark hadn't seen us leaving, Junior drove around aimlessly for ten minutes or so, but once we were sure he wasn't following us, she drove to the piece of land Oliver had told us about. I was glad we were in Byerly instead of Boston. At three in the afternoon, it would have already been starting to get dark in Boston, but we still had plenty of daylight left.

"According to this map, the dirt track should be coming up soon," I said.

"There it is." Junior turned down the road.

"I think the phrase *well-cleared track* means something different to realtors," I grumbled as we bumped along. "If I were any further along, this would bounce the baby clean out of me."

"Please, no labor jokes," Junior said. "My nerves can't take it."

"It would help if you weren't going so fast."

"Fair enough," she said as she slowed to a crawl. "Keep an eye out. Seth may have left a marker of some kind."

We had gone maybe five minutes farther, well out of view of the main road, when I saw something flapping on a tree. "What's that?" I said.

A red plastic strip was tied around an outstretched limb.

"That might be it," Junior said. "If we're reading the map right, the pond is on that side and this is the closest the road comes to it." She stopped the car, then reached past me to unlock her glove compartment and pull out a shoulder holster and gun.

"Do you think we'll need that?" I said.

"If I thought we'd need it, I wouldn't have let you come along," she said, "but there's no reason not to be careful."

I let Junior lead the way, though she was kind enough to slow down so I could keep up. It was surprisingly quiet in the woods. Years' worth of pine needles covered the ground, soaking up most of the noise we were making, and at that time of year, there weren't many bird sounds.

"It should be somewhere around here," I said, consulting the map. "What exactly are we looking for, anyway? I've never seen a still."

"I've seen plenty, but no two look alike. Just look for a good-sized clearing. I expect that's where we'll find it."

A few yards farther on, we found the pond Oliver had told us about, and we traced the edge until we stepped into a clearing maybe twenty or thirty feet around. In the center was a metal contraption.

"Is that it?" I asked Junior.

"That's it."

It wasn't what I'd expected. I'm not sure what I had expected — maybe something out of Willy Wonka — but this wasn't it. Junior explained the workings. The part that was the cooking chamber was a stainless steel drum that had been painted mud brown to make it harder to see. It was set up over a fire pit, a hole lined with rocks. Condensing coils on top of the drum were attached to a funnel on top of a metal bucket; that's what the moonshine would drip into. Nearby was a stack of firewood.

Junior touched the side of the still and peered into the fire pit. "It doesn't look like it's been used for a few days. I guess Jake's been too busy with the play."

Off to one side of the clearing, placed where the trees would hide it from anybody flying overhead, was a small storage building, the kind Sears sells for people to put their lawnmowers in.

"I don't see a lock," I said.

"I guess they figured they didn't need to bother," Junior said. "If somebody found it, they were screwed anyway." She drew her gun. "Why don't you step back?"

I obeyed, making sure a nice, thick tree was between me and the door to the storage building. Only then did Junior push the door open with one foot. She waited, but when there was no reaction, she peeked inside without exposing much of herself. Finally she straightened up and reholstered her gun. "All clear."

We searched the shed together, but it was a disappointment. While there were plenty of supplies like sugar, yeast, cornmeal, malt, and empty jugs, there was nothing that pointed to Seth Murdstone or his killer.

I did get excited when I found a box of shotgun shells, but Junior said, "That's probably just to sweeten the moonshine."

"To do what?"

"Don't ask me why, but unless shine has a little lead in it, it won't sell. Supposedly it makes it sweeter. Some folks use lead apparatus, but I guess Seth added shot so a little lead would leech in."

"Isn't that dangerous?"

"Of course it's dangerous; people get

poisoned all the time. But moonshiners still add lead to increase the market value."

When we gave up on the shed, we poked at the woodpile to see if anything was hidden there.

"Nothing," Junior said in disgust. "Not a damned thing."

"They must have left fingerprints," I said. "Or something!"

"Maybe they smeared some DNA on the equipment," Junior said sarcastically.

"Junior, we are *not* giving up. There has to be something here!"

"I didn't say we were giving up," she said. "I'm just . . . Never mind. Let's keep looking. You circle around that way, and I'll circle around this way."

We moved away from each other, looking at the ground, in the trees, anywhere there might have been some trace of Seth or Jake. I went faster because I couldn't come up with as many places to look as Junior, and I ended up back at the still first. So I had time to notice that there was a blackened circle on one side of the fire pit, as if something had burned there.

"Looks like they had an accident," I said.

Junior came over. "Somebody must have spilled some moonshine into the fire. Seth must have made some potent stuff for it to go up like that. Look at the scorch pattern."

"They're lucky nobody got hurt out here in the middle of nowhere." Then my eyes widened as a couple of things came together. "Junior, maybe somebody did get hurt out here. Maybe this was where Barnaby had his accident."

"What are you talking about?"

"You remember when I was out at the Murdstone house? I saw where Barnaby supposedly burned himself. The carpet was burned, but there wasn't nearly as much damage as I'd have expected, considering how badly hurt he was."

"Are you sure? The report said the carpet was ruined and soot all over the walls and ceiling."

"Who wrote the report?"

Junior's face turned grim. "Mark. Lord knows how many other things he's lied about."

Mark's perfidy was the last thing on my mind. "Jesus, Junior! That's what Barnaby meant in his letter to Santa when he said he was trying to earn enough money to buy Jake a Christmas present. Seth must have been paying him to work out here." I was suddenly furious. "A nine-year-old boy messing with a still! That's why Seth didn't call an ambulance for him."

I thought about the bumpy road Junior and I had driven down to get there, then imagined the pain driving over it must have caused that poor burned boy. If Seth had been standing in front of me right then, I think I would have hit him myself. "Could this be why Seth was killed?"

"I don't see how," Junior said. "That would mean Jake did it, but Jake knew that Seth was in charge when Barnaby was hurt, and I never saw any sign that he blamed him. Why would he suddenly decide to take it out on him?"

"We're still missing something, Junior. I just don't know what."

"We'll get there," she said, patting my back. "Now that I know where this place is, I can come back with a fingerprint kit and everything else I need to prove it's Seth's."

I realized she was smiling. Heck, she was beaming. "You're looking mighty pleased with yourself."

"I'm feeling pretty pleased with myself. Finding this place has taken a long time."

I was feeling pretty smug, too. Maybe we didn't know who'd killed Seth or why, but finding his still felt like a step forward.

Junior said, "I can't wait to tell Daddy. Maybe I'll bring him out here for a Christmas present."

"Beats the heck out of a tie."

"Cheaper, too," Junior said. "We better get going. It's getting late, and I don't think Richard would appreciate it if we get lost."

I followed her back to the Jeep, but just as we reached the dirt track where it was parked, the baby started kicking in an extremely inconvenient place. "Junior? I have to go to the bathroom."

"We'll stop at the first place we see," she said, unlocking the car.

"I can't wait that long," I said.

It must have been an effort for her to resist snickering, but she managed. "I'll wait while you head for the bushes. Be sure to go on the other side of the track from the still. Jake will probably be able to tell we were here, but let's not make it worse than it is."

"Just let me get my pocketbook from the car."

"Why?"

"Kleenex."

"Of course."

Despite my days as a Girl Scout, I absolutely hated going to the bathroom outside. I liked my privacy, especially since I was as big and as graceful as a beached whale. So I went a ways into the woods before I found just the right spot: hidden, with a nearby stump I could hold on to when I squatted.

Even so, I wasn't so far away that I couldn't hear Junior's voice. I had just pulled my pants up and was making a hole in the ground with my sneaker to hide the used Kleenex when she spoke. I froze instantly.

"What the hell are you doing here?" she said.

There was an answer I couldn't quite make out, but the voice sounded familiar.

"Are you crazy?" Junior said.

There was another mumble, and then quite clearly I heard Mark Pope say, "I said, drop it! Don't think I won't shoot you, Junior."

I stayed where I was, trying desperately to figure out what I should do. I didn't want to go toward where Mark had the drop on Junior, because with him armed there was nothing I could do. I didn't want to run the other direction either, because I was sure Mark would see me if I moved, and he'd shoot. The sheer frustration of knowing he had Junior made me sick to my stomach.

"Where's your friend?" Mark asked.

"She's not here."

"You're lying. Stay there while I take a look."

I heard the car door open. I thanked the powers that be for reminding me to take my pocketbook, because if I hadn't grabbed it, it would have been on the front seat, letting Mark know I was nearby.

"You think I'd bring a pregnant woman out to the woods?" Junior said. "I dropped her off before I came, but she knows where I am, and if I'm not back there in half an hour, she's going to call for help."

"Who's she going to call?" Mark said, and I could almost hear the sneer. "I'm the law, remember?"

"She'll call her family," Junior said calmly. "And mine. That's an awful lot of men to come looking for you, Mark. Are you ready for that?"

"Shut up!" he snapped. There was a pause, and then he said, "Put these on." I heard metallic clicks and guessed he'd made Junior put on handcuffs. "Now get in." There were rattlings and the slam of a car door. A minute later the car drove off, leaving me crouched in the woods alone.

CHAPTER
THIRTY-FIVE

Only when Mark and Junior had been gone at least five minutes did I stand up, nervous as a cat that a shot would ring out. There was nothing, so Mark must have really driven off. But where had he taken Junior, and what was he planning to do with her? As I started back toward the dirt track, I realized the more important question was, what was I going to do about it?

Junior's car was gone, and I decided that Mark must have parked his own somewhere else and walked in. Unfortunately, I didn't have any idea of where to look for it, and even if I'd found it instead of getting hopelessly lost in the woods, I wouldn't have been able to drive it without a key.

"Baby," I said to my tummy, "when Mama gets back home, the first thing she's going to do is learn how to hot-wire a car."

It was getting dark and colder, and for once I was glad that being pregnant kept me so warm. "All I've got to do is follow the track back to the main road," I told myself. "Then I can find a phone and call for help." I started walking, my feet already sore and swollen. "On second thought, the first thing I'll do is get a cell phone. Then I'll be able to call somebody to hot-wire a car for me."

I didn't remember coming more than five or ten minutes away from the main road, but that had been in a car. On foot, in the dark, it seemed to take forever, and the bushes and tree limbs looked like something out of *Snow White* as they pulled at my arms and hair.

My mind was moving much faster than the rest of me. Obviously, Junior had been right about Mark. He must have killed Seth and tried to kill Jake. Why else would he risk kidnapping her and . . . I didn't want to think about what else he might risk. There was nothing I could do to stop it if I didn't reach civilization soon. I walked as fast as I could without falling.

An eternity later, I saw headlights, and at first I thought I'd reached the main road. Then I realized the headlights were coming toward me, along the dirt track. Had Mark realized I was out there after all? I bolted into the woods, diving behind a bush as full and round as I was.

The headlights came closer, and I saw it was a pickup truck, not Junior's Jeep or Mark's squad car. The driver was going slowly, even more so than the rough going called for. As the truck got closer, I saw that the driver's window was open, and I heard a voice call out, "Laurie Anne! Are you out there? It's me. Jake Murdstone."

More relieved than I could have said, I stood up and started waving. "Jake! Over here." I stumbled toward the truck.

"Are you all right?" he asked anxiously.

"I'm fine," I said, though I must have looked pretty bad.

He reached over to open the passenger door for me. "Climb in and we'll get you out of here."

I gratefully clambered aboard and tried to catch my breath while he turned the truck around.

"Is Junior all right?" I asked.

"Junior?"

"She sent you after me, didn't she?"

He shook his head. "Nope, it wasn't Junior."

I reached for the door handle, wondering what my chances of survival — and, more important, my baby's chances — would be if I jumped from a moving truck. "Did Mark send you?"

But he shook his head again. "I got a call from a friend of mine. She said you were out in the woods all by your lonesome and could use a ride." He eyed me sideways. "I didn't know you knew Clara Todger."

"Clara?" I blinked. Junior had said the Todgers kept a close watch around the area, but I hadn't realized how close. For a moment I wondered if they'd seen me squatting to do my business, but I shook it off. "What else did she say? Was there anything about Junior?"

"No, just that you needed help, and I should come right away. You ought to get yourself a cell phone before you go traipsing off alone, in your condition and all." Then, all too casually, he asked, "What were you doing out in this neck of the woods anyway?"

"We found a still," I said carefully.

"Is that right?" he said, and I thought he was gripping the steering wheel more tightly.

Just because Mark hadn't sent him didn't mean that he'd be happy about my knowing how he made his money, so I said, "Of course, there's no telling who's been running it, out here in the middle of nowhere. I've heard that hunters run into them all the time and never do find out who they

390

belong to."

"I've heard that too," he said, and his hands relaxed.

I went back to the important part. "Didn't Clara say anything about Junior?"

"What's the matter with Junior? Is she out in the woods, too?"

"Mark's got her!"

"Mark Pope?"

I took a deep breath, not wanting to waste the time to explain, but knowing that I had to. "There's no way to break this to you gently, Jake. Mark killed your father."

"That's impossible."

"I know it sounds crazy, but hear me out." I explained why Junior had become suspicious, and how Mark's actions had only made him look more and more like a killer. "We weren't sure, but he must think we know more than we do or he wouldn't have kidnapped Junior. We've got to find her before it's too late."

"You really think he's going to hurt her?"

"He took her gun and handcuffed her, Jake. What do you think he's going to do?"

He shook his head slowly, but I could understand why he was having problems taking it all in.

I said, "I'm sorry I had to spring it all on you this way, but we've got to figure out where he's taken her."

Jake was quiet for a long time, and by the time he spoke, he'd turned onto the main road. "I think he's heading for my house."

"You might be right," I said. "He's already tried to kill you once. Maybe he's planning to take care of you and Junior at the same time."

"Tried to kill me? What are you talking about?"

"Last night, with the gas."

"That was an accident."

"Mark wanted it to look like an accident — or even suicide." I half laughed. "The funny part is that until that happened, Junior and I thought you might have killed Seth yourself."

"I did," he said quietly.

I think my heart must have skipped a beat, and I put my hand on the door handle again. "What did you say?"

"I did kill Daddy. Mark's been trying to help me hide it, but I'm the one who killed Daddy."

I don't know how many questions ran through my head, but the one that came out was, "Why?"

"Haven't you figured it out? Mark must have thought you had."

I went over all we'd heard and the facts

we'd learned, thinking so hard it almost hurt. "Did it have something to do with your son's death?"

"That's right."

"But that was an accident, wasn't it?"

"Yeah, it was an accident, but it should never have happened. Barnaby shouldn't have been at the still."

"Hadn't he been there before?"

"Never," he said, shaking his head vigorously. "Barnaby didn't know what I did for a living, and I didn't want him to know. Moonshining's caused me nothing but trouble. I know worrying about it is part of the reason my mama got so sick when she was so young, and it messed up my marriage, too. I decided it was going to be different for Barnaby. I was stuck with it, because I didn't know how to do anything else, but I wanted Barnaby to take after my brother. To go to school, and get a good job, and make something of himself — maybe even marry a good woman like Florence. That meant he wasn't ever to know anything about the moonshining. Daddy knew how I felt, but he took him out to the still anyway."

Jake was watching the road in front of us, but I wasn't at all sure that was what he was seeing. "It shouldn't have happened,

Laurie Anne. Barnaby shouldn't have been there. I might have been able to forgive Daddy for that, and even for the accident, but I couldn't forgive him for lying to me. He looked me right in the eye and told me that Barnaby got hurt at the house — even made me think it was that space heater I bought that did it to him. Those days and nights I spent with Barnaby at the hospital, wishing I could make it quit hurting, and thinking I'd done it to him myself . . ." He took a sobbing breath. "Then to find out that Daddy had lied . . ."

"How did you find out? Was it Barnaby's letter to Santa Claus?"

"Mrs. Gamp gave it to me that day at rehearsal. She thought it was so sweet that Barnaby had been working to get me a present, but I realized that Barnaby had been working for Daddy. I wanted to believe that it was with the chairs, but I had to know for sure. I saw Daddy going to take a cigarette break, and I went with him. Before I got a chance to say anything, Daddy handed me the cane he was using for Scrooge and asked if I could sand it down because it was rough on his hands." He snorted, as if amazed that anybody would care about anything like that. "I asked him about Barnaby, and that's when he told me how my boy really got hurt."

He looked at me, but I was too appalled to speak.

Jake took a ragged breath. "You know he even got Barnaby to lie for him? Daddy told him that if he told anybody the truth, the police would put Daddy and me in jail, and Barnaby would have to go to an orphanage. They don't even have orphanages anymore, but Barnaby believed him, just like I always did. So he lied, even though he was afraid Santa Claus would hold it against him. Daddy said he was sorry, like that was enough. He expected me to forgive him, right then and there. Can you imagine that?"

"So you . . ." I couldn't bring myself to actually say it.

"So I took that cane and I hit him. As hard as I could."

"Did you mean for him to die?"

"I don't know, Laurie Anne, I swear I don't. But I didn't call for help afterward. I just left him there. So I don't guess it matters what I meant to do, does it?"

I wasn't sure of the answer to that one myself.

"I should have gone ahead and told Junior what happened, but I couldn't."

"Because you were afraid?" I said.

395

"Afraid? What did I have to be afraid of? My boy was gone. My daddy was gone. What else could anybody do to me that would matter? I wasn't afraid. I was ashamed."

"Of what you'd done?" I said, not quite understanding.

"No, not of what I'd done. I was ashamed of what Daddy had done." He made a sound that might have been a laugh if it hadn't been so sad. "David was always ashamed of Daddy's moonshining. He tried not to be, but I know he was. Not me. I was proud of the way he pulled the wool over everybody's eyes. I knew we had to keep it quiet because of the law, but if it hadn't been for that, I'd have shouted it from the housetops. But I couldn't stand the thought of people knowing how Daddy had let his only grandchild get hurt. How when Barnaby was in all that pain, all Daddy could think of was covering his tracks so nobody would find the still." He looked at me. "Would you want folks knowing that about your daddy?"

I couldn't even imagine being in that situation, but I said, "I guess I wouldn't."

He was quiet then, as if he'd explained everything, but I still had questions. "How did Mark get involved?"

"Didn't y'all figure that out? Mark said you would if we weren't careful."

"Figure out what?"

"That Mark was part of it. Of the moonshining, I mean."

"What?"

"He didn't do any of the work himself. He just told us when to lay low and when it was safe to deliver. When Andy Norton took a notion to watch us, he'd tell us that, too."

"Why?"

He looked at me as if I was crazy. "For the money, of course. Daddy paid him the first of every month."

"Mark's been taking bribes?" I leaned back in my seat, both aghast that he would do such a thing, and aggravated that Junior and I had suspected Mark of the wrong crime. "How much did he want for helping you cover up your father's murder?"

Jake looked shocked. "That didn't have anything to do with money. After I saw Daddy's — after I saw what I'd done, I meant to come clean. So as soon as I could, I told Mark what had happened. He said he didn't blame me, that no court in the country would convict me. The thing was, if it went to court everybody would find out about Daddy's moonshining."

"Not to mention finding out about Mark

being on the take," I added. That would have quashed his hopes of being police chief forever, in Byerly or anywhere else.

"That wasn't it. We were worried about David and Florence. How would it be for them if everybody found out?"

"Mark cared about that?" I asked suspiciously.

"Of course he did. He said that there were some things people didn't need to know."

I wriggled uncomfortably at that. I'd held on to more than one secret myself — things I'd decided people didn't need to know. Was I any better than Mark and Jake?

"Mark said we were lucky that Junior was on vacation, because she wouldn't understand. He figured he'd pretend to investigate until things died down, and nobody would be hurt. He even hid the cane where nobody would find it."

"It didn't bother him that a murderer would be walking around?" Then, remembering that I was sitting next to the murderer in question, I said, "I mean . . ."

"I know I'm a murderer," Jake said. "I killed my own daddy — there ain't nothing on earth lower than me."

"Then you did try to kill yourself last night."

"I keep telling you," he said, irritated,

"that was an accident."

"But . . ." I couldn't understand why he'd admit to murder but not suicide. "How could it have been an accident, Jake? My aunts didn't leave the stove on. I saw Aunt Nora use it to make a pitcher of iced tea, and I was there when she turned it off. Unless you did it yourself when fixing dinner . . ."

"I didn't exactly eat dinner," he said sheepishly. "I meant to, but I got to drinking and fell asleep."

Passed out, in other words. "Then how did the stove get turned on, and how did the pilot light go out? I'm telling you, it was Mark. He must have decided that killing you was the only way to cover his tracks. Once you were dead, he'd have produced evidence proving you killed Seth. Didn't you say he's got the cane you used? It's bound to have your fingerprints and bloodstains from Seth. All he'd have to do is plant it nearby. He'd probably have claimed to have found out about your moonshining, too. What would that have done to David and Florence?"

"Mark wouldn't do that," he said, shaking his head over and over.

I couldn't really blame Jake for being taken in by Mark. How many years had he been fooling everybody in Byerly? "What now?" I asked. "Are you going to kill me, too?"

The car swerved sharply, then he pulled back into the lane. "Jesus, of course not. What do you think I am?"

I couldn't think of an answer other than the obvious one, and saying that might change his mind. "Then what are we going to do? Where are we going?"

"We're going to talk to Mark. I can't let him do anything to Junior, not on my account. He's done enough to keep me out of trouble."

I spent the rest of the drive trying to talk Jake into stopping so I could call somebody else for help, but he wouldn't do it. He kept saying that he'd handle it himself, and when I pointed out that Mark was probably waiting for him and had likely set a trap, all he would say was that Mark had no reason to hurt him. It didn't matter how much logic I spouted, how convincing my arguments were, or how fast I talked. He just kept shaking his head. I even tried pretending that there was something wrong with the baby. Maybe a visitation from Marley's ghost would have convinced him, but nothing less than that would.

If we'd passed close enough to one single

car, I'd have pounded on the car horn or waved for help through the window, but the roads leading to the Murdstone house were empty that night.

Finally we turned into the long, dark driveway to the house. I'd expected Jake to drive all the way down, but he stopped about halfway, where a slight bend in the road blocked anybody in the house from seeing us.

"You better wait here," he said. "Just in case."

"You're starting to realize what Mark's been up to, aren't you? That's why you don't want me to come with you."

"No, it's just that — I figure we can't be too careful, not with you in the family way." Darned if he didn't reach over to pat my tummy. "You don't ever want to lose a child, Laurie Anne." He started to get out.

"Can't you leave me the keys so I can keep the heater running?" I said plaintively. It was lame, but I figured it wouldn't hurt to try.

Jake shook his head. "You wait here. If I'm not back soon . . ." He paused, and I think he couldn't stand to consider why he wouldn't come back. "Just wait until I get back."

He pushed the door closed and silently

401

picked his way down the gravel driveway
toward the house.

CHAPTER THIRTY-SIX

Needless to say, I had no intention of waiting for Jake. The question was, what could I do to help Junior? Even if I hadn't been waddling, I wouldn't have known what to do against an armed police officer. Mark might be crooked, but even Junior had said he was competent.

What I really needed were reinforcements, but the Murdstone house was so isolated that I might as well have been back in the woods. The Todgers had played guardian angel once already; I couldn't count on them doing it again. I still didn't have a cell phone and I still hadn't learned how to hotwire a car.

Maybe I didn't have to, I thought. Surely Jake had a spare key somewhere. I climbed out of the truck and wasted five minutes searching both bumpers to see if he'd hidden a spare set before I gave it up as a lost cause.

So I couldn't drive anywhere, and in my current condition, I wasn't likely to get to the nearest neighbor fast enough to do any good. What did that leave?

I looked speculatively down the driveway. There was a phone I could reach — if I was lucky. Though I wasn't about to try to sneak into the house, I remembered seeing a phone in Seth's workshop. The door had been unlocked the previous day. Dared I hope that it was still unlocked? And that Mark hadn't cut the phone lines? And that . . . ?

I stopped myself. There was no point in imagining all the things that could go wrong, because there was nothing I could do about any of them anyway. So, just as I had known I would, I followed Jake to the house. Later on, I wondered if Jake hadn't also known that I would eventually come after him.

I did make a quick stop. I was trying to decide whether my pocketbook would be a hinderance or a help when I thought of something. Richard had joked for years that my bag was so heavy it must be full of rocks. Though I hated to do it to a brand-new D'Arcy bag, a bag of rocks could make a formidable weapon. I upended the bag on the seat of Jake's truck and then filled it up with gravel from the driveway. It was a testimonial to the designer's workmanship that the shoulder strap held.

Carrying it didn't slow me down much, because if I'd gone any slower, I'd have been going backward. As much as my nerves wanted me to hurry, I knew that I couldn't afford to be heard. That meant taking my time.

Once I got within sight of the house, I glued myself to the shadows, thankful that Seth had never felt the need to knock down trees and create a featureless lawn where I would have stuck out like a sore thumb. Junior's Jeep was parked in front of the door, and there were lights on in the house, but with the curtains drawn I couldn't tell where anybody was — or, more important, what condition they were in. I was tempted to creep closer just to see if I could peek in a window, but I resisted. There would be plenty of time to peek once I had a brace of my cousins and Junior's brothers-in-law at my side.

Instead, I kept going toward the workshop in the backyard, wincing each time I stepped on a twig or rustled a fallen leaf. Only when I made it to the door without being discovered did I relax. I reached for the knob. The only thing that saved me from walking right in was a loud thump from inside. I'd read about people's hearts jumping into their throats, but that was the first time I knew what it meant. I inched away from the door and to the side of the building farthest from the house. I don't think I even breathed until I was around the corner, where I couldn't be seen.

There was a small window on that side, and since it was only a workshop, Seth hadn't bothered to put up curtains or blinds. He had stacked half-finished chairs in front of it — not enough to keep me from looking in, but enough that I felt somewhat concealed from whoever was inside.

It wasn't just curiosity, though I had enough of that to burn. I needed to see who was inside so I would know if there was anybody left in the house.

The first thing I saw was an oddly familiar assortment of tubing and pots set up in the center of the room. It was the camp stove underneath it that helped me recognize it as a still. Before I could even begin to guess why it was there, I saw Mark dragging Junior across the floor. She was so limp that, for one horrible second, I thought she was dead. Then I heard her moan as Mark dropped her like a sack of potatoes.

Jake was in there, too, watching Mark lean

down to unfasten the handcuffs from around Junior's wrists.

"You shouldn't have hit her like that, Mark," Jake said.

"I had to," Mark said matter-of-factly. "We can't let her body be found wearing handcuffs, and I couldn't take them off with her awake. It's got to look like she got caught in her own trap, which is exactly what she deserves for trying to plant a still on your property. If I hadn't followed her out here and caught her, she'd have put you in jail for moonshining, and then it would only have been a matter of time until she sweated the rest of it out of you. Then you'd have a murder rap on top of everything else."

What was he talking about? Mark hadn't followed Junior to the Murdstone house. He'd kidnapped her. And Junior hadn't planted that still. The man was laying down lies in layers, like Richard's lasagna. Surely Jake didn't believe him, not after what I'd told him.

"I can't go through with this, Mark," he said. "There's got to be another way."

"I'm telling you, this is the only thing that's going to save us. Not to mention your brother. Isn't David worth more to you than her?"

"What about Laurie Anne?" Jake said. I tensed, afraid he was about to tell Mark that he'd left me in the truck. But all he said was, "She'll never believe this, even if everybody else does."

"Then we'll take care of her, too," Mark said, sounding pleased at the idea.

"Mark, the woman's carrying an innocent baby."

"So what? What's one Burnette brat more or less?" Then he must have realized that hadn't been the best thing to say to a man who'd recently lost his son. "We probably won't have to worry about her anyway," he added quickly. "She and her husband will be back in Boston in another week or two."

"But Junior —"

"Forget Junior!" Mark boomed. "It's her or us. With her gone I'll be police chief, just like I should have been all along, and I'll make sure the record shows she accidentally ignited the still she was setting up and burned to death. Nothing could be simpler. We won't even have to fake the evidence this time."

Mark went to fiddle with the still, so he didn't see the look on Jake's face. If he had, he would never have turned his back on the man.

"Mark," Jake said softly, "did you know

408

Daddy lied about where Barnaby got hurt?"

"Of course not," Mark said, still not realizing his slip of the tongue. "I told you that."

"You say a lot of things, Mark, but I'm not sure I believe you anymore. What did you mean, 'this time'?"

"What are you talking about?"

"You said we won't have to fake the evidence *this time*. Did you fake it before? Was it you who made it look like Barnaby hurt himself here, instead of at the still?"

Mark finally turned to face the other man. "You know I wouldn't have done that, Jake. It was Seth."

"That's what I thought, but when did he have a chance? Daddy was wrong to take Barnaby out to the still, and wrong to lie about it, but at least he got Barnaby up to the hospital as fast as he could. He stayed there with him until I got there, and then he stayed with me. When did he have time to burn that hole in the playroom floor?"

Mark's eyes widened for a second, then I could almost see what he'd decided to do. "The pressure is really getting to you," he said. "Tell you what, Junior's not going anywhere. Let's go to the house and work this out. Okay, buddy?"

Jake nodded, and this time he was the one

to turn his back on the wrong man. Mark yanked his nightstick from his belt and whacked Jake across the back of his head. Jake dropped like a rock.

Mark looked down at the man as he replaced the nightstick, not looking apologetic or sorry, just irritated. Then he went back to messing with the still and the camp stove underneath.

Every muscle in my body was screaming for me to do something — anything — to save Junior and Jake, but I couldn't think of what I should do. Maybe I could make it to the phone in the house without Mark catching me, but what then? Nobody would be able to get there in time to do any good. The only one who could do anything to help was me, and I'd never felt so helpless in my life.

Mark had pulled out a jug and was splashing the contents around the workshop, taking particular care to slosh some on both Junior and Jake. Next he pulled a gun that had to be Junior's out of his waistband and placed it in her holster. Presumably he knew it would look suspicious for her body to be found without it. Then he glanced around the room, with the same expression Richard always had when blocking an act on stage. Clearly, he was making sure the scene was set properly. Then he picked up an open can of Sterno from the camp stove, walked toward the door, and pulled a lighter from his pocket.

Without really thinking, I ran toward the workshop door, carrying my rock-filled pocketbook. Mark must have seen the movement out of the corner of his eye, because he started to turn my way, but I'd already swung the bag, and it hit him across the shoulder blades. The breath rushed out of his mouth, and he stumbled forward, dropping the Sterno and his lighter.

Unfortunately, he was still standing, and he fumbled at his holster. I hefted the pocketbook to take another swing, but he drew his gun first, and I froze as he aimed the barrel right at my midsection.

"I should have known," he gasped. "The bitch lied to me, and —"

I never found out what he was going to say or do next, because Jake erupted out of the workshop and slammed into Mark. The gun fired, but the shot went wild as the men rolled around on the ground. Mark still had the gun, but Jake had a grip on his wrist, keeping him from aiming it.

I headed toward them, ready to use my pocketbook again. I knew I had just as good a chance of hitting Jake as Mark, but I didn't care if I had to knock both of them out to make sure Mark was out of commission.

Then I smelled something burning. I saw flames erupting from the workshop, and I realized that Mark's stray gunshot must have gone inside and set the fire he'd intended all along. I dropped the pocketbook, raced into the workshop to where Junior was, and wasted precious seconds trying to rouse her. As the air grew hotter, I gave up and grabbed her under her arms to drag her from the building. I didn't know what was going on outside, but anywhere had to be safer than in that firetrap.

Junior started coughing as we went, but though I had to pat out a burning cinder that landed on her side, we made it out all right. Between the coughing and the cold air hitting her, she started to come to.

Jake and Mark were still grappling, but it looked like Mark was winning. Jake must have been weakened from the blow to the head, and my pocketbook hadn't done nearly as much damage to Mark as I'd wanted it to. Once I was sure Junior was safe for the moment, I looked around for another weapon.

But then Junior croaked, "Laurie Anne, get out of the way!"

She had her gun in her hand — I'd forgotten Mark had given it back to her. I obeyed instantly, and Junior fired into the air above Mark's and Jake's heads.

They both jerked, and Jake's grip on Mark's arm slipped. Mark pushed him off and twisted around toward Junior. A shot cut through the night, but for an endless second I didn't know who'd been shot. Then Mark fell to the dirt while Junior stood motionless.

My knees gave way and I sank to the ground, my arms wrapped around my belly. Junior waited until she was sure Mark was no longer moving. Then she walked toward him, not letting her aim waver as she kicked the gun away from his hand. Only when she'd reached down to pick it up did she look back at me.

"Laurie Anne, are you hurt?"

"No, just — I'm fine."

"Is the baby all right?"

"Kicking up a storm."

She nodded and turned her attention toward Jake. "Are you all right?" she said.

"Junior, I didn't mean for —" he said. "I didn't know what Mark had —"

"Jake, I don't know what all happened in there or what's been going on between you and Mark. With him gone, I might never find out for sure. What happens next is up to you."

She and he looked at each other for a long moment, their faces transformed into angles and shadows by the light of the burning building behind us.

Finally Jake spoke. "I always told my boy to tell the truth, and now it's time for me to act the way I taught him to."

She held up one finger, and said, "Let me say something first. Jake Murdstone, you have the right to remain silent. If you give up that right . . ." She went through the rest of the Miranda warning. "Now go ahead, if you still want to."

He took a deep breath. "Chief Norton, I'd like to confess to the murder of my father, Seth Murdstone."

CHAPTER THIRTY-SEVEN

If anybody had been watching the Murd-stone house from above that night, it would have looked like nothing so much as an ant hill that's been stirred up with a stick. Junior held off on arresting Jake until he could take a hose to the still burning workshop while she used her cell phone to call the fire department. Then she called her brother Trey, and since it would have been awkward for either of them to be in charge of the crime scene, he brought along the county police.

Meanwhile, I went inside to use the phone to call Richard at the recreation center, where dress rehearsal had just ended. He hightailed it over to the house, pushed past the county police, who were trying their best to secure the scene, and grabbed hold of me. He kept asking if I was all right, if the baby was all right, and though I insisted that we were, he said he wanted a doctor to look at me immediately.

Dr. Connelly, the medical examiner, had just arrived, so he postponed examining Mark Pope's body in order to check me out. Since Dr. Connelly had a general practice in addition to his duties as medical examiner, it wasn't as grim as it sounded. He confirmed what I'd told Richard, though he sternly ordered me to eat a hot dinner and get a good night's sleep, and suggested that I avoid attacking armed men with my pocketbook.

I guess the rumors started when Richard tore out of the recreation center, because it wasn't long before David and Florence showed up. I wasn't there when David found out what really happened to his father. Nobody was, other than David and Jake. Junior put them into a room alone and let them work it out for themselves. Whatever was said, when they came out, David had his arm around his little brother's shoulders, as if to protect him from the world. Florence took one look and announced that she would be representing her brother-in-law.

One of the county officers took my statement, and once that was done, Junior came over long enough to give me the abandoned contents of my pocketbook, and to tell Richard and me to leave. I wanted to hug her, but I figured she wouldn't want anybody to see. Darned if she didn't hug me instead.

Richard and I drove slowly out of the Murdstone's driveway, partly because of all the police cars and such parked along it, and partly because Richard wanted to hold my hand. Otherwise, we wouldn't have noticed the man sitting in a car in the back of the line.

We pulled up alongside, and I rolled down my window while the driver of the other car did the same.

"Tim? Is that you?"

"Laurie Anne, are you all right?"

"I'm fine."

"I heard somebody was shot."

"Mark Pope. He's dead."

"Jake?"

"He's fine." I hesitated, but knew it was better for him to know. "Jake killed your father, Tim." I quickly explained what I knew. "I'm sorry."

"Me, too. I just wish . . . I guess it doesn't matter now. Thanks for telling me."

"You take care," I said.

We left him sitting there alone.

I talked Richard into going through the drive-through at Hardee's on the way back to Aunt Maggie's, which was silly. Half the

Burnette family was waiting for us, and of course Aunt Nora had brought more food than even I could eat. She plucked the Hardee's bag out of my hand and made me sit down to a real meal.

Richard wanted to put me to bed as soon as I'd swallowed the last bite of apple pie, but I stayed awake long enough to tell everybody what had happened. Then I went to sleep, knowing that they'd spread the word to any family members who weren't there — not to mention the rest of the town.

Richard wanted me to stay in bed the next day and even volunteered to stay with me, but I promised to take it easy and shooed him off so he could go to the recreation center. Otherwise, he probably would have exploded. He was so excited, he was nearly vibrating. Though there was no rehearsal, he had plenty of things to do to get ready.

To Richard's immense relief, David and Florence were still going to play their roles, and everybody pitched in to take over Jake's job. Though Oliver tried not to show it, he was clearly delighted that he was going to get to say the charity collector's lines.

Come curtain time, I'd expected Richard to stay backstage where he could issue last-minute instructions, but instead he was sitting next to me in the front row. Admittedly, he was holding my hand a little too tightly for the first few minutes, but eventually he relaxed, and I think he honestly enjoyed the show. I know I did, and I cried at the end when the audience gave a standing ovation. Richard nearly cried, too, when the cast and crew presented him with a copy of *The Annotated Christmas Carol,* inscribed by everybody.

The play was a huge success. There were so many curtain calls over the three-night run that, assuming one night out a week, Aunt Maggie was going to be eating dinners with Big Bill Walters for the next two months.

Vasti was ecstatic, both because of adding another feather to her cap and because Sally's Holiday Follies turned out to be all too appropriately named. Apparently, Sally had caught Bitsy's cold the day she came over to torment Vasti, and had managed to give it to half the people in her show, meaning that she had to cancel some of the best acts at the last minute. Dorcas Walters caught it, too, but refused to stay home, and her voice gave out in the middle of her dramatic reading of *A Visit from St. Nicholas.* She blamed Sally for the humiliation, which was hardly fair, but Vasti didn't mind.

Especially when it came out that Sally

really had been playing practical jokes. Not the dangerous ones, but she had set up the merely annoying pranks, and she'd been the one to leave the boxes of costumes outside the recreation center after all. When she saw Mark Pope as she was driving away, she thought he'd seen her, but since nothing ever happened, she decided she'd gotten lucky. Still, it had scared her enough to make her stop playing pranks.

It turned out that Mark had seen her. He told Jake he was going to start playing jokes himself, and that was when they turned nasty. He'd gotten a skeleton key for the building and set up some of the pranks at night, and arranged others while supposedly investigating Seth's murder. As Vasti had suspected, the tricks really were intended to stop the show or, failing that, to distract Junior and me.

But Vasti wouldn't cancel the show, and Junior and I wouldn't stop investigating. Mark was afraid we were getting close, which was why he'd followed us to the mall that day. Then he realized that I might have seen him when he rigged the scenery flat to fall. He'd been afraid all along that Junior was suspicious, so he decided the only way to protect himself was to kill Jake. At some point in his dealings with Seth, he'd gotten a key to their house, and he knew that Jake had been drinking heavily since his father's death. All he had to do was wait for Jake to pass out, and then sneak in to turn the gas on.

When that didn't work, he planned to booby-trap the Murdstone still, but he ran into Junior on his way there. It wasn't until a week or so later that his car was found nearby, hidden in some bushes. Scrooge's cane, the one Jake used to kill Seth, was in the trunk. Junior might never have found it had it not been for an anonymous phone call. I guessed Clara Todger was practicing her peculiar brand of civic-mindedness again.

At any rate, it's hard to know exactly what Mark meant to do that night at the Murdstone house. Junior, who'd still been conscious at the time, said he'd been mighty surprised when Jake arrived, so he'd probably planned to set a trap that would kill both of them. Thinking on his feet, he'd convinced Jake that Junior was his only target, but when Jake balked, he went back to the original plan. At least, until my pocketbook and I interfered.

As Vasti had hoped, Tim Topper invited the cast to Pigwick's for a party following the last performance. After I happily ate a heaping plate of pulled pork and hush puppies, Richard and I called Tim over to talk.

First, of course, Richard and Tim had to congratulate themselves.

"Richard, I don't think I've ever had as much fun in my life as doing that play. I don't mean to downplay the bad parts, but as soon as that curtain went up, all of that went away."

"You did a terrific job," Richard said.

"I couldn't have done it without you."

"No, you had the part down cold, and the stage presence is yours alone."

"Thanks, but you —"

"You were both great," I interjected. "Awesome, wonderful, incredible, amazing, whatever adjectives y'all want to use."

"Sorry," Richard said. " 'He that is proud eats up himself; pride is his own glass, his own trumpet, his own chronicle.' "

"*Great Expectations?*" Tim asked.

"*Troilus and Cressida.* Act Two, Scene Three." With the play over, Richard had happily gone back to his usual source of quotes.

"I wouldn't mind trying out some Shakespeare, too, if you'll come back to direct," Tim said. "Maybe *Othello.* I think I've got greasepaint in my blood."

Before they could start patting each other on the back again, I said, "Actually, it's your blood I wanted to ask about. Have you told the Murdstones yet?"

"I didn't think it was the right time, Laurie Anne — not with Jake's situation and all the talk about Seth. The last thing they need is to have an illegitimate brother showing up."

"Then again," I said, "it might do them good to have more family around right about now. You can't have too many shoulders to lean on."

"You think?"

"Yes, I do. Besides," I said with a grin, "at this point, you're the white sheep in the family."

Everybody in the room turned to see what had made Tim laugh so loudly, but we wouldn't explain. A few days later, I heard through the grapevine that the Murdstones had welcomed Tim with open arms. I was glad. Maybe Tim hadn't gotten the father he wanted, but at least he had two brothers and a sister-in-law who wanted him. That made a pretty good Christmas present.

What with the play wrap-up, the finishing touches on our Christmas preparations, and then the big day itself, it wasn't until the day after Christmas that I had a chance to

423

go see Junior. She was back on duty, of course, and I found her at the police station. She was sitting behind her desk, and though there were papers in front of her, I suspected she was really just enjoying being back where she belonged.

"Hey there, Laurie Anne," she said. "Did you get everything you wanted for Christmas?"

"Pretty much. Richard even got me another D'Arcy pocketbook. How about you?"

"No complaints. Though I could have used a new deputy in my stocking."

"I am sorry about Mark. How it all turned out, I mean." Though I didn't think him much of a loss, I knew that shooting him hadn't come easily to her.

"I'm sorry I never realized who he really was. Daddy's feeling even more got away with, after having hired and trained Mark himself. Here Mark had been on the take all these years, and we never had the first clue." She shook her head. "You remember how Seth told the Todgers he left Mr. Gamp's body because he thought he heard sirens? According to Jake, he really did hear a siren. Mark was there that night and offered to forget what he'd seen. That's how far back it went."

"I take it that Jake's cooperating."

"Oh, yeah. Florence is making a case for temporary insanity or diminished capacity, because of what happened to Barnaby. So the more Jake cooperates, the better that's going to look to the judge and D.A."

"You realize that he could have turned me over to Mark, and Mark only hit him because Jake wouldn't let him kill you."

"I know. Maybe I won't add him to my Christmas card list, but I can't blame him for what my own deputy did. You can bet I'm going to be more careful about who I hire next time." She looked at me. "I don't suppose you're interested in law enforcement, are you?"

"Me?" I laughed. "Thanks anyway, but I'd never be able to keep up with all the rules you've got."

"Just a thought," she said. "If you ever do decide to turn professional, I'd be proud to have you work with me."

"Junior, that's the nicest thing you've ever said to me."

She looked alarmed. "You're not going to hug me again, are you?"

"Hey, it was you who hugged me last time."

"So it was," she said. "I never thanked you for what you did that night."

"You don't have to. In fact, I ought to

apologize for not helping when Mark kidnapped you."

"Laurie Anne, don't you ever think that," she said firmly. "There was nothing you could have done to stop Mark. He was armed, he was trained, and he was desperate. The only reason I was talking so loud was to warn you. I wanted you to stay where you were."

"I know, but if Clara Todger hadn't sent Jake to come get me —"

"But she did. By the way, when I spoke to her the other day, she asked after you. And she says she loves your pocketbook."

I laughed. "Maybe I'll get her one as a thank-you."

Junior's face turned serious. "Laurie Anne, even though I appreciate your saving me more than I can say, I don't want you ever to put my welfare ahead of your baby's again. The day I let anything happen to a Burnette baby is the day I'd have to leave town. Because if your family didn't get a hold of me, my own mama would."

"I'll make a New Year's resolution to be more careful." Then I asked, "Do you think I should stop these investigations? For the baby's sake?"

"I don't know, Laurie Anne. It wouldn't hurt for you to be more careful, but that's true of anybody. Having a baby changes you, but it's not supposed to change you into somebody else."

"You lost me."

"Would I still be myself if I quit being a cop?"

"Lord, Junior, I can't imagine you doing anything else."

"Then what you have to ask yourself is this: can you imagine yourself not getting into these situations?"

I tried to picture myself no longer asking questions and tracking down answers, all the while knowing that solving problems made me feel special in a way nothing else did. I felt as if I was really helping people, making a difference, and other Peace Corps slogans. It wasn't that I *looked* for dead bodies, but I couldn't seem to ignore any that came my way. "I don't think I can, Junior."

"That's what I thought."

I got another hug out of her before I left, and as I walked out to the car, I rubbed my tummy and said, "Baby, we're going to have some interesting times together."

The employees of Thorndike Press hope you have enjoyed this Large Print book. All our Thorndike, Wheeler, and Kennebec Large Print titles are designed for easy reading, and all our books are made to last. Other Thorndike Press Large Print books are available at your library, through selected bookstores, or directly from us.

For information about titles, please call:
(800) 223-1244

or visit our Web site at:
http://gale.cengage.com/thorndike

To share your comments, please write:
Publisher
Thorndike Press
295 Kennedy Memorial Drive
Waterville, ME 04901